A CHRISTMAS LOVE

A CHRISTMAS LOVE

Kathleen
Creighton

Thorndike Press • Thorndike, Maine

Copyright © 1992 by Kathleen Creighton

Published in 1995 by arrangement with
St. Martin's Press, Inc.

Thorndike Large Print ® Romance Series.

The tree indicium is a trademark of Thorndike Press.

The text of this Large Print edition is unabridged.
Other aspects of the book may vary from the original edition.

Set in 16 pt. News Plantin by Rick Gundberg.

Printed in the United States on permanent paper.

Library of Congress Cataloging in Publication Data

Creighton, Kathleen.
  A Christmas love / Kathleen Creighton.
    p.   cm.
  ISBN 0-7862-0540-7 (lg. print : hc)
  1. Large type books. I. Title.
  [PS3553.R368C48   1995]
  813′.54—dc20   95-35378

This book is for Mrs. Leona Pleasant Lee, granddaughter of slaves, in honor of her one hundredth birthday; and in loving memory of my grandmother, Hattie Merriam Hand, who would have celebrated hers next year; and for Cyndy Hall, organist and director of the children's choirs of the United Methodist Church of Camarillo, California; . . . three extraordinary and beautiful women who believe, as Miss Leona and I do, that all God's Children can sing.

Prologue

The week before Christmas, John Clayton Traynor came home from his usual afternoon walk in the woods, put his coat and rifle away in the closet where they belonged, and went into the kitchen singing out, "Miss Leona, I'm home." At ninety-two Miss Leona was getting a little hard of hearing, and didn't like surprises.

He found her standing by the stove, which, since she wasn't close to five feet tall, came nearly to her chin. She cocked her head to look at him over her shoulder in the way she had that reminded him of a little brown bird and snapped, "John Clayton, wipe your feet."

"Yes, ma'am," Clay said cheerfully as he went to see what she was up to. "What's that you're making now?"

"Scones."

"*Scones?*" He burst out laughing.

Using a potholder, Miss Leona nudged a metal jar lid with what looked like a doll-sized biscuit sitting in the middle of it over in his direction. "Here — the tester's done. See if it's right."

"Miss Leona, you don't need a tester," Clay

said, knowing she wasn't going to listen to him this time any more than she had all the other times he'd explained it to her. "That's not a wood stove like the one that burned your house down. That stove's gas — it's got its own thermostat."

Miss Leona's snort told him how much faith she put in such newfangled notions. He gave up and poked the jar lid with his finger. "So that's a scone, huh? Looks like a biscuit to me."

"The recipe book says they's scones, then scones they is." Miss Leona had her chin poked out in a way Clay knew well, so when he took a nibble of the scone and it tasted pretty much like a biscuit to him, only sweeter, he didn't say so. Instead he mumbled good-naturedly through his mouthful, "What are you doing poking around in cookbooks again, Miss Leona?"

"Christmas," she said, as if that were the whole explanation.

Clay nodded as if he understood it, which he did. Even under normal circumstances Miss Leona considered it her mission in life to feed any living thing that might need feeding, human or animal, and Christmas required some extra special effort. Of course, he didn't understand the whole craziness about Christmas himself, but if it made Miss Leona happy, he didn't mind it.

"What's wrong with plain old down-home cookin'?" he inquired with a deep Southern drawl, half teasing, half serious. Last season's pre-Christmas cooking binge had been French and Cajun, and it had taken him till spring to get his stomach back to normal.

"Ha!" said Miss Leona. "Southern cookin'll kill you."

"Well," said Clay matter-of-factly, "we all got to go sometime."

"Not me," retorted Miss Leona. "I'm goin' to raise chickens next year."

He didn't have any answer for that kind of optimism, so he gave it up and said meekly, "Well, it sure is good, whatever it's called, Miss Leona. And the oven temperature seems just fine. I guess you can go ahead and cook the rest." He polished off the biscuit while Miss Leona independently wrestled a new panful into the oven.

When she'd straightened up and was facing him again she remarked casually, "Someone's moving in across the gully." But her eyes were sharp and yellow as a raven's.

" 'Cross the gulley?" Clay said. "You don't mean the *summer* house? The old Robards place?" Miss Leona nodded sagely. "How do you know?"

"Miz Robards wrote, that's how I know.

9

Now what do you suppose they'd be doin' over there this time of the year, wintertime, and so close to Christmas? They don't have kinfolk here anymore, I know that for fact." Miss Leona pulled out a chair and sat in it, hooking her feet over the bottom rung, like a child. Her eyes squinted up and her voice got far away.

"Let's see now . . . I sold that piece a' land to those Robards folks in nineteen hundred and forty-two, same time I sold this place to your granddaddy. That was right after I got the letter that my Thomas been killed in the war. Sold off most my land then. Didn't mean nothin' to me, you know, without my Tom. Your granddaddy, of course, he settled right down here and raised his family, but that Jack Robards, he always thought he was too good for country folks." Miss Leona snorted and shook her head. "And his wife, well, she always had to be in the middle of things in town, you know. Came out in the summertime, which always seemed like the waste of a good home, to me. Rich folks got some strange ideas 'bout what makes a good life."

Clay mumbled agreement, and Miss Leona got up to check on her scones. When she came back she smacked the potholder down on the table and lifted up one crooked brown finger as though she'd just had a revelation. "You know, I never did care much for that boy of theirs. That Russell — most spoiled-rotten white boy I ever saw. Married late, as I remember — found him a nice wife, though. Got a sweet little baby girl, too. Used to spend summers here, just like his folks did up until they passed on." She stabbed Clay in the chest with the same finger. "*You* remember — the first time they come was the summer right before you went North." Miss Leona always said "north" in capital letters.

"I don't know," Clay said doubtfully. "That was a long time ago. Fourteen years."

Miss Leona cocked her head and squinted up her eyes again. "Well," she admitted, "time gets by me, you know. Seems like just yesterday you were goin' away to school. . . ." Her face had the sad, cracked look of forgotten heirlooms. "And then, you met that Northern girl up there and never came back. You never came home. . . ."

"Sure I came back, Miss Leona," he said, gently patting her hand. "I'm here now."

She beamed at him like a good-natured baby just woken up from a nap. "Why, yes you are. Yes you are — you're a good boy, John Clayton. Always were. Made your mama and daddy so proud, you know — you being a policeman, gettin' those medals." She gave his hand a good hard squeeze and went

11

back to the stove.

Clay didn't say anything, just got up and went to help her.

This time Miss Leona allowed him to remove the potholder from her hand and the pan from the oven. She had other things on her mind now. Though she came back quickly enough when he tried to help himself to another scone, pouncing on his hand like a raven on a grasshopper.

"Here, John Clayton, you let those biscuits cool first! And don't you eat all those now — you know I got to have plenty for the church baskets. God's chul'ren got to eat, too." God's children being what Miss Leona called anybody she thought might be in need of feeding, human or animal.

She tilted her head and gave him a sideways, crafty look he'd learned to dread. It meant she was cooking up more than food for God's chul'ren. "John Clayton, I want you to go on over there tomorrow mornin' and see about things, you hear me? That summer house is in no fit shape for a woman and chile, especially in the wintertime."

"Woman and child?" Clay frowned. "I thought you said it was Robards coming with his family."

"Said no such thing," Miss Leona countered, managing to look both righteous and evasive. "What I said was, Miz Robards wrote. Looks like she shed that no-good man of hers, because she's comin' alone, with her little girl. And you goin' to go over there tomorrow like a good neighbor and see if they need anything, you hear?"

Clay sighed. It wasn't the first time Miss Leona had tried to set him up with somebody, and although he'd had some pretty interesting dates come out of her meddling, a divorcée with a kid was the last thing he had any desire to mess with. However, he knew better than to argue.

"Yes, ma'am," he said, "I will, I'll go be a good neighbor — if you'll just let me have another one of those scones of yours."

Miss Leona snorted and waved the pot-holder. "Biscuits. That's what they is. That English cookbook can call 'em what it wants, they's still *biscuits.*"

Clay laughed, popped one in his mouth steaming hot, and went to put on his chore boots.

Going out the back door he stumbled — mostly from habit — over the old roasting pan that had been the farm dogs' feeding dish for as long as he could remember. Every evening Miss Leona filled it up with scraps and leftovers — also from habit, because the last Traynor dog, good old Buster, had succumbed at the end of last summer to old age aggravated by snake bite. And every morning, "God's children," miscellaneous four-legged varieties, would have licked it clean.

"Miss Leona," he'd tease, "you putting food out for the possums again?"

Miss Leona would always just shrug and say, "Keeps 'em out of my chickens."

From the kitchen came the crash and clang of a cookie sheet hitting the floor, followed, since she thought he was out of hearing range, by some mild swearing from Miss Leona.

Clay shook his head and went on out to the barn, smiling to himself. It looked like *all* of God's children were going to eat scones tonight.

Chapter 1

Carolyn Robards sat in the silent car and watched oak leaves scuttle across the open porch — like mice, she thought, frightened away by unexpected arrivals.

"It's creepy," her daughter Jordy complained. "I don't remember it being like this, all cold and bare."

Carolyn said cheerfully, "We were always here in summer before, honey. This is December. It's supposed to be cold and bare in the wintertime."

"Maybe it'll snow," Jordy said hopefully. Her thirteen winters had mostly been spent in Southern California, and snow was still a source of entertainment to her.

"I don't think it snows much around here," Carolyn told her. "This is the South, after all." She turned to look into the back seat. "How's Harriet?"

"Drunk as a skunk," Jordy reported, after a brief glance beneath the towel covering the cat carrier. "Her eyes look all weird."

"Let's leave her in the car, then, while we unload." Carolyn opened the car door and the December cold came inside.

"It sure feels cold enough to snow," Jordy grumbled as she gathered up her Walkman and the assortment of paperbacks, snacks, and pillows she considered essential for surviving car trips with her mother. She paused to add in an aggrieved tone, "If we *have* to be someplace away from home for Christmas, it seems like it could at *least* snow."

Christmas. Carolyn took a deep breath, inhaling the rich brown smells of moist earth and decaying leaves and remarked, "If it's snow you want, you can always go to Aspen with your dad."

From the back seat came a snort. "Yeah, right — and the Strawberry Tart? No thanks."

"Jordy!" Carolyn barely managed to cover a gust of shocked laughter. Valiantly she put on her sternest expression and in her "I'm your mother and I'm not fooling around" voice warned, "I won't have you talking about Crissy like that. After all," she added, trying out the words for the first time, "she's probably going to be your stepmother eventually."

"Ooh goody," Jordy cooed as she yanked open her door. "Then I'll have somebody close to my own age to play with." The sarcasm was punctuated by the slamming of the car door and the crunch and swish of angry footsteps.

Carolyn fought down shameful bubbles of

laughter, knowing it wasn't really funny, and that, unlike her own, Jordy's wounds hadn't yet begun to heal. She stayed where she was for a moment longer to watch her daughter plow through drifts of oak and poplar leaves, adolescent clumsy in her jeans and Nikes and hot-pink ski jacket, blond, baby-silk hair still retaining the warm glow of the California sun.

Maternal love rushed stinging to the backs of her eyelids. Oh Russell, she thought, feeling no rage at all, feeling only tired remnants of the grief that had evolved long ago into a strange kind of compassion. You poor idiot. You have no idea, do you, what you've thrown away.

Jordy was calling impatiently from the porch. Carolyn twisted around to look once more at the tranquilized cat, still crouched in her carrier staring with glassy intensity at nothing, then got out of the car and went to unlock the trunk.

"You start bringing things in," she instructed as she joined Jordy at the front door. "I want to make sure we've got power and propane while it's still light." The assortment of keys gave way to the right one, and the knob turned. The door creaked inward upon the cold, lonely odors of mildew and mice.

"Oh yuck," Jordy said, wrinkling her nose.

Carolyn said briskly, "Well, what do you

17

expect? It's probably been years since any-one's been in here." She stepped into the kitchen, footsteps crackling on warped lino-leum, and put her car keys and purse gingerly down on the chrome and Formica tabletop. On her left, just as she remembered, were the metal sink and fifties-style appliances. To the right was the "living room," dark and charm-less with its bank of small-paned windows overlooking the front porch, and only a de-partment-store braided rug to give it warmth and set it off from the unpartitioned kitchen.

With all the enthusiasm of one entering a bat-infested cave, Jordy followed her. "Looks more like a century," she grumbled. "I thought you said the neighbors were looking after it. Mom, are we really going to stay here? This place is a *dump*."

"Oh, honey, it's not so bad." Carolyn straightened her shoulders as she looked around in the dim, wintry light, giving herself the appearance, at least, of self-assurance. "It'll warm right up once we get the power turned on and the furnace lit. The smell will go away after a while. It's just that old empty house smell . . ."

It wouldn't, though. In all the summers they'd spent here, no matter how she'd scrubbed, cleaned, laundered, and disinfected, she'd never been able to get rid of that smell.

It was buried deep in the wallboard, the wood, in the cupboards and pipes, in the fibers of that awful old rug she'd hated the moment she'd laid eyes on it, and which Russell would never hear of replacing. It was the smell of the heat and damp of fifty South Carolina summers and the emptiness and abandonment of fifty winters. The smell of a house that had never been anyone's home.

"Mom," Jordy said, her tone outraged and accusing, "there's no TV."

"We'll buy one," Carolyn promised. "A *small* one. Though as I recall, there wasn't much to see. I wonder if cable's gotten this far . . ." She tried a light switch. "Darn — the breakers must be off. I'll go check the box. It's around back. While I'm doing that you can be getting a load out of the car — go on, hurry up."

"I bet there's spiders in there," Jordy said with a sniff as she peered into one of the three shadowy doorways that opened off the living room. "And *mice*."

"Well then," Carolyn remarked lightly, but with waning patience, "maybe you should bring Harriet in."

"Harriet is eighty-seven years old in cat years," Jordy shot back. "How would *you* like to have to kill mice if *you* were eighty-seven?"

Carolyn gave her daughter's flushed face

and too-bright eyes a glance. All she said was, "Let's get busy, shall we? You can put your things down right here for now, on this table. It doesn't look too dusty."

But outside in the cold shade of the abbreviated December afternoon she blinked away tears, wondering what had happened to her relationship with her only child. It wasn't just that Jordy was growing up, changing before her eyes, she knew that. It was something missing in *her*. In his abdication Russell had stolen something precious from her, and she didn't know how to get it back.

The fusebox was on the downhill side of the house, on the wall next to the basement door. Rounding the corner of the house, Carolyn stopped suddenly, distracted by the unexpected glimmer of sunshot water through the skeletons of trees. Strange — she hadn't realized before that the lake could be seen from here. In the lazy, humid depths of summer the woods had always seemed to enfold the little house like sheltering wings, giving it a coziness and sense of security she now knew she'd been looking forward to. Instead, here were unexpected vistas of lemony sky and sun-dappled water, a bright, beckoning world beyond the lacy black curtain of winter branches. She didn't know whether to rejoice, or be sorry.

Familiar scufflings drew her attention, and she watched a squirrel go bounding through the leaves and up the trunk of a nearby hickory tree. From the topmost branches she could hear it scolding in fear and foolish bravado. Silly creature, she thought, recalling that Russell had used that very sound to locate squirrels so he could shoot them with his twenty-two.

She heard other scuffles much closer by, and realized with a small jolt of uneasiness that the basement door was slightly ajar. On tiptoe she stepped up to it and gave it a tentative push, like one touching a hot surface. The scuffles, furtive, panicky, and unmistakable, came again. She jumped back, then hovered there, rooted in indecision. Beyond her own dry mouth and pounding heart her senses gave her an odd impression of something crouched, waiting . . . frozen in terror and dread.

"What's goin' on?" Jordy, her natural buoyancy restored, had come crunching up with the cat in her arms, in blithe ignorance of any sinister auras.

Carolyn gave a short, relieved laugh, indefinably bolstered by the presence of another person, even a small one. "I don't know. I think there's something in the basement."

"No kidding," Jordy said in an awed voice, "look at Harriet. She's freaking out, Mom."

It was, for her, a fairly mild exaggeration. A low, feline growl issuing from the cat's throat lifted the fine hairs on Carolyn's arms.

She murmured dryly, "Good thing she's still tranquilized." The cat was staring fixedly at the half-open doorway, her eyes fully dilated, round and dark as ripe currants.

Jordy peered over Harriet's head, her own blue stare avidly mimicking the cat's. "What do you think it is, Mom?"

Carolyn gave an offhand shrug. "Oh, I don't know, probably just a raccoon or a possum." But she edged carefully away from the open doorway, just in case. "Either one would make short work of a cat, though, even one who *isn't* eighty-seven years old and drunk as a skunk. So you'd better keep a good tight grip on her. Better yet, take her in the house."

"What are you going to do?"

"About whatever's in there?" Carolyn gave a shuddering laugh. "Well, I'm not going in after it, that's for sure! For right now we'll just . . . we'll leave the door open, that's what we'll do. Whatever it is," she added firmly as she turned back to the fusebox, "I'm sure it's going to be only too happy to leave, now that we're here."

She pulled the breaker switch and heard the stutter and hum of power returning to the various appliances scattered through the house, the grinding whine of the water pump starting up over in the well shed. Relief flooded her. At least everything seemed to be in working order.

From the murky depths of the basement there was only silence.

"Mom," Jordy said in an uncharacteristically subdued voice, "do we have to stay here? Can't we go to a motel or something, just for tonight?"

For a moment Carolyn hesitated, keeping her back to her child, her eyes on the metal fusebox. For a moment she let herself think about it, the antiseptic austerity of a motel room, safe and familiar; the lighted bustle of a restaurant dining room, the warm, cholesterol-rich smells of charbroiled meat and french fries. At last she said without emotion, "Now what would be the point in that? We'd just have to go through all this again tomorrow."

Jordy said nothing as she sullenly watched the toe of her Nike scrape a trench in the damp red ground. Then she blurted out, "I know why we had to leave California. It's because of the money, isn't it? We don't have enough money since Dad —"

"We have plenty of money," Carolyn said calmly. "Just not enough for California. It will cost us a lot less to live here, Jordy, I explained

23

that. This house is all ours, so we don't have to pay rent or a mortgage while I'm writing my book. And after that . . ."

"Yeah, Mom, what about after that? What are you going to do, get a *job?*"

"Well, you needn't say it like *that.*" Carolyn gave a short laugh, then glanced at her daughter and said with a casual shrug, "I might go back into practice."

Jordy snorted. "Yeah, right, Mom. Who's going to go to a marriage counselor who's been divorced?"

"Ooh, smarty pants," Carolyn said lightly. "Did your father tell you that?"

"No," Jordy retorted in an insulted tone, "I thought that up all by myself. What *Dad* said was, nobody in the South would ever admit to being messed up enough to need a shrink. Mom, don't you think it's weird?"

"What is?" Carolyn said gently, because with the question Jordy's tone and expression had abruptly switched from nasty smart-aleck to bewildered child, a transformation Carolyn had seen all too many times lately.

"Dad's the one that's from South Carolina, but he's in California and we're here. It's not fair."

"Fair's got nothing to do with it. A little ironic, maybe . . ." She put her arm around Jordy's shoulders and gave them a reassuring squeeze. "Listen, your dad doesn't like to be reminded that he came from a small Southern town, which is why he was happy to let me have this house as part of the divorce settlement. It's going to work out very well for us, you'll see. It's going to be all right."

"I just wish it wasn't Christmas," Jordy said in a mournful tone, burying her face in Harriet's fur. "It doesn't seem like Christmas here."

"Oh, I know," Carolyn said with a wry smile. "How can it be Christmas without eighty-degree, forty-mile-an-hour Santa Ana winds blowing Christmas trees all over the parking lots?"

"There were decorations up in the malls," said Jordy wistfully.

"Well, we'll just have to put up some decorations of our own," Carolyn said briskly. "I know there's holly in the woods — I used to blunder into it all the time. We'll pick some — you know, 'Deck the Halls'? And tomorrow morning first thing we'll go over and say hello to our neighbors — that'll help. You'll like the Traynors. They're everyone's idea of the perfect grandparents. They have this lovely little farm, just like a picture book, with a big barn and all sorts of animals —"

"I remember," Jordy said suddenly. "Sort of. I remember every time we went over to visit, Mrs. Traynor would tell me to go out and gather the eggs, like it was some great privilege, or something."

"It was," Carolyn said. "You used to love doing it."

Jordy shrugged dismissively. "Yeah, well, I was little then. Dumb things like that are fun when you're little."

Carolyn didn't answer. Defeated, she let her arm drop away from Jordy's shoulders, and they trudged up the hill together, side by side, in silence.

A pale haze lay soft on the lake when Carolyn stepped outside the next morning. The air was cold and smelled of wood smoke, and from somewhere far off a mourning dove was calling, evocative as a train whistle in the night.

She found Jordy standing motionless on the porch, shoulders hunched with the unaccustomed cold, hands withdrawn inside the sleeves of her pink jacket, puffs of breath feathering into the quiet air.

"Ready to go?" she asked as she hastily zipped up her own jacket. "Did you eat breakfast?"

"I had some Cheerios," Jordy said absently, without turning. And then, in the carefully toneless voice she used when she didn't want to sound excited, "Mom, what kind of bird is that? Over there in the bushes — that red one. Is that a cardinal?"

"Oh —" Carolyn gave a little gasp of delight. "Yes, it is — I'll bet you've never seen one, have you? They don't have cardinals in California."

"Yeah, well, I bet they don't have condors in South Carolina," Jordy muttered sourly, making it just loud enough for her mother to hear. She was in a bad mood this morning, even for Jordy.

Carolyn sighed inwardly and clumped down the steps, saying brightly, "You know, I used to have a book of all the trees and birds and animals in this part of the country. I'll bet it's still here somewhere — I'll look for it when we get back. Then we can look up all the different things we see, learn their names . . . Won't that be fun?"

"I'm not really into bird-watching, Mom," Jordy said with withering scorn.

Carolyn folded her arms across her middle and bit down on her lower lip and they crunched down the driveway in silence. After a while she cleared her throat and tried again. "How's Harriet this morning?"

"Hiding in the closet," Jordy muttered, watching her feet turn cold-crisped leaves to brown dust.

27

"Well, that's normal," Carolyn said comfortingly. "Especially after she kept us awake all night growling and stalking whatever's in the basement. I don't think I've ever seen her act like that before."

"Except around dogs," Jordy reminded her. "She *hates* dogs. If there's one within two miles, she gets all wild-eyed and weird, and her hair stands on end, just like last night. I'll bet anything that's what's down there, Mom. I'll bet it's a stupid *dog*."

"Now what would a dog be doing in our basement?" Carolyn said logically. "There's nobody around to feed it. No, honey, I'm sure it's just a possum or a raccoon. Harriet's never met either one before, so to her it would probably smell like some exotic breed of dog. Anyway, since she's sleeping now, that probably means it's gone. We'll look when we get back. Oops — let's turn here. Don't you remember? There's a shortcut."

Without protest or reply, Jordy veered to the right. The gravel track that wound away through the woods was badly overgrown, pocked with dormant anthills and treacherous with hickory nuts and acorns. Thorny tentacles of wild berry vines caught at their pantlegs, and branches left dusty remnants of last summer's spiderwebs in their hair.

"This path used to go to Miss Leona's

cabin," Carolyn said, panting a little from the slightly uphill climb. "It doesn't look as if it's been used for quite a while. I guess Miss Leona must have died. She was very old."

"I remember her," Jordy said grudgingly. "She was that little tiny black lady, wasn't she? And she lived in this little tiny cabin with a wood stove. Dad took me to see her once, and she made us lunch. She cooked it on this big stove, and it was so *hot* in there we almost died. She kind of reminded me of a bird."

"What else do you remember?" Carolyn asked, pleased to have finally gotten that much response.

"I remember —"

Jordy was walking along with her head down, forehead furrowed, so it was Carolyn who saw the man first. He was some way off, on the hillside across the narrow gulley that ran down to the cove, the gulley that separated her property from the Traynors', standing among the cold black skeletons of trees, so tall and thin and still he might have been one of them.

"— Dad and I used to go walking in the woods. I remember I used to pick flowers, and acorns. And sometimes we'd go along the lake, and we used to find these little tiny clams . . ."

Jordy's voice faded. For Carolyn, the air

had suddenly grown warm and humid, and smelled of summer rain.

. . . He was braced comfortably on the steep slope as if in arrested stride, downhill leg straight, uphill leg bent, one hand resting on the bent knee, head turned to watch her. He seemed as relaxed on that mountainside as a stag in the forest. As if, she thought, he owned the forest and everything that was in it, as if he knew exactly where his place on this earth was, and would always be . . .

"Mom?"

Carolyn felt a jab in her ribs and looked down, frowning. "What?"

"Who *is* that? Is he our neighbor?"

"I don't know," Carolyn murmured, half to herself. "I suppose he must be . . . maybe one of the Traynors. They had a bunch of kids."

"Well, why were you staring at him like that?"

"Staring? I was not."

"Yes you were, Mom. Like you'd seen a ghost, or something."

Carolyn shrugged. "Well, if I was, it was only because —" *Because for a moment I thought I knew him.* But she didn't say that, because déjà vu was such an ephemeral thing, and trying to explain it was like telling someone about a dream when the memory of it was already fading. "Because I didn't expect to see anyone here," she finished. "That's all."

"He's just watching us," Jordy said in an undertone. "Don't you think we should wave, or something?"

"Uh . . . yes," Carolyn said hesitantly, "I suppose we should." This was the rural South, after all, where people waved at each other when they met in their cars on the road.

"Well, I'm going to," Jordy said, and gave a huge, uninhibited child's wave.

After a moment's hesitation the man lifted a hand in acknowledgment, then came on down the hill. Carolyn saw that he carried a rifle loosely cradled in the crook of one arm.

" 'Mornin'," he called, nodding politely as he came toward them. His head was bare, his jacket unbuttoned. Under it he wore a brown plaid flannel shirt, and jeans tucked into the tops of leather boots. He looked freshly shaven and his brown hair was cut short and neatly combed. All in all there was nothing special about him, really, although something — maybe the steely, glint-eyed gaze or the rolling, sort of bow-legged walk — reminded Carolyn of someone, a movie star whose name she couldn't at the moment recall.

Maybe, she thought, that's all it was.

But if it was a movie she was remembering, why had she *smelled* it? Why had she felt it so unmistakably . . . the soft and sweltering embrace of summer?

"Good morning," she and Jordy both called out in response, drawing unconsciously closer together in the presence of the stranger.

They met on the footbridge at the bottom of the gulley.

"I'm your neighbor — John Clayton Traynor." Clay shifted his rifle to his left hand and held out his right, smiling a big, good-neighborly smile that felt about as comfortable to him as a pair of three-dollar shoes. "Folks generally call me Clay."

"Mr. Traynor." The woman's hand was stiff and cool, and so was her voice. Pure California. "How nice to meet you. I'm Carolyn Robards, and this is my daughter, Jordan." She let go of his hand as quickly as she could and used it to haul the kid up beside her, kind of like calling up reinforcements, Clay thought. From the kid he had a brief impression of California-cutie looks — blond hair, blue eyes, and winter tan spoiled by a sulky, sullen mouth — before the mother's polite voice continued, "We were just on our way over to say hello to John and Hannah Lee. I guess that would be —"

"My folks, yes," Clay helpfully confirmed, still trying to be neighborly. "They're gone now, though. I live on the place with —"

Lines of acute distress appeared between Mrs. Robards's eyebrows, like wrinkles in silk. "Oh," she whispered, "I'm so sorry."

"Not dead — just *gone*," Clay said kindly. "Dad got tired of farming and Mom's arthritis was getting worse, so they moved to Arizona and took up golf."

"I'm so glad," she breathed, her forehead smoothing out again. "I mean — I am disappointed they're gone. I was looking forward to seeing them again. I'll miss them."

It made him warm up to her quite a bit, knowing she'd thought so much of his mom and dad. He let his voice show it, and his smile grew less strained. "Well, don't worry," he said dryly, "they'll be coming for Christmas." There was an awkward pause. Clay shifted and said, "It's a good thing I decided to take the shortcut, or I guess we'd have missed each other. I was just on my way over to see if you folks needed anything."

The woman shook her head. Straight, heavy brown hair with streaks of sunshine gold in it bowed against, then brushed the tops of her shoulders. "That's very nice of you," she said in that cool, polite California voice. "But we don't need a thing. We're fine. Thank you."

"Oh," Clay said, and cleared his throat, any warm feelings he'd been starting to have cooling off again in a hurry. He was wondering what he was going to say next when he remembered the foil-wrapped package tucked inside the front of his jacket. He pulled it out and handed it to her with a careless shrug.

"Well, Miss Leona was worried about you," he said. "Sent you some of her fresh-baked . . . uh, biscuits."

"Miss Leona!" Carolyn Robards cried, smiling unexpectedly. "Oh — then she's still alive? I thought surely —"

Clay suddenly found himself looking at a stunningly beautiful woman. He sucked in air as if a sweet spring wind had hit him full in the face and managed to mumble, "Oh yes, ma'am, she's very much alive."

"But I thought, since the road was so overgrown . . ."

"Her cabin burned down last winter."

"Oh, how awful." She was frowning again.

"She lives with me now."

And the smile reappeared, just like the sun after a spring squall. "Oh — that's nice."

It was her eyes, he decided. Well, maybe her mouth, too. Wide-set hazel eyes touched with the same gold that was in her hair . . . a curiously unformed, almost childlike mouth, with a full upper lip that had very little indentation in it. Somehow those two features combined to give her a look of . . . well, *hope-*

fulness, a kind of wistful joy that tugged at his heart in unexpected ways.

Also unexpected was the way she kept looking at him, in a puzzled, searching way, as if she didn't know what to make of him, or was trying to think where she'd seen him before. Maybe that was what got him to wondering, too. Because all at once he found himself spinning backward through fourteen years of memory to the summer before he'd left to go North, the last summer of freedom before college, and Gillian. It was a sensation a lot like falling down a rabbit hole. It had been a long, long time, and he couldn't for the life of him remember . . .

It took a pointed "Ahem!" from behind Carolyn Robards to remind Clay that there were three people on the footbridge. He glanced at the kid standing there at her mother's elbow, shifted uneasily and said, "Well —"

Carolyn cleared her throat and threw her daughter a quick, almost furtive glance, then looked down at her feet and jammed her hands into her coat pockets. At about the level of her shoulder, a pair of steady blue eyes were blatantly giving him the once-over, and with a look Clay Traynor knew well. It was the street-tough, punk-kid look that says, Listen, mister, I've heard everything you've got to say, and don't believe a word of it.

Clay's good-ol'-boy Southern charm was a thin veneer at best, and it wouldn't take much from a smart-mouth kid to wear clear through it. He could feel his smile stiffening up and starting to slip already, so he nodded and murmured politely, "Well, ma'am, as long as you don't need anything . . ."

He'd turned and was about to make good his escape when the kid suddenly blurted out, "There's something in our basement."

He turned back, his boots scraping on the rough log planks of the bridge. Mrs. Robards was shaking her head, making motions with her hand as if to erase her daughter's words from the air. "Oh — no, really, I'm sure it's nothing. Just a possum, or a raccoon . . ."

"Personally," the girl said, affecting boredom now that she had his attention, "I think it's just a dog."

Clay frowned. "Whether it's a dog or a possum, it'd be dangerous cornered. You say it's in your basement?"

The girl shrugged. "Well, *something* is."

"I'd better have a look," Clay said in a resigned tone, and clumped back down the bridge toward the Robards side. The two women scrunched against the handrails to let him pass, then fell in behind him.

"If you're sure you don't mind," Carolyn said when they were on solid ground, a little out of breath from hurrying to catch up with him.

Clay glanced down at the top of her head, then quickly away again, surprised by a bump in his breathing. He coughed and said without expression, "No, ma'am, of course I don't mind. It's what I came over here for — to see if you needed any help."

"What are you going to do, shoot it?"

The kid had moved up on his left. He looked down and met her bright, avid stare, ignoring Carolyn's soft, dismayed, *"Jordan —"*

"With this?" he drawled, hefting his dad's old hunting rifle. "Honey, this thing ain't even loaded. All us Southern country rednecks take guns when we go out walkin' in the woods, don't you know that? It's kind of a cultural thing — maybe even genetic."

From Carolyn's direction came a gust of startled laughter, quickly smothered. Clay felt an odd sort of lightness inside his chest, and realized — much to his surprise — that he'd like very much to join in with that laughter. But the kid was still giving him that measuring, skeptical stare, and he didn't like to let go of it. He wasn't sure why. He sure as hell didn't feel like he had anything to prove, especially not to a smart-mouthed kid.

"I'm sorry," Carolyn said huskily, but her lips were still quivering and her eyes shining with that held-back laughter. He found himself wondering what it was about his remark that had tickled her so; it hadn't been *that* funny.

"Mr. Traynor —" She stumbled, and his hand shot out automatically to steady her.

"Call me Clay," he growled impatiently. But he'd liked the feel of her elbow in his hand.

Miss Leona, he said to himself, what in the world are you trying to do to me? The last thing in the world I need in my life is a divorced woman with a smart-mouthed kid!

Nobody said anything more until they got to the Robards place. Then Carolyn muttered, sort of self-consciously, "It's around back, down here . . ." and went slip-sliding around the corner of the house.

Clay followed, pausing to take in the nice view of the lake and the pair of Canadian geese he could see settling onto the surface of it. When he caught up with Mrs. Robards she was standing in front of the basement door, her head turned toward him, an odd, troubled look on her face.

"It's shut," she said in a hushed voice. "I'm sure I left it open last night."

"Draft probably blew it shut." Clay reached past her and turned the doorknob. But it occurred to him as he pushed the door open on its stiff rusty hinges that it would have had to be one heck of a draft for that to happen.

He looked down at Carolyn and said softly, "Ma'am?" She sidestepped hastily out of his way.

"Are you sure you know what you're doing?" the smart-mouthed kid asked him, strolling up with her hands in her hip pockets.

Clay ignored her and went on squinting into the darkness beyond the doorway.

"Who knows," the girl said in a hushed, gleeful voice, "maybe it's a bear, or a mountain lion in there."

He threw her a look over his shoulder. She was all wide-eyed innocence, but with a gleam in those baby blues that suggested it might please her greatly if there was a bear in the basement, especially since he'd told her his gun wasn't loaded.

"There's worse things," he muttered, and stepped into the gloom.

Inside the door he paused, listening. He couldn't hear a thing, not even the telltale scurryings of mice. But he could feel his heart pounding, and he could feel the cold, clammy film of sweat on his forehead. Easy, he said to himself. Take it easy . . .

The basement was large, covering the whole length of the house and dug back into the side of the hill. In the half-darkness he could see that it held a number of unidentifiable objects big enough to hide undesirable creatures of varying sizes, including bears, or worse. Wishing he had a flashlight, he leaned against the wall and shut his eyes while he waited for his night vision to take effect.

It was a mistake. The minute he closed his eyes his ears filled with sounds: city sounds, distant and muted — horns honking, voices calling, sirens wailing; the small, crisp, close-up sounds of tension and stealth — water dripping, the betraying creak of a floorboard, the sounds of frightened breathing. His nostrils were filled with the oily, fetid smells of poverty, of too many people crammed into too little space. He heard a baby crying down a dark hallway, smelled cooking, and human waste. He felt his heart pounding, and the cold trickle of sweat between his shoulder blades.

He fought to open his eyes, but they refused to obey him. Against the backs of his eyelids he saw the room clearly, as clearly as the image on a television screen — just like the one that had been there that morning. In its flickering silver light he saw the pallet on the floor, the pile of blankets, the meager, pitiful Christmas tree. And just beyond it, the shadow on the wall, the shadow in the shape of a head, shoulders, arm . . . and a hand holding a gun.

His own gun was heavy in his hand. His finger was on the trigger, sweat-slippery but steady. His jaws ached with tension. *Come on . . . come on . . .* His finger tightened, a heart-beat away . . .

Nausea overwhelmed him. Ice-cold and trembling, he fought free of the nightmare, groping for the basement doorway like a drowning man reaching for the light.

Chapter 2

"Mr. Traynor, are you all right?" He could hear Carolyn's voice, tight with concern.

"I'm fine," Clay ground out between clenched teeth. "Nothing in there that I can see. Whatever was in there, it's gone now." He took deep, determined breaths, pressing his back against the wall, feeling the rough, reassuring texture of wood siding through his jacket.

The smart-mouthed kid chirped with obvious relish, "Wow, you look awful. You look like you've seen a ghost."

"Mr. Traynor —" Carolyn's fingers brushed his coat sleeve, a brief, anxious touch.

He looked down, his forehead creasing as he met those oddly set golden eyes. He cleared his throat and said it again more firmly. "I'm *fine*." But his voice was harsh and rough, and she snatched her hand away as if he'd slapped it. Regret washed through him unexpectedly. He tried his best to make amends, adding with a crooked half-smile, "Just a little touch of claustrophobia. Comes when I least expect it."

"You should have said something." She sounded accusing, almost angry.

He pushed stiffly away from the wall. "I would have, if I'd thought it was important. It's no big deal — don't make one out of it."

At that the smart-mouthed kid kind of rolled her eyes and said cryptically, "See, Mom? Looks like Dad was right."

Clay gave her one quick, hard look as he pulled the basement door closed, but he wasn't really interested in knowing what it was her dad was right about. Because he was thinking again that there wasn't a wind short of a hurricane that could have blown that door shut, and it didn't make him happy that what- or whoever had been in the basement yesterday had so thoughtfully closed the door behind him when he left.

Carolyn shoved her hands into her coat pockets and said breathlessly, "Well, I guess that's that," ending what had become an awkward little silence. "Whatever it was, it's gone. See, honey? Just like I said it would. Harriet knew it before we did."

Jordy snorted. Clay said, "Harriet?"

"Our cat," Carolyn explained. "She spent most of the night carrying on about the thing in the basement, but she seemed to settle down okay this morning. I think she knew the minute it was gone. Right around daylight, wasn't it, Jordy?"

"Daylight?" Clay liked that no better than

he liked the closed door. As far as he knew, most critters likely to move into a vacant basement — the four-legged ones, anyway — were nocturnal. They'd be out and about during the night and holed up during the day, not the other way around.

But he didn't mention his concerns, not wanting to scare the lady out of feeling safe in her own house. Anyway, he thought there was a good possibility it was just him. Nine and a half years with the Chicago Police Department couldn't help but leave a blight on his soul, and he knew it did tend sometimes to warp and darken his thinking. He reminded himself that this wasn't Chicago, this was lake country, western South Carolina. God's Country. He'd grown up in these woods, in the foothills of the Great Smokies. And while there'd been one or two unfortunate incidents way back in the sixties, since then about the only danger around here had been to the deer and wild turkeys that called these woods home. Some of Miss Leona's relatives weren't above poaching.

Anyway, even if he was still feeling uneasy about things, there didn't seem to be anything else he could do for Carolyn Robards. Whatever had been in that basement, it wasn't there now. So he cleared his throat and said, "Well if you're sure you have everything you need

44

. . . power and propane all okay?"

Carolyn nodded and smiled in a gentle way, as though she found his concern rather quaint. "Yes, thank you, we've managed."

Clay frowned. "Telephone?"

"They've promised me it will be connected today."

"Well, okay." And then he couldn't think of any excuse to stay, or, for the life of him, think why he should want to. The lady and her smart-mouthed kid didn't need him, and he sure as hell had things he needed to be doing. Annoyed without knowing quite why, he picked up his rifle from where he'd leaned it against the wall and shifted it to his left hand.

"I guess I'll be going," he said gruffly, then cleared his throat and slipped with relief into familiar if half-forgotten rituals of hospitality. "Ya'll come on over when you can, you hear? Miss Leona will be glad to see you." He lifted his right hand to his temple in a careless gesture of farewell.

Since he was looking right at her just then he saw it happen — saw Carolyn Robards's face suddenly change and that *look* come into her eyes. The same look she'd worn when he'd met her on the bridge, the half-puzzling, half-eager look of recognition. It unnerved him, made him feel awkward and uncertain, which he wasn't used to and definitely didn't like. He kind of checked, half-turned, then pivoted back again with an unformed question hovering on his lips.

Her lips parted and she made a small sound, as if she'd started to say something and caught it back just in time. Annoyed, Clay frowned and began again to turn away.

"Mr. Traynor —"

He did an exasperated about-face. "Yes, ma'am?"

"I was just . . . would you like to come in for a cup of coffee?"

The smart-mouthed kid muttered something under her breath which her mother and Clay both ignored. He studied Carolyn's face for a moment, then drawled softly, "Well, ma'am, I might consider it, if you'd do me one favor."

"What's that?" Her voice had a hushed, breathless quality that softened the California brittleness and touched something dormant deep inside him.

"Could you stop calling me 'Mr. Traynor'? Every time you do it I want to look over my shoulder, expecting to see my dad standing there."

She smiled, and his loins stirred. "Well," she said huskily, "I might consider it . . . if you'd do *me* one favor."

He almost chuckled, but caught himself. "What's that?"

"Could you stop calling me 'ma'am'?"

"Carolyn," he drawled, "you've got yourself a deal." He stuck out his hand and they shook on it. Her hand didn't seem stiff at all now, or cold, either.

It was strange, Carolyn thought, how different the house seemed with Clay Traynor in it. More crowded, for one thing. He was so very tall, taller than he'd seemed out in the open with the trees looming all around. Indoors he moved in the slow and careful way big people often do, a habit probably born of a thousand small but embarrassing mishaps. But it was more than that, more even than the sudden case of nerves that had afflicted her the moment she'd opened her mouth and blurted out the invitation to have coffee, surprising no one more than herself. (Goodness only knew what *Jordy* was thinking!)

No, the difference in the house was something else, something not easy to define or pin down. It just seemed . . . *less empty* with Clay in it, Carolyn decided. Which wasn't the same thing as *more crowded*. Not the same thing at all.

She invited him to sit down in one of the chrome and plastic chairs that went with the chrome and Formica kitchen table, then dithered at the sink, trying to decide how much coffee to make. It would brew more quickly, she reasoned, if she only made enough for her guest. But then — would it be awkward if she didn't have a cup too? Things seemed awkward enough already, and it certainly didn't help matters that Jordy had plunked herself down in the chair opposite Clay, elbows on the tabletop, fingers laced beneath her chin, and was subjecting him to her Harriet Impression — a silent, unblinking, eerily catlike stare. Which he was valiantly ignoring.

Carolyn was suddenly filled with painful embarrassment, and a shaming sense of inadequacy. She knew Jordy's manners were appalling, but she couldn't say anything without humiliating the child in front of company, and no doubt creating an uncomfortable situation for her guest as well. She was a professional counselor — why was it so hard to know what to do about her own child? All the advice she gave so freely to others seemed to elude her. Parenthood, which had always seemed so natural and fulfilling, had lately become like a maze through which she stumbled daily, taking wrong turns and getting nowhere.

To her great relief, Harriet chose that moment to voice her displeasure at finding herself on the wrong side of a closed door. Clay looked startled. Jordy said loudly, "Oops, Harriet's awake," and jumped up to answer the summons. The door to her bedroom opened and closed, and the kitchen filled with silence.

Carolyn found that she had to try hard to concentrate on the simple task of making coffee. I'm nervous, she thought in surprise, and instantly wondered why. Professionally, she'd faced silent strangers every day, and had always felt confident and in control. What was it about this particular stranger that made her feel vulnerable and uncertain in her own kitchen? Oh, how she regretted, now, the impulse that had made her invite him into her house. Why had she done that, when she was barely moved in herself, and so ill-prepared for company?

Oh yes, she remembered — it had been that moment of recognition. Of realizing at last just where it was she'd seen him.

"Do you take cream or sugar?" She threw the casual question over her shoulder as she measured coffee into the drip basket, enough for two cups, and was bemused at the breathlessness in her own voice.

"A little cream, if you have it."

She waited for the "ma'am," and smiled to herself when it remained unspoken, remembering the moment the bargain had been sealed, the handshake . . . "Is milk all right?"

49

"Milk'll do fine."

She filled the glass pot to the correct line with water straight from the tap, poured it into the coffee maker, then took the carton of milk out of the refrigerator and placed it on the table, noticing as she did the long-boned, weathered hands that rested there. Quiet, relaxed, confident hands. Strong, work-hardened hands. She remembered suddenly, vividly how those hands had felt wrapped around hers, and frowned as an unexpected thrill wafted through her, like a cool breeze over naked skin.

She didn't sit down, choosing instead to maintain the distance between them, leaning against the counter and folding her arms across her waist. Behind her the coffee began to trickle slowly into the glass pot.

"So, Mr. Traynor —" she began in what she knew was a stilted, overpolite voice, then self-consciously amended, "*Clay* . . . you've taken over the farm, then? When did John and Hannah Lee move away? I'm sorry, I guess it's been longer than I realized since I was here last. It must have been . . ." She thought about it and was surprised herself. "Oh heavens, at least six years." So much had happened to her in those six years. She'd changed so much, and yet . . . She forced a smile and finished the thought out loud. "You really don't expect things to change when you're not around to see them."

"Yes," Clay said, politely noncommittal, "I know what you mean."

Which seemed to be another conversational dead end. Carolyn coughed and changed the subject. "I believe I've met your sisters — two of them, anyway. The older ones. They were married and living . . . let me see . . . one in Atlanta and the other in Greenville, wasn't it?"

"Still are," Clay confirmed with a nod.

"And of course, I remember the little girls, too — goodness, they must be grown up now. And I thought there were three boys in between, but. . . ." She paused, annoyed with Clay for being of so little help, for letting her flounder when he knew very well what she wanted to know and was too polite to ask. *Which one of the Traynor brood are you, and why don't I remember you?*

"There are," said Clay. His gaze was light and soft, and there were curving lines of amusement bracketing the corners of his mouth, like parentheses. "I've been away. Living up North — Chicago. I just came back two years ago."

"Oh," Carolyn murmured, distracted by the way the parentheses multiplied and the fan of creases at the corners of his eyes deepened

51

when he smiled. It made him seem more attractive than she'd first thought. A lot more. "Then I guess it couldn't have been —"

"Couldn't have been . . . ?"

She shook her head, smiling a little at her own sense of disappointment. She'd been so sure. That little gesture, the hand raised to the temple, the relaxed, easy stance . . .

"Oh, it's nothing," she said. "I just thought I'd seen you before." She made a gesture with her hand, dismissing the notion. "It was a long time ago."

And her emotional state at the time had been precarious, at best. So, she'd been mistaken. It had been another Traynor, perhaps, a brother or a cousin. Someone else as tall, lean, and cocksure, someone else who walked the woods like the lord of all he surveyed.

"How long ago?" Clay asked, frowning. "If I'd met you, I think I'd have remembered."

"Not necessarily," Carolyn said, laughing now to cover a pleasant surge of warmth to her cheeks, because the glint in his eyes when he said that made it unmistakably — though she thought probably unintentionally — a compliment. "It was fourteen years ago — well, fourteen and a half — and we didn't exactly *meet*."

"Fourteen years?" Clay's keen blue eyes were resting on her, thoughtfully squinted.

"Summer, right? Then it could have been me. That would have been the summer before I left for Chicago."

"It was July," Carolyn said, hearing her own voice as if it were someone else's, and far away. "It was the first time Russell — my husband — brought me here. I . . . had gone for a walk, and I found the footbridge, the one at the bottom of the gulley. I was standing there, wondering if I should cross it . . . wondering who owned the woods on the other side, and whether they'd mind if I trespassed. . . ." *Wondering if I could somehow cross that bridge and just keep right on going.*

She'd been eighteen years old that summer, newly married and realizing already what a terrible mistake she'd made, feeling trapped and helpless, and desperately alone. And then she'd looked across the gulley.

She'd seen him standing there, braced on the steep slope as if in arrested stride . . . as relaxed on that mountainside as a stag in the forest, as if he owned the forest and everything that was in it, as if he knew exactly where his place on this earth was, and would always be.

He'd seen her, too, and lifted his hand to his temple in a jaunty salute, grinning with engaging arrogance, openly flirting. And in response to that wave and that grin her eighteen-year-old heart had taken wing. For the first time in a very long time she felt young, attractive . . . desirable. Oh, but she *was* young! Her life was just beginning, all things were possible, and mistakes could be corrected.

With that smile and wave the young man in the woods had gone on his way, and Carolyn had returned to the summer house, all set to tell Russell she wanted a divorce. But before she could, the telephone call had come from the hospital in California with the test results that had changed everything. Eighteen and on her own, all things might indeed be possible. Eighteen, alone, and pregnant was something else entirely.

"I do remember," Clay said slowly. His eyes were narrowed, now, and very intent. "I remember you. My God, I was so full of myself that summer. I was going away to college. Up North. Chicago — Northwestern, on a basketball scholarship." He shook his head and his voice grew very soft. "I couldn't wait to go."

"And you stayed away twelve years?" Carolyn found that she was hugging herself, containing strange little shivers.

Clay shrugged and looked away. His lips took on an odd, bitter twist. "Well," he drawled, "what happened was, I met my wife in college. She was a Northerner and wanted to stay in Chicago, so I did, too. We were both sociology majors. She became a social worker, and I became a cop."

"A cop! Really? No kidding?" Jordy had returned to the kitchen with her arms full of grouchy, round-eyed feline, just in time to catch the last part. The effect of her entrance was like a large rock dropped into a quiet pond. She flopped ungracefully into a chair and leaned forward to inquire with ghoulish excitement, "Did you ever, you know, *shoot* anybody?"

Carolyn uttered a small, shocked gasp, then pressed her fingertips to her lips to hold back a reprimand. Clay looked over at her, eyes quizzical . . . waiting for her response. She opened her mouth, then shook her head in mute apology, and the hard blue gaze swiveled slowly back to Jordy.

"Little girl," he said in a soft, dangerous voice that had no trace at all of the South in it, "having met your mother, I've got to believe you were taught better manners."

How, Carolyn wondered, was it possible to burn with shame and feel frozen at the same time? She felt as stiff and cold as Jordy's face, felt the stab of a child's humiliation in her own heart. The shame, of course, was hers, but that didn't keep all her maternal instincts from rushing in trembling fury to her child's defense.

She said "Jordy —" and put out her hand, but Jordy's chair had already hit the floor with a metallic clang. The slamming of her bedroom door left an echoing silence, irreverently broken by the belch and gurgle of the coffeemaker coming to the end of its brewing cycle.

Carolyn turned abruptly to the counter, wielding mugs and coffee pot with jerky, uncoordinated hands. "I wish you hadn't done that," she said in a low voice, struggling for self-control.

"Ma'am, I wish I hadn't had to." Clay's voice was just as low as hers, and seemed to achieve without apparent effort the calm that eluded her. "It wasn't my place."

"No, it wasn't." She set a steaming mug carefully in front of him, avoiding his eyes.

After what seemed like a long, long silence he said softly, "I'm sorry." She could feel him watching her, the awareness like the brush of fingers across her skin.

He's nice. The thought came to her with mild surprise — though why she couldn't imagine. She knew a brief surge of resentment. Why shouldn't he be nice? He came from a very nice family, with wonderful parents, a big, noisy house full of children . . . the kind of family she'd always envied, and dreamed of being part of.

But . . . it had been very nice of him to come over and offer to help — although of course she didn't *need* any help. Fourteen years of marriage to Russell Robards — not to mention her childhood — had taught her how to manage very well on her own. No, she thought as she poured herself a cup of coffee, I'm the one who's sorry. Sorry for spoiling whatever it was that was happening between us. Friendship, maybe? She didn't need help, but she could have used a friend.

She poured herself a cup of coffee and turned with it, leaning back against the chrome edge of the counter and curving her hands around the cup for warmth — and courage. "So it's 'ma'am' again, is it?" She kept her voice light and put a touch of a smile in it, hoping to repair the damage, or at least end the silence. It had never worked with Russell; when he was miffed, his silence could go on for days. "I thought we had a deal."

"Yeah, we did," Clay said, giving her a quick glance as he sat up straight and reached for the cream pitcher. "I just figured since you're mad at me, all bets might be off."

"I'm not mad at you."

"Well, if a stranger yelled at my kid I would

be," Clay said, then paused. "Even if she did deserve it."

Carolyn sipped coffee while she tried to decide whether she really was angry and maybe repressing it. It was the kind of thing she asked her patients a lot. But she was pretty sure that all she felt was embarrassment for Jordy's rudeness, and frustration at her own inability to do anything about it. She had a sudden urge to ask Clay for advice, which confused her, since she was supposed to be the expert on troubled teenagers, and she didn't even know whether Clay had children. Come to think of it, she didn't even know whether or not he was still married.

"I want you to know," she said in a low voice, after a quick glance toward the bedroom, "she's not usually like this. She, um . . . she was very badly hurt by her dad's — by the divorce. She feels . . . betrayed. Abandoned." She stopped and looked hard at her coffee cup.

Clay said, "If it's hard for you to talk about, don't. You don't have to explain anything to me."

Her eyes flew upward and found his. "Oh, but I do," she said softly, and instantly wondered why that should be so. After a long moment both the silence and the eye contact began to feel weighted with a significance she didn't really understand, so she ended both, looking down at her cup once more and clearing her throat. When she continued, it was in her professional voice.

"You see, she's very resentful and suspicious of men right now. She's confused. She's at an age where she wants attention and affection from the opposite sex, but she feels she can't trust them."

"Smart girl," Clay said dryly. He stood up and carried his empty mug to the sink, pausing close by her side to look down at her. The lazy, half-closed eyes held the unmistakable gleam of irony. "We men are definitely not to be trusted."

Carolyn murmured, "What makes you say that?" Air seemed suddenly to be in short supply, perhaps because he was taking up so much of the supply in her immediate vicinity. She felt a sultriness, reminiscent of thunderstorms. She heard the crack and rumble of laughter, a remarkably pleasant, faintly exciting sound.

"Carolyn, ma'am, if you don't mind my sayin' so, you sound an awful lot like a shrink."

"Oh, really?" she replied coolly; she'd never cared for being referred to as a "shrink." "Have you had so much experience with shrinks?"

"Oh yeah . . . a bit." This time his chuckle

was less pleasant, the gleam in his eyes frankly sardonic. "Like I said, my wife was a social worker. I'm accustomed to psychobabble with my morning coffee."

He turned abruptly back to the sink, splashed water in the coffee mug, placed it in the drainer and wiped his hands on the dish-towel, then folded the towel carefully and hung it neatly over the edge of the sink. Not the habits, Carolyn noted, of a married man.

"Was?" she ventured.

He shook his head and spoke without turning, in a voice utterly devoid of expression. "My wife died almost three years ago — three days before Christmas, as a matter of fact. She was stabbed to death by one of the people she was trying to help — a homeless Vietnam vet, strung out on drugs. He was apparently having a flashback and thought she was the Viet Cong. Knowing her, she'd probably have said he was 'confused.' "

There was a long pause while they stood there side by side, Clay's hands resting on the edge of the counter, Carolyn leaning against it. Silence filled up the space between them, thick as a cushion.

Finally Carolyn cleared her throat and said, "I'm sorry."

His shrug made it plain that the subject wasn't one he wanted to pursue — a real conversation stopper, in fact. Carolyn made a mental note to avoid the subject of Clay's marriage like the plague in the future, which was fine with her; she didn't much like to talk about hers, either.

"Well, thanks for the coffee," he said as he turned from the sink and hooked one finger under the collar of his jacket, lifting it off the back of his chair. "I'd better be getting on back."

Carolyn stayed where she was and watched as he lifted his arms and swung the jacket around his shoulders, noticing the long, lean lines of his body, the jeans riding low on narrow hips . . . She pushed away from the counter abruptly and followed him to the door, murmuring polite things in a curiously breathless voice. "Well, if you're sure you . . ."

He paused suddenly, turned and leaned against the doorframe. "Now I'm curious," he drawled, and she saw that the spark of amusement was back in his eyes. "You're *not* a shrink, are you?"

In spite of his insistence on the word "shrink," Carolyn found herself smiling. "Well, not quite. I'm a licensed MFC."

"Oh yeah? What's that?"

"Marriage and Family Counselor."

"Ah." He shook his head and made a clicking sound of chagrin. "And I just thought everybody out in California talked that way. Sorry — I was out of line. You planning to go into practice around here?"

"I might," Carolyn said. "Eventually. Right now I'm writing a book."

"Oh yeah?" He straightened up and looked more than just politely interested, which was about the sort of response Carolyn was coming to expect to that announcement. There was something about saying you were writing a book that always touched a chord in people, maybe, she thought, because nearly everyone had thought about doing it at one time or another. "What about?"

"My subspecialty — job burnout."

"Huh," said Clay. He was silent for a moment, then slapped the doorframe. "Well — I've got things to do, and I'm sure you do, too. Listen, I meant what I said. You come on over when you get a chance and say hello to Miss Leona."

"I will," said Carolyn. "I promise."

Halfway out the door he turned back. "You need anything, you give me a call, you hear?"

"Yes, thank you, I will." And then, when it was almost too late, remembered something she should have mentioned before. "Oh — by the way. . . ." He turned back once more, a question and a smile in his eyes, and suddenly there didn't seem to be enough air to go

62

around again. "Thank you again," she said breathlessly, "for checking out the basement. I'm sorry about the claustrophobia. You really should have said something."

His face closed and he didn't reply, just touched his temple in that way that already seemed so familiar.

After he had gone she went on standing there for a few moments, staring at the place where he'd been. *So that's my neighbor.* She felt a little dazed, thoughts and impressions filling her head like dry leaves in a whirlwind. A Southern farm boy who'd become a Chicago cop, and now was home again . . . a nice man, but one who didn't like to talk about his past . . . a strong, confident man who nevertheless suffered from claustrophobia so acute it made him physically ill . . . What an intriguing mix! And from the sound of things, just possibly an ideal case study for her book.

But Carolyn was too much a psychotherapist to allow herself to escape the truth — and the whole truth — about her own feelings. She wasn't kidding herself. She knew perfectly well that her reaction to Clay Traynor had been something a lot more basic than professional curiosity. The fact was, she couldn't remember ever having felt such a strong physical attraction to a man. She found that very disturbing, in more ways than one. The timing couldn't have been worse; right now she had to concentrate on Jordy, and on getting her own life put back together again. And even when she'd managed that, she didn't think she wanted a man in it, not on a permanent basis, anyway. She had a chance to start over, to be her own person for the first time in her life, and she didn't want to blow it this time. She didn't need anybody. No — she didn't *want* to need anybody. Ever again.

Presently she formed the word "Oh —" with her lips, huffed out air and finished it with a whispered, "— *boy*." Then she resolutely crossed the room and tapped on Jordy's bedroom door.

"Honey?"

Jordy was lying on her back on her unmade bed, knees drawn up and crossed, one arm pillowing her head, the other hand idly stroking Harriet, who lay like a limp sphinx across her stomach. The cat's tail was twitching, the expression on her face resembling that of a miffed owl. Jordy's expression was unreadable.

"Is he gone?" she inquired without looking up.

"Yes, he is." Carolyn sat down on the edge of the bed and waited. When Jordy remained stubbornly silent, she prodded gently, "Jordan, is there anything you'd like to say —"

"Before I pass sentence?" Jordy intoned in a sepulchral voice. She heaved a deep, solemn sigh. "I suppose . . . I have been unforgivably rude."

"Rude, yes," Carolyn said, smiling in spite of her best intentions. The old Jordy always had been able to make her laugh. "Unforgivable . . . no. Do you have any idea why you were behaving like such a . . ."

"Brat?" Jordy offered helpfully. Her head moved slowly from side to side. "Uh-uh."

Treading carefully, Carolyn said, "Was it something about Clay? Did you just . . . not like him?"

Jordy shrugged. "He's okay." Keeping her eyes on the cat, she said in a light, neutral tone, "You liked him. And he couldn't keep his eyes off you."

So that was it.

"Jordy, for heaven's sake," Carolyn exclaimed, briskly rumpling her daughter's already mussed, cornsilk hair, "I was only being neighborly. And so was he. *And* might I remind you, lovey, *you* were the one who asked him to check out the basement, remember? *I* was trying to tell him we didn't need any help. Come on —" She stood up and bounced the bed hard enough to dislodge Harriet, who vaulted to the floor and crouched there, tail twitching, looking royally unamused. "Get up

65

— the haze has burned off and it looks like it's going to be a nice day. Spruce yourself up a little, and let's go shopping."

"Shopping?" Ah, the magic word. "Where? Is there a mall —"

"*Grocery* shopping."

Jordy's face fell. "Oh, yippee."

But the drive into town did seem to go a long way toward lifting her spirits. And Carolyn's, too. She was surprised to discover how little had changed and how much she remembered, and was inordinately pleased when she found the Bi-Lo Market with only one wrong turn.

Jordy was thrilled to discover that all her old favorite snack foods were available here too, and went up and down the aisles greeting them like long-lost friends. ("Where did you think we were going?" Carolyn asked her when she found her cooing over Twinkies. "Tibet?")

They found Christmas, too, alive and well — flourishing, in fact — at the Wal-Mart next door. "See?" Carolyn said as they wheeled their cart up and down aisles and aisles of tree lights and tinsel, tubes of wrapping paper and pyramids of potted poinsettias, listening to canned carols on the loudspeaker. "There's everything we need for Christmas right here, all under one roof, just like a mall."

"It's a lot more fun going to the mall with your friends," Jordy said wistfully, her mouth beginning to droop again. With a pang of guilt, Carolyn suggested buying funny Christmas cards to send to all her friends, which perked her up a bit. She even went so far as to pick out a particularly outrageous "Far Side" card for her dad and "the Strawberry Tart."

While her daughter pored over the greeting-card racks, Carolyn prowled the aisles, buying dishtowels, wastebaskets, a rug for the kitchen, a small color TV, and, since she had no intention of wasting valuable writing time cooking — something she'd never gotten much satisfaction out of anyway — a microwave oven. In addition to the cards, Jordy bought two new *Star Trek* paperbacks with her week's allowance, and appealed to her mother to add an "economy-sized" box of microwave popcorn packets to the already overflowing shopping cart.

They also looked over the assortment of Christmas trees in the chickenwire enclosure next to the garden shop, but Jordy dismissed them all as either too tall or "too weedy."

"We shouldn't wait too long," Carolyn warned, "or they'll all be gone. We can't really afford to be choosy."

"We have Christmas trees in our woods," said Jordy. "I saw them. Why can't we just cut one of them down?"

"Cut our own tree?" Carolyn considered that idea with mixed feelings. She'd always rationalized the annual destruction of millions of living trees by telling herself that they were a farm crop grown for that sole purpose, providing employment and livelihood for a lot of people. There was no such justification for cutting down a tree growing in happy isolation in the forest. But still . . . visions of herself and Jordy dragging a vanquished pine tree through snowy woods filled her mind like Currier and Ives Christmas cards. "I'm not sure we can," she mused regretfully. "It's probably illegal."

"Ha," Jordy argued, "it's our woods, so they're our trees. We should be able to do anything we want with them."

Carolyn wasn't convinced that was so, but promised to look into it. "Clay would know," she said thoughtfully. Jordy lapsed pointedly into silence.

By the time they got home after a late lunch at McDonald's it was mid-afternoon, and the weak winter sunshine was already losing its warmth. Harriet met them at the front door, quite restored to her bad-tempered, imperious self and complaining bitterly about having been left home alone all day with an empty food dish.

As soon as the car had been unloaded, Jordy put on her jacket and went out, saying she was going to scout for Christmas trees in the woods. Carolyn spent the rest of the afternoon scrubbing cupboards, putting away groceries, and reading instruction manuals for the microwave oven and the TV set. She was attempting to fine-tune the latter when Jordy returned, rosy-cheeked, red-nosed, and smug, to announce that she'd found a perfect tree, and not far from the house, either. Carolyn glanced distractedly at the windows and pointed out that it was already getting dark outside, and she would have to wait until tomorrow to inspect it.

"Look, what do you think?" she said proudly, standing back from the television and wielding the remote control with a flourish. "We get three channels . . . sort of. This one . . . this — no, wait. That's not it. There — see? Through the snow — isn't that —"

"No cable," Jordy said bleakly. "That's great, Mom." She made herself a bowl of microwaved popcorn and retired to her room with her *Star Trek* novels, Harriet twining and scolding around her ankles.

Carolyn sighed and turned off the TV, then sat for a moment, listening to the silence. The wonderful smells of butter and popcorn permeated the house, but although her stomach rumbled in predictable response, she found that she lacked the energy even to get up off the couch. It was the stress of the past few days — weeks, even — catching up with her, she supposed. Closing her practice, packing, putting her furniture in storage, getting ready for the trip, keeping up a positive front for Jordy's sake while her own doubts and fears kept her awake at night. She'd come so far . . . And now, hovering on the brink of a new beginning for both herself and Jordy, she suddenly felt drained, exhausted, weighed down.

With a masterful exercise of willpower she picked up a seven-year-old copy of *Reader's Digest* and thumbed through it, wishing she'd followed Jordy's example and picked up something to read from the paperback book rack at Wal-Mart. Her briefcase, which she could see out of the corner of her eye, was a silent reproach and a reminder of what she'd come here to do, but opening it up and facing her notes and tapes was far beyond her capabilities at the moment.

One day at a time — that was how she'd gotten through more years than she cared to think about. One day at a time, and this one was all but over. She'd feel better tomorrow. Tomorrow she'd start working on the book, when she felt fresh and rested.

She pulled a faded afghan over her legs and settled into the dusty couch cushions, determined to lose herself in the gripping account of one woman's survival following an Arctic plane crash . . .

"Mom! Mom, wake up."

"I'm awake." Carolyn found herself sitting upright, with adrenaline coursing through every vein and trembling in every muscle. "What is it? What's wrong?"

Jordy was standing beside the couch, clutching Harriet to her chest. "Mom —" she hissed, "you know that thing in the basement? It's *back*. I heard it. Oh God, Mom — it's making noises!"

Chapter 3

"The first thing we have to do," Carolyn mumbled, "is keep calm." She stood up and groped for her jacket.

"What are you going to do?" Jordy asked tensely. She sounded genuinely frightened. "You're not going down there!"

Carolyn frowned, pausing in the middle of an unsuccessful struggle to shove her arm into a coat sleeve. "Well, what do you suggest I do?"

"I don't know — call somebody. Call the police!"

"The police? For a possum?"

"I don't think it's a possum," Jordy said in an awed tone, slowly shaking her head. "You should have heard it. It sounded like a *ghost*."

"Great," Carolyn said with gritted teeth. Now it was her zipper that wouldn't cooperate. "I'm sure it would make the police feel a lot happier about coming all the way out here if they knew it was for a ghost, and not just a plain old possum. Where did I put the flashlight?"

"Mom —" Jordy gave a squawk as Harriet suddenly vaulted from her arms, hit the floor with a thud, and streaked for the bedroom. A moment later they heard the ghastly, ululating yowl that only a very angry cat can produce. "See?" said Jordy. "I told you. She hears it, too. Come on, Mom — you've got to listen to this."

Carolyn followed Jordy into the bedroom, both of them, for some reason, tiptoeing. "What are we —" she began in exasperation, then stopped as if the words had been choked off.

Jordy had picked Harriet up and was attempting to soothe and comfort her, and as the cat's racket subsided to low, menacing growls Carolyn heard another sound. A sound that prickled her scalp and raised goosebumps on her arms. Not ghostly sounds — at least, she didn't think so — but something much, much worse. It was muffled and distant, to be sure, but she'd heard it too many times before to be mistaken. Something — or someone — was weeping.

"Mom — where are you going?" There was real panic in the question, because Carolyn was already on her way out of the room. Jordy lunged after her and caught her by the arm. "Please — you're not going down there!"

"I certainly am. Honey —"

"Mom, *please* don't go. Please . . . I'm really *scared*." Jordy looked around frantically for some source of aid and finding none handy blurted out in desperation, "Look — you could call somebody. You could call a neighbor — what's his name — Mr. Traynor."

Carolyn hesitated. "Clay?"

"He'd come, I know he would. And he has a gun, Mom."

A gun that's not loaded. "Oh, I don't think —" She took a deep breath, held it while she thought about it, then let it out in a rush. "I don't know his number."

Jordy gave her that "parents are so dumb" look. "Try information, Mom. I'm sure he's listed."

"I don't even know if the phone's hooked up yet!" But when she picked up the receiver, there was the dial tone, loud and clear. Sending up a silent thank-you to utility companies that kept promises, she spun out the three digits on the old-fashioned rotary dial and waited, trying not to fidget. After several rings a cheerful voice with an accent thick as molasses said, "City an' listin', please."

"I'm not sure it's a city," Carolyn said doubtfully. "It's Harkness County — near Mayville. Traynor."

There was a brief pause and then the voice said, "Ma'am, we have several Traynors listed."

"Clay," said Carolyn. "No, wait — it's John

Clayton. Try that."

"We have a J. C. Traynor, ma'am. Would that be it?"

"I guess I'll find out," Carolyn muttered. She repeated the number twice under her breath and hung up the receiver.

Before she picked it up again she wiped her hand on her pants and briefly closed her eyes, struggling for calm.

"Mom," Jordy said, eyeing her closely, "you want me to call?"

"No," Carolyn said. The worst of it was, she knew her sweaty palms and pounding heart weren't for fear of the thing in the basement. Oh God, she thought, I hate this. *I hate needing . . . anyone.* But she had Jordy to think about. After a moment she took a deep breath, picked up the phone, and began once more to dial . . .

Clay was in his office doing the weekly bookkeeping, which he hated, so he let the telephone ring four times before he picked it up, just out of orneriness.

"Yeah," he said, more impatiently than usual because he had a column that didn't add up right. Besides, he couldn't think who'd be calling him at eight o'clock on a Thursday night except one of his brothers or sisters. His parents always called on weekends, when the rates were low.

It was a woman's voice, soft, breathless, and familiar. Pure California, cool and accentless as a news broadcaster's. "Oh, I'm sorry. Did I wake you?"

He chuckled and tipped his chair back. He hadn't really noticed it before, but the voice was damned attractive. "Hello, there, California. No, ma'am, not hardly. I'm too old to be put to bed at eight and too young to fall asleep in my chair. What can I do for you?"

There was a soft gasp and then a rustling sound, as if she'd rearranged the phone to look at her watch. "Is *that* all it is? I didn't realize . . ."

Clay's chair creaked upright and his feet scraped the floor, because he'd just heard a certain note of anxiety in the voice that made him quit flirting in a hurry and sit up straight and let all his senses go on full alert. Old cop habits die hard.

"Carolyn," he said in a calm voice, listening hard, listening to more than her words. "Everything okay over there?"

"I'm so sorry to bother you —"

"No bother. I told you to call if you needed anything. You got a problem?"

"Well, I'm not really sure —" She broke it off, and he could hear some whispering going on in the background before she came back to him, trying to keep her voice light, not too concerned. "Clay, you know that . . . possum, or whatever it was in our basement? Well, it seems it's not gone after all."

"You're sure about that?"

"Oh, yes. We can hear it down there right now. It's . . . making noises."

"What kind of noises?"

There was another pause before she said, almost reluctantly, as if she didn't really expect him to believe her, "Crying . . . noises."

"*Crying* noises?" He shoved his chair back and stood up. "Sounds to me like you might have a sick or injured animal down there. You did right to call me. Stay in the house, now, you hear? I'll be right there. And don't you try and do anything until I get there."

He hung up the phone, but stood and looked at it for a second or two while he clamped his back teeth together hard and worked a muscle in his jaw. *Crying noises.* He kept thinking about a door no draft should have blown shut.

On his way out he stuck his head into the living room, where the TV was going full blast. Miss Leona had fallen asleep in her chair watching *Cosby*, as usual, though of course if he woke her up and suggested she ought to go on to bed, she'd deny it. He decided not to disturb her. He didn't expect to be gone long.

Out on the back porch he took his coat and rifle out of the closet, then on second thought went back into the kitchen and got a good-sized flashlight out of the drawer. Passing by the closet on his way out a second time he hesitated, then stopped, reached up to the box on the top shelf and took out a handful of rifle shells. He stood there for a moment staring at the shells, then slowly closed his fingers around them and shoved them into his jacket pocket. He snapped the pocket flap, straightened his shoulders, and went through the screen door into the night.

Carolyn was waiting for him on her front porch, hugging herself and shivering slightly, though she seemed to be wearing a warm enough coat. She had a flashlight in her hand, too, and switched it on when she saw him.

"Thanks for coming," she whispered, her teeth chattering.

"No problem."

Her daughter, the smart-mouthed kid, was there filling up the doorway. Funny, though, she seemed a lot younger — and quieter — than he remembered, standing there with the cat in her arms and the light from the kitchen making a halo out of her blond hair. Whatever it was down there in that basement, it had everybody worried, not just him.

Clay jerked his head in the general direction

of the back of the house. "Still making noises?"

Carolyn shook her head. "It's quiet right now." She seemed about to say more, but apparently decided against it.

"Well, okay," Clay said in a gruff mutter, "I'll go have a look." At the bottom of the steps he stopped, turned around, and growled, "Where do you think you're going?"

Carolyn stopped too, just in time to keep from climbing up his back, and said breathlessly, "I'm coming with you."

"The *hell* you are. Go back in the house and stay there."

"The hell I'm *not.*"

Standing there on the top step, she was just about on a level with him. He tried glaring her down, but she just glared right back at him, eye to eye and nose to nose, and he could see that, short of hog-tying her, there wasn't any way he was going to keep her from coming along.

"Suit yourself," he snapped. "But the kid stays here."

"Jordy, stay here," she called obligingly over her shoulder. "And for heaven's sake, shut Harriet in your room!"

But as they made their way down the slope to the back of the house Clay distinctly heard the slap of adolescent Nikes on the wood porch steps. "Kid minds as well as you do," he muttered under his breath.

"*Minds?*" Carolyn murmured with dangerous emphasis.

"Look," Clay said patiently, "I just don't want anybody getting hurt. You both stay back, you hear me? Stay out of my way."

"I plan to," Carolyn said. "I assure you." She glanced down at the gun in his hand. "Is that loaded this time?"

"No, it isn't."

"Is that wise?" she asked. Clay grunted in response. "Don't get me wrong," she said in an airless, broken whisper, "I'm not crazy about guns. It just seems to me . . . that if the situation calls for one, it would be a good idea to have . . . bullets in it."

Clay stopped, swearing softly, wishing devoutly that the woman and her kid had stayed in California. But she was right, dammit, he knew she was right. It was time he got over the past. High time.

He could feel those golden eyes of hers studying him, even in the dark. He could feel her watching him as he unsnapped his pocket, took two cartridges out, and inserted them into the chamber of the rifle. What was she thinking about him? he wondered — and then wondered why he cared.

"Satisfied?" he murmured as the chamber clicked shut.

80

She didn't answer. They went on down the hill together, side by side, the rifle between them like a wall. It seemed a lot heavier to him now.

As they approached the basement he put out his hand, holding her back. With his back to the door and his hand on the knob he paused for a moment to listen, then set his jaw and pushed. The door creaked inward. Over the echo of its protest he heard scuffles . . . and a distinctly canine whimper.

I'll be damned, he thought. The kid was right — it's a *dog.*

Knowing that didn't make him relax, though. There was still the possibility the dog was sick or hurt, and even if it wasn't, it was bound to be scared to death, and a frightened dog is a dangerous dog. And he hadn't forgotten that closed door, either. He didn't know of very many dogs who could open and shut doors by themselves.

Ah God, he thought disgustedly, leaning his head against the door panels, feeling the cold trickle of sweat between his shoulder blades. I thought I was done with this stuff. Two years, and it feels like yesterday. *Yesterday.*

Gritting his teeth, he switched on the flashlight and eased through the door. The whine came again — louder, more frightened. "Easy, boy," he crooned softly. "What are you doin' in here, huh? Come on, now, nobody's going to hurt you."

The flashlight's beam swept the room, sending shadows leaping and dancing across whitewashed walls and over the low, rough-board ceiling. It almost missed the tiny, greenish gleam in the farthest corner, then wavered and jerked back, steadied and focused on the feral glow of animal eyes. Soft shine of a coal-black nose. Shaggy, toffee-colored fur. Pale glint of canine teeth.

"Easy, boy," Clay said again. He started forward, and the whine became a low growl of warning. "Take it easy . . ." His fingers shifted, cradling the rifle more securely on his hip. He didn't want to . . . not unless he had to. He didn't want to . . . but there was the woman to think about. And the kid. He took another step, the gunmetal cold and slippery in his hand.

The growl grew louder, and there was a sudden flurry of movement in the shadows. He felt the deadly fit of the rifle in his hand, his finger on the trigger. The shadow leaped out of the corner of his eye, and every nerve in his body leaped with it. Adrenaline surged through him like a charge of electricity and an instant later recoiled, leaving him cold, trembling, and sick.

A tear-streaked face appeared in his flashlight beam, like a pale, pinioned moth. "Please, mister," cried a small, desperate voice. "*Please* don't shoot my dog!"

Carolyn gasped from the doorway, "Oh my God — don't shoot! It's a child!"

Clay lurched past her, knocking her against the doorframe in his haste. She heard him mumble, "Sorry," as he stumbled into the night. She started to call to him, started to go after him, then turned instead to the dark basement.

"It's all right," she called urgently, then repeated it more softly, pleased to hear the calm assurance in her voice, relieved to hear no trace of the trembling in her legs, or her wildly pounding heart. "It's all right. No one's going to hurt you, or your dog. What's your dog's name?"

There was a pause, then a loud sniff. "T-Traveler, ma'am."

"Traveler, huh? That's a good name. Does Traveler bite?"

"No, ma'am, he's a real good dog. He didn't mean to growl. He was just scared."

"I know," Carolyn said softly. "I don't blame him. I'd have been scared too. But nobody's going to hurt you, I promise."

"I *knew* it was a dog." Jordy's voice quivered with excitement.

Clay was there again, suddenly, right behind her, one hand braced on the doorframe above her head. She glanced up at him, but the darkness told her nothing. "Ask him if there's anybody else in there," he murmured hoarsely in her ear.

"Honey," she called, her voice breaking, "who's with you? Are you all by yourself?"

"No, ma'am." The reply was emphatic. "I got Traveler with me."

Carolyn sagged against the wall, shaking with silent laughter. Reaction was beginning to set in.

Clay put his hand on her shoulder and gave it a squeeze, then spoke in a voice she hadn't heard before. A quiet, controlled voice, with the ring of authority. A cop's voice. "Okay, buddy, time to come out of there, now. Nobody's going to hurt you. Come on — you can bring your dog with you."

There was no reply, but Carolyn could hear reluctance and dread in the slow progress of shuffles and scrapes and bumps across the shadowy basement. She still had her weak flashlight beam trained on the far corner, so she jumped when something large and furry brushed her leg, and a small voice spoke breathlessly from very close by.

"Are you gonna put me in jail?"

"Of course not," Carolyn gasped. A cold, damp nose bumped her hand, then nudged its way under it.

"We didn't take nothin', I swear."

There was a rustling sound as Clay crouched down, balancing on his heels. "Son, you want to tell me what you *were* doing in there? Where are your folks?"

Carolyn felt the dog lean . . . subtly intruding his body between the man and the child.

There was a long pause, then a grudging, "Got no folks. I told you — it's just me and Traveler."

Carolyn's hand found a shoulder — a terribly thin, bony shoulder covered only by a light sweatshirt. Her heart turned over.

"What's your name, son?" asked Clay.

"William."

"William, huh? Folks call you Willie, or Bill?"

"No, sir. I'm *William*." The pride in that pronouncement sent an unexpected rush of emotion to the back of Carolyn's throat and eyes, a stinging sensation, like an approaching sneeze.

"Okay, William, do you have a last —"

"It can wait," Carolyn interrupted, pushing words through cramped jaws. It suddenly seemed too much, too incredible; she was beginning to shiver, and she wanted very much to sit down. Shock, she supposed. And the child . . . oh God, the child. Her mind shut down. "It's cold out here," she said angrily. "Can we continue this interrogation inside?"

There was an audible exhalation. Then Clay said, "Sure — you're right," and stood up. Carolyn gave the scrawny shoulder a reassuring squeeze, and a small, cold hand crept into hers. Her throat began to ache.

The moon had risen, and away from the house's dense shadow the night was bright. They trooped uphill in the milky glow of moonlight, without flashlights and in silence, like miscreants. Clay led the way; Carolyn followed, still holding the child's hand, with the dog sandwiched jealously between them, getting in the way of her feet. Jordy trotted almost forgotten in their wake, hands and chin withdrawn inside her ski jacket.

Carolyn thought, My God, he's so *small*. What can he be doing here, all alone? What am I going to do with him? I can't believe this is happening . . .

To her, of all people. Throughout her life there had been times when she didn't know whether she believed in God at all. And other times, such as now, when she thought He — or She — must have a strange and ironic sense of humor.

When they reached the porch, Jordy thumped up the steps past them and threw herself at the door as if she meant to barricade it with her body. "You're not bringing that dog in the house!"

"Honey," Carolyn said carefully, "just put Harriet in your room and be sure the door's shut. It'll be fine."

"She'll have a heart attack," Jordy warned.

"Hey, you're a *kid*," William said in surprise, evidently noticing the fourth member of the party for the first time.

"Huh," Jordy said with a bark of miffed laughter, "look who's talking."

"Harriet," said William in an interested, friendly way. "Who's that? Is that your cat? That's okay — my dog likes cats."

"Well, it's not okay," Jordy snapped, not friendly at all, "because it just so happens my cat *hates* dogs."

"For breakfast," added William, absolutely deadpan.

"Mo-ther?" Jordy said in a warning tone, and slammed into the house while Carolyn and Clay exchanged surprised glances over William's head.

"Feisty little devil," Clay muttered under his breath.

"Well, William," Carolyn said winningly, in an effort to make up for Jordy's lack of hospitality, "would you like to come inside?"

William swiveled his head around and looked up at Clay, then sighed and mumbled,

87

"Yes, ma'am." Evidently he'd decided he wasn't realistically going to have a choice in the matter.

Carolyn gave his hand a reassuring squeeze and motioned him inside. There was a brief traffic jam when Traveler refused to unstick himself from William's side even long enough to go through the doorway, causing Carolyn to step backward into Clay, who was following too closely to stop in time.

"Sorry," she muttered, rattled by the unexpectedness of solid, warm male against her back.

It occurred to her suddenly that she should be very glad Clay was there, glad she didn't have to cope with this incredible development by herself. But the truth was, she wasn't. She hadn't wanted to call him for help in the first place, and now she wished she hadn't. She knew exactly how William was feeling — nervous, anxious, suspicious, a little scared, a little hopeful . . . She knew, more than anyone else could possibly know. Incredible, she thought. Twenty years, and it seems like yesterday. *Yesterday.*

Meanwhile, William was checking out the kitchen in a critical, appraising kind of way, trying to look cool. When Carolyn suggested he might like to sit down, he nudged a kitchen chair around with his hip, then hitched half his bottom onto it and perched there, one foot braced against the floor as if in preparation for a quick getaway. Any ideas of which were unwittingly foiled by Traveler, who promptly sat down on William's foot, and from there watched, alert and quivering, as Clay pulled out another chair nearby.

"Easy, boy," Clay said as he settled into the chair. The dog whined softly. "Good ol' dog . . ." Clay held out his hand for inspection, then casually fondled the dog's drooping brown ears. Traveler whined again, and licked his hand.

"William," Carolyn said, "would you and Traveler like something to eat?" She said it carefully, sensing tremendous pride in that stiff little neck and hunched, defensive shoulders.

William lifted one of those shoulders in an offhand shrug and said matter-of-factly, "Well, ma'am . . . I guess Traveler's pretty hungry. I think that's why he was cryin'. 'Cause he smelled the popcorn."

Crying. Carolyn threw one beseeching look at Clay and turned blindly to the sink. For in just that terrible moment she saw another child, huddling in a dark alley among the cold hulks of trash cans, crying because the smell of pizza made her stomach hurt. Oh, it hurt so bad . . .

Behind her she could hear Clay's voice, his cop-voice, asking more questions. She wanted to yell at him, to tell him the child needed questions like he needed a hole in the head. That what he needed was food, and warm clothes, and a safe place to sleep. Especially that . . . *a safe place.*

Anger made her hands jerky; she had a tendency to bang cupboard doors and thump things on countertops as she got out the biggest mug she could find, filled it a third full with water, and put it in the microwave. By the time the water was hot she was calmer. Carefully she dumped in a packet of hot cocoa mix, the kind Jordy had picked out, with tiny marshmallows in it, and stirred it until the marshmallows looked partly melted. Then she filled the mug the rest of the way with milk and set it on the table in front of William. He gave her a quick, startled look and touched one of the bobbing marshmallows with a fingertip as if he expected it to vanish into thin air, like a soap bubble.

"Go on — drink it," she said encouragingly. "It's good."

"Yes, ma'am," said William. And then, hesitantly, "Could . . . Traveler have some, too? He likes marshmallows."

Carolyn began to laugh, and was instantly afraid it might become something else before she could stop it. "I don't think marshmallows are good for dogs," she said huskily. "Let me see if I can find him something better, okay?"

She got out the package of wieners she and Jordy had bought just that afternoon and slit it open. Traveler whined and ducked his head, wriggling all over and licking his chops. The first wiener she held out to him disappeared as if by sleight of hand. The three more that followed vanished as quickly, and thereafter the dog's soft brown eyes followed her worshipfully wherever she went.

"I like hot dogs, too," said William pointedly.

"I thought I'd put yours on a bun," Carolyn told him. "You like ketchup and mustard?"

"Yes, *ma'am*," said William, and grinned for the first time.

It was an urchin's grin, complete with dimples and an irrepressible twinkle, daring and sassy . . . and utterly irresistible. Well-fed and secure, Carolyn thought, the kid would be an imp — a real handful.

Oh God, she thought, why this, why now? She could take anything but this — anything.

"How long's it been since you ate?" Clay asked, as casually as it's possible for a cop to ask questions, getting down to business again while Carolyn, fighting an indefinable resentment, popped two hot dogs into the microwave.

Unperturbed, William thought about it while he licked his upper lip, managing to do so without noticeably damaging his chocolate-milk moustache. "Yesterday, I guess." He dove back into his cocoa while Carolyn and Clay looked at each other in surprise. When he came up for air again he added sorrowfully, "We were afraid to go back. Almost got caught this mornin' . . ."

Clay said carefully, "Afraid to go back where, William? Where have you been getting food?"

"It wasn't stealing," William said quickly, sitting up straight and shaking his head emphatically. "No *sir*. There's this lady — she always puts stuff out for the dogs, see? Only, there isn't any dog. I know — I checked. And Traveler's a dog, so that means it ain't stealing . . . right?"

"Of course not," Carolyn said, giving William's shoulder a reassuring squeeze as she set a plateful of hot dogs down in front of him. She glared at Clay, daring him to contradict, but he was shaking his head and chuckling, and muttering under his breath what sounded like profanity. Puzzled, she asked, "You know what he's talking about?"

"It's Miss Leona," Clay explained. "She has

this . . . she puts food out for the wild animals — calls them God's children."

"We were gonna go back there this mornin'," William offered, looking at Carolyn but indicating Clay with a jerk of his head. "Only *he* came along. So we had to come back. And then you and . . . that girl came, and me and Traveler had to hide under the bridge. I heard . . . *her* . . . tell you about somethin' bein' in the basement, and then I saw him go in . . ." He paused to take a huge bite of hot dog, chewed once or twice and gulped. "I figured it was time for me and Traveler to move on, but then . . ." He took another bite.

"But you came back," Carolyn prompted softly. "How come?"

William shrugged and looked down at his plate, as if he'd suddenly lost his appetite. "Traveler didn't want to go," he said in a small, forlorn voice. "I tried to make him, but he just wouldn't leave." He swallowed hard once more, though there wasn't anything in his mouth, and finished dejectedly, "I guess maybe he's just tired."

"Been on the road a long time?" Clay asked sympathetically.

But William wasn't fooled. He sat up straight and said evasively, "A while." He suddenly became very busy dividing up what was

93

left of his hot dog, feeding half of it to his dog and wolfing down the rest.

"Kind of tough for a kid your age, being on your own," Clay persisted in a friendly tone. "What are you, about ten?"

"Hey," said William, looking affronted. "I'm older than I look."

"Yeah? How old are you?"

William's eyes slid sideways. "Fourteen."

Clay chuckled. "Come on, William. Try again."

Leave him alone! Carolyn wanted to shout, suddenly furious with Clay, with his sleepy, all-knowing cop-smile and the Clint Eastwood gleam in his eyes. Leave him alone, for God's sake, he's only a child!

She folded her arms across her stomach and kept her mouth shut. William shrugged, looking unabashed. He jerked his head toward Jordy, who had just emerged empty-handed from her room — curiosity having evidently cured her sulks — and said, "How old is *she?*"

"I'm thirteen," Jordy informed him grandly, advancing like a promenading princess.

"Really?" William was clearly impressed. He swung back to his remaining hot dog and told Clay reluctantly, with his mouth full, "I'm gonna be eleven."

"Uh-huh," said Clay, still skeptical. "When's that?"

"Come summer . . ." William's chewing slowed as he watched Jordy take a box of Cheerios out of the cupboard and a carton of milk from the refrigerator, then return to the cupboard once more for a bowl.

"Can I have some of that?" he asked, valiantly swallowing the last lump of hot dog.

Jordy gave him a look but got another bowl out of the cupboard and two spoons out of a drawer, then collapsed into the nearest chair, at the same time dumping everything in her arms onto the table. William snaked out one skinny — and very grubby — hand and snagged a bowl and spoon for himself, which he hugged possessively to his chest while he waited for Jordy to finish pouring Cheerios and milk into hers.

"Here, help yourself," she muttered ungraciously, shoving the box and carton across the table. William wasted no time doing so, including a handful of dry cereal for Traveler. The sounds of earnest crunching filled the kitchen.

Carolyn glanced at Clay across the two bowed heads and found him watching her with the frowning intensity that meant he had things he wanted to say to her — in private, if possible. But she knew what he wanted to say, and she didn't want to hear it, so she shook her head slightly and gave a helpless shrug, pretending not to understand.

"I'm sorry, what I said about your cat," William said to Jordy, with his mouth full, as usual. "I didn't mean it. Traveler wouldn't hurt her."

"Well, I meant it about my cat hating dogs," said Jordy. "Harriet would make mincemeat out of your old dog."

"Wouldn't," William said stoutly. "I wouldn't let her. Me and Traveler, we watch out for each other. We're a team."

"Yeah?" said Jordy. "So, what were you doing in our basement, huh?"

William ducked his head and mumbled, "Weren't doin' nothin'. Just sleepin', that's all."

"Don't you know that's trespassing?" said Jordy with casual arrogance. William's alarmed glance bounced off Clay and sought Carolyn with mute appeal.

"It's all right, William," she said soothingly, with a look of warning for Jordy, and went to stand behind him with her hands resting protectively on his shoulders. "Nobody is going to do anything to you — I promise." And she looked straight at Clay. For a long moment his gaze dueled with hers, and then he snorted softly in frustration and got up from the table, leaving her tremulous and shaken inside, knowing she'd won only a reprieve, a small skirmish at best, and that the outcome of the war was still very much in doubt.

"Weren't you cold?" Jordy asked, with more curiosity than sympathy.

Look at him — he doesn't even have a jacket, Carolyn thought, staring down at the back of William's neck, at the knobs of his spine above the neck of his sweatshirt, the spikes of straight brown hair . . . The image swam, and she blinked and angrily looked away, feeling the pain of cold in her own bones.

The bony shoulders moved beneath her hands. "Traveler keeps me warm," said William stoutly.

"Well, William," Carolyn said decisively, "you and Traveler are sleeping here tonight — in my room," she added pointedly, as Jordy started to voice a loud protest. "I'll sleep on the couch."

She turned to glare at Clay, daring him to voice the objections she could see written in every long, lean line of him, from the rigid set of his neck and shoulders to the cant of his narrow hips, the angry hook of his thumb through a belt loop, the jut of his elbow, the impatient drumming of his fingers against the doorframe. But there was only the silence, and again she was shaken and unnerved by the victory.

"William, if you're finished eating, I'm going to run you a bath," she said briskly, and laughed when William spun around with a look of dismay. "Jordy, you go see if you can find a pair of sweats that aren't too big. Okay, William? You come with me — yes, Traveler can come too."

"Yes, ma'am," William mumbled, looking down at his shoes, and slouched ahead of her into the bathroom like a condemned man walking his last mile, Traveler pacing unperturbed at his heels. In the doorway he paused and turned, his expression woeful but resigned — the condemned making his last request. "I got my things . . ."

"Are they down in the basement, William?"

He nodded, a spark of hope in his eyes. "Can I go get 'em?"

"You get your bath — I'll get your things," Clay growled, and dove out the door.

William's face fell.

When Clay came back from the basement he found Carolyn in her bedroom, turning down the bed, plumping up the pillows, fussing over it like a mother hen. Jordy's door was closed. So was the bathroom door, and judging from the noises coming from behind it, William was having a lot more fun in the tub than he'd expected to.

Clay marched right into the bedroom and dropped the torn and dirty nylon backpack full of the kid's worldly possessions on the shag throw tug at Carolyn's feet. He was suddenly, unreasonably furious with her, which surprised him.

Chapter 4

"You can't keep him," he said flatly. "You do know that, don't you?"

"It's just for tonight," Carolyn said in a muffled voice, keeping her face turned away from him.

"For the Lord's sweet sake, Carolyn —"

"Look, it's *late,* dammit." She kept on with what she was doing, angrily punctuating words with a tug on a sheet, the slap of a pillow. "He's *exhausted.* Can't you wait until tomorrow?"

In spite of himself, in spite of everything, he found that he was noticing the arch of her back, the nice round shape of her bottom as she bent over the bed, and that he was curious about what the rest of her body looked like inside the baggy sweater she was wearing. Well, hell, why not? It had been a long time. He tightened his jaw muscles until they hurt.

"Sure," he said softly, "*I* can wait, and *he* can wait, but what about his parents? Did you think about them? Waiting . . . worrying, wondering if he's alive . . . How would you feel if it was your kid?"

Her hands were still for a moment. "He says he doesn't have any parents."

"And you believed him? Carolyn, that kid didn't just come out of nowhere. *Somebody* has to be missing him."

She turned on him suddenly, her golden eyes dancing fire. "Well, wherever he came from, he's not very anxious to go back there, is he? Did you think about that?" Her voice was a hoarse, angry whisper. "For God's sake, Clay, that isn't some teenager in there, pissed off because his parents grounded him. It's a little boy. A *little* boy. Do you know what it takes to make a child like that run away from home?"

"Not very much, if I remember right," said Clay, smiling wryly. "I ran away a time or two myself. So did most of my brothers and sisters."

"Yes, and how far did you go? And how long were you gone?"

Clay grinned. "We usually went straight to Miss Leona's. And she'd feed us up and send us right on back home."

Carolyn nodded, but she didn't even begin to return his smile. "Okay then, you tell me — is William from around here? Do you know him?" Her voice was tense and angry; for reasons he couldn't begin to understand, she seemed to be taking this whole thing very personally. "That child has been on his own for

101

a lot more than a couple of hours, dammit. A lot more than a couple of days. He doesn't want to go home, that's obvious. Don't you even care to know *why?*"

"Of course I care."

"No you don't! All you want to do is call the authorities and have them come and collect him like . . . like an unwanted parcel. And then what, huh? You know as well as I do what will happen to him. Unless his parents are convicted criminals or homeless and destitute, they'll send him right back to them. And maybe that's not the best thing, did you ever think of that? Maybe that little boy had a damn good reason for running away!" Her voice broke and she turned abruptly away.

"Ah hell, Carolyn," Clay said, getting good and exasperated himself, now. Where did she think this was, the moon? "They'd have the Department of Social Services check out the parents first, they wouldn't just send him home to a bad situation."

"Oh, yeah?" Her voice was hushed and trembling. "Well, let me tell you something, that's no guarantee, no guarantee at all." She whirled on him, stabbing herself in the chest with a pointing finger. "You're looking at someone who knows. Parents can lie. They can cover up. They can make themselves look like saints to the rest of the world, so no one believes —" She stopped suddenly, but Clay knew the word she'd broken off was "you." Not "the child," but . . . *you.*

"Hey, Carolyn," he began uneasily. Her face had a pale, pinched look about it that gave him the panicky feeling she might be about to lose control. If there was one thing he didn't need, it was a weeping woman.

She stood there looking at him, arms folded on her chest as if she were trying to hold herself together. It didn't seem to be helping much; her voice sounded tight and trembly. "Even if they don't send him back they'll send him to a foster home. And it's almost Christmas — he'll be with strangers."

"Geez, Carolyn," Clay said helplessly, "*we're* strangers!"

"And what about Traveler?" she rushed on, ignoring him. "Do you think for one minute they're going to let him keep that dog?" Her voice broke once more, and this time she pushed past him and ran out of the room. A moment later he heard the front door slam.

There was a ringing silence that seemed to go on for a long time before it was broken up by some incongruously gleeful whoops and splashes from the bathroom next door. Clay muttered, "Ah, *hell,*" and threw up his arms in frustration and went after her.

She hadn't gone far. He found her on the

porch, standing with her back to him, hands on the railing, squeezing it hard. He stopped and closed the door behind him carefully and with some noise, so she'd know he was there. He wasn't at all sure, now that he was here, just what he ought to do. It seemed like the kind of situation that called for him to go over and take her in his arms, rub her neck a little, maybe run his hands up and down her back and murmur comforting things to the top of her head. That was certainly his first instinct. The trouble was, he didn't feel like he knew her well enough to do that yet, and he wasn't sure how she'd take to having her privacy and her space suddenly intruded upon by a stranger. It surprised him a little to find his Southern reserve still so healthy and strong.

Finally he went to lean against a post in the corner of the porch, hands in his jacket pockets, close enough to be there for her and far enough away so she could ignore him, if that was what she wanted to do. He wished he could offer her a cigarette, or something, to relieve the tension, but he'd quit a long time ago, back in college — Gillian had refused to go out with him unless he did. Another thing he wished was that he could come right out and ask Carolyn the questions that were chasing each other around in his mind like tree squirrels. But she seemed to be sort of touchy about his cop background, and he didn't know whether he knew her well enough that she'd consider he might possibly be asking her questions just as a friend.

"I'm sorry," she said presently, without turning.

He waited for more, but that seemed to be it, so he cleared his throat and said, "Well, I am a little bit surprised."

"About what?"

"You being so upset about this. You told me you were a family counselor. For some reason that made me think you'd run into this sort of thing before. All the time, even."

"I have." She took a big breath. "And . . . you're wondering why I'm not dealing with this like the professional that I am." She turned around suddenly, tipping her head back so that her hair caught in the collar of her jacket and belled out onto her shoulders. "What I'm wondering is why you're still acting like a cop, when you're not." Her voice was clipped and brittle, pure California, and harsh to his ears.

"I'm not acting like a cop," he said coldly, losing patience and getting thoroughly pissed off again, "so much as I'm acting like a responsible adult. Look — in a situation like this, you call the authorities — it's that simple. They have systems in place to deal with it."

"The *system*." She said the word as though it choked her. After a moment she went on in that sharp, bitter voice, looking away from him, into the darkness. "Don't forget, I have, on occasion, been called upon to be part of that system. I know how it works. The system is dedicated to preserving the Family at all costs. And that sounds great. But it's a sad fact that some families just shouldn't be preserved." She turned shadowed, accusing eyes on him. "You, of all people, should know that."

"I know it," Clay said evenly. "And we try our best to weed them out. Carolyn, nobody's going to send that kid in there into a bad situation, I promise you that."

"*You* promise me? How can you? How do you know that?"

"How do you know he'd be going into a bad situation? You don't know that, either!"

In the silence he heard her draw a long and not very steady breath. Then she said softly, "That's just it, Clay. We don't know. But once you make that telephone call, for better or worse we've lost him. He's going to disappear into the system — it's irrevocable. Whatever happens. And dammit, sometimes 'our best' just isn't good enough!"

"You know that," Clay said slowly. "Don't you? From personal experience, not professional." He didn't know why he hadn't figured it out before.

It was a long time before she nodded and whispered, "Yes."

He frowned, again not knowing how far he could go without treading on her privacy, how many questions he could ask without her accusing him of acting like a cop. In the end he just went with gut instinct and waited.

She made soft, distressed sounds in her throat, as if the words were rusty, and she was having trouble getting them started. Finally, in a voice so low he could barely hear it, she said, "I've been there myself, Clay — where that little boy is."

"You . . . were a runaway?"

She nodded. "And I don't mean like you, to a kindhearted neighbor's house. I tried . . . earnestly and very, very hard . . . to escape."

He uttered a soundless whistle and settled himself against the porch railing, kind of half sitting on it. After a moment she did the same, adopting a stance identical to his — arms folded, legs stretched out and crossed at the ankle — except her legs only stuck out about half as far as his did. And there they stood, side by side, listening to a hoot owl call in the night, Clay thinking that he really would like to put his arm around her and pull her in closer, and that life — and people — sure were full of surprises.

"I used to dream," she said, in a voice he had to bend down to hear, "that I'd be sent to live with some nice family, where the children laughed and played, and the grown-ups were kind, and no one yelled or hit . . . anybody. And every time, they just sent me right back. After a while —"

"Every time?" said Clay incredulously. "You mean to tell me you ran away from home more than once —"

"More times than I can count."

"— and nobody caught on there was something wrong? I find that pretty hard to believe."

She made a soft, bitter sound that couldn't really be called laughter. "No, see, you don't understand. My parents were nice, upstanding, upper-middle-class people. My father had a good job, made lots of money — he was a record-company executive — so we lived in a very nice house. My mother could be very charming, when she wanted to, and gave great parties . . . They were also alcoholics, and very, very good liars." She was silent for a moment, rubbing at the rough floor planks with the toe of her shoe.

Then she shook her head and said, "You know, I don't think I ever even tried to tell anyone what hell it was, living in that house. I think I knew in my heart no one would believe me. I just found ways to live with it . . . and when that became impossible, I'd run away again." There was another long pause, and then in a whisper, "I didn't want to cause trouble. I just wanted to be . . . rescued."

Clay didn't know what to say. Again, there were things he wanted to know, questions he wanted answered he knew he didn't have the right to ask. Besides that, he was beginning to feel uncomfortable, because he could see where this was leading, and it was someplace he didn't want to go.

"Carolyn," he said gruffly, "that was twenty years ago. You might very well have been believed even then, if you'd tried, and you'd be a lot more likely to be now. Things have changed. People are more aware —"

"You think so?" Her head whipped around, and he could feel her eyes blazing at him even in the half-darkness. "You want to know how many times I've written recommendations for removal from parental custody, how many times I've gone before a judge to testify to what I felt was an unsafe environment, only to have the judge overrule me? It's just a matter of luck, which judge you happen to get, what his priorities are, what attitudes he or she has about families, what mood she happens to be in on a given day. *Luck,* Clay. Once you go in there and make that phone call to the sheriff, or whoever, it's like you've just spun the roulette wheel, and William becomes just another little ball, bouncing around and around. . . ."

"Damn it, Carolyn, what do you want me to do?" It was the one question he could ask, and the one he dreaded the most, because he already knew the answer to it.

"Please don't call yet," she whispered, confirming his worst fear. "Let him stay here, just for tonight. And tomorrow. . . ."

"Tomorrow?" said Clay grimly. "What about tomorrow? You think it's going to be any easier then? What difference do you think one night's gonna make?"

"Find out who he is. Just . . . find out where he came from before you send him back there. Please, Clay, that's all I'm asking."

"All you're asking?" Clay exploded. "My God, lady, you don't even know what you're asking. Hell, all you want me to do is go against everything I believe in! Not to mention the *law.*"

"You're not a cop anymore — it's not as if I'm asking you to violate an oath!"

"Oh, right, what are a few principles, anyway? Look, just because I'm not sworn to uphold the law anymore doesn't mean I don't believe in obeying it."

"It's not that cut and dried, Clay, and you know it!"

Clay didn't answer. He was looking down at Carolyn's hands, which he'd suddenly realized were holding on tightly to his forearms. She looked down, too, but didn't take her hands away, as he'd thought she would. For some reason he found himself thinking of Miss Leona, maybe because that was her favorite way to get his attention, being one of the few parts of him she could reach. He found himself thinking about "God's chul'ren," and the pan full of dog scraps that had kept a boy and his dog from starvation. In this particular fight, he had no doubt whatsoever which side Miss Leona would be on.

"Clay . . . *please.*" Carolyn's voice had a certain quality to it that made him devoutly glad there wasn't much light on the porch. If there was one thing he couldn't stand it was a weeping woman. And those eyes of hers had a strong enough effect on him dry — he didn't like to think what they'd do to him all drowned in tears.

"You hardly know me," she went on in that liquid whisper. "I know I have no right to ask you to do something like this. I wouldn't, if . . . it wasn't so important. Please — he's safe here. What difference will one more day make?"

He could think of a lot more arguments to that, but up against thoughts of Miss Leona and Carolyn's tear-drenched eyes, they didn't seem to amount to much.

"One day," he growled, just as a loud whoop came from inside the house, almost simultaneously with what sounded like a whale breaching. That was followed in rapid succession by a dog's excited barking, a cat's outraged yowl, and an equally outraged *"Mother!"*

"Oh — thank you!" Carolyn breathed, with a moist little chuckle of sheer relief. "Thank you so much —" She stood on tiptoe, stretched up as high as she could and kissed him. Right square on the mouth.

Then she darted into the house to salvage the situation, leaving him with the taste of her on his lips and a sense of foreboding in his heart.

"Miss Leona," he murmured to himself as he started home in the moonlight, "what in the world is this you've gotten me into?"

I shouldn't have done that, Carolyn told herself over and over again, lying chilled and sleepless on a couch that smelled of loneliness and dust. *I should never have told him.*

She couldn't think now how it had happened, or why it should have come popping out like that, when it had lain undisturbed for so many years. She thought she'd buried it — oh, she had, she *had!* She just hadn't realized it was in so shallow a grave.

But why Clay? What on earth had possessed her to blurt out to a neighbor, practically a stranger, things she'd never even told her own husband? Not that she was ashamed of her past, of course; it was just that her childhood was something she preferred not to think about at all, like a closet full of nightmare shadows. As long as she kept the door closed she could feel safe. *Safe.*

But she'd opened the door for Clay. And even with the door open and all the shadows revealed, for those few moments with him she'd still felt safe. It was only now that he was gone and she was alone with the shadows flying all around her that she felt like that cold, hungry runaway child again.

Oh, but I wish I hadn't told him, she thought. *I wonder what he must think of me . . .*

I wonder why she did that, Clay thought to himself, lying wide awake with his stomach growling and the smell of Miss Leona's latest baking in his nostrils. *What on earth got into her, to kiss me like that?*

It sure had come as a surprise to him. Here he'd been worrying about intruding on *her* space! Maybe, he thought, it was just some kind of California thing. He had an idea people were a lot more casual about hugging and kissing out there. Maybe she hadn't even thought twice about it.

But he sure as hell had. The fact was, he hadn't been able to think about much else, which was the most surprising thing about the whole day, and it had been a day full of surprises. Who would have thought finding that kid would dredge up so many old nightmares . . .

Carolyn knew what had brought it all back, of course. Finding William like that, seeing him . . . it had been like seeing herself in a small, cloudy mirror. But — who would have believed such a thing could happen, and to *her*, of all people? Almost as if —

No. She didn't believe in Fate, or Divine Intervention, or whatever you wanted to call it. Things happened, that's all. It was just a matter of luck, or happenstance. And, of course, timing.

Yes, she thought, that's what it was. Just a matter of timing. Wasn't that the way it had always been for her? All her life she'd longed to be rescued, and then, just as she'd reached the age of consent, along had come dashing Russ Robards, with his golden hair and Prince Charming smile. And, as she'd learned later, an ultimatum from the senior partner of his law firm, telling him in no uncertain terms that his playboy lifestyle didn't fit the firm's image, and that if he ever hoped to become a partner he'd better be thinking about finding a wife and settling down. And so, instead of being just another notch on Russ Robards's bedpost, Carolyn was picked to become his wife.

It had been months before she'd found out that the row of notches hadn't ended with hers.

Timing. She'd made that discovery while she'd been packing for the trip to Russell's family home, the summer house on the lake in South Carolina. It had hit her hard. She'd been only eighteen, and back then had imagined herself very much in love with her husband. Why not? She'd been desperately hungry for love, and since she'd never known the real thing, Russell's Southern charm and sexual expertise had been convincing substitutes. But finding out about her husband's infidelities had made her see for the first time how empty the sex really was without the love, and how lonely, and for the first time she understood that with her marriage she had only traded one brand of hell for another.

Timing. And so, for the last time in her life, she'd decided to run away. In the depths of her despair she'd looked up and there had been the boy on the hillside, the tall young man with the flirty grin and the cocksure attitude of someone with all the answers . . .

I wish I knew what to do, Clay thought. Dammit, I wish I knew what was *right*. It didn't feel good to him, what she'd asked him to do, going against the law and everything he believed in. But when he thought about it the other way — turning that kid over to the sheriff's deputies in spite of her, that didn't feel any better. Especially after what she'd told him about herself. She was right — it wasn't all that cut and dried, and the fact was, sometimes there just weren't any easy answers.

Though there'd been a time when he'd thought differently, when he'd seen the world in black and white, and the difference between right and wrong had been crystal-clear to him. But that was before Chicago. In Chicago it had seemed like everything was shades of gray. Gray — the color of dirt and grime and corruption and sadness. And before he knew what was happening, it had rubbed off on him and he hadn't been able to tell anymore where he left off and the gray began.

He hadn't been prepared for Chicago, that was the trouble. Maybe nothing could have prepared him, but growing up on a South Carolina farm with six brothers and sisters and a momma and daddy who believed in hard work and good food and a whole lot of love and church on Sunday sure as hell hadn't! He'd even accused his parents once — only half joking — of letting him down, doing him and his brothers and sisters a disservice by protecting them from the ugliness and the cruelty of the world.

Which hadn't been true, of course. Farm life could be very cruel. And his parents, being Baptists, had believed wholeheartedly in sin, which he thought Southerners probably engaged in as much as anybody else. In fact, most of the folks he knew considered sin — especially other people's — to be a great source of entertainment. Better than television.

But in Chicago he'd learned that there was a vast difference between sin and evil. He had never gotten used to it, and when he found himself on the edge of becoming a part of the evil himself, he'd left it all and run back home as fast as he could go, to the sweet green grass and thick red clay of Carolina, where gray was only the color of the sky when it rained . . .

I'm scared. The thought came to Carolyn as she lay listening to the stillness, watching the moonlight shadows of tree branches play across the walls that separated her from the two sleeping children, one large dog and a very old cat. It was a lot like running away again, wasn't it — this thing she'd done, leaving behind her home and all that was familiar to her and striking out into the unknown? That was why this thing — finding William — had hit her so hard. She might not be a child anymore, but she knew the child was still there inside her, still vulnerable, still frightened. Still hoping . . .

But I'm not a child, Carolyn reminded herself. And she wasn't alone. There was Jordy to think about. It was all up to her. Somehow she had to find a way to make this place a home, and to mend a little girl's broken heart. Somehow she had to find a way to make this Christmas happy for her, and all the Christmases and other holidays and special times that came after that. It suddenly seemed an overwhelming responsibility.

And now, incredibly . . . there was William. His face swam before her in the half-darkness — pointed chin and sharp-honed features, too-large eyes and cheeky, dimpled grin. She saw him standing in a soapy puddle, clutching a towel around washboard ribs and trying to look chastened while commas of brown hair dripped water onto his nose. Emotions crowded into her, squeezing her heart. Familiar emotions, like the ones she'd felt when she'd first held Jordy in her arms.

"You're safe now," she whispered aloud to the child snoring softly in the other room, in her bed, with his arms wrapped around a big shaggy dog.

And she'd keep him safe. She would. But she was going to need Clay's help.

Clay. So it turned out that she did need him, after all. She leaned on the idea, like pushing on a loose tooth, and was surprised to find that it didn't bother her nearly as much as she'd thought it would.

I was right to tell him, she thought drowsily, as her body relaxed and warmed beneath the dusty comforter. The little boy's image in her mind faded and the man's took its place — a tall, angular body with broad shoulders and big, warm hands; the glitter of hard blue eyes, thoughtfully squinted, a fan of lines at the corners; twin creases in his cheeks, like parentheses bracketing his mouth . . .

I kissed him.

It was her last thought before she fell asleep.

Was it really so much she'd asked of him?

Clay wondered. Just to find out who the kid was and where he'd come from before handing him over to the people who'd decide his fate? Carolyn was right — he wasn't a cop, and this wasn't Chicago. So what the hell — tomorrow he'd go down to the sheriff's station and call in a few favors.

Her image came easily to his mind, so sharp and clear he could almost count the unexpected freckles on the bridge of her nose, smell her hair, feel the imprint of her mouth, still moist and salty from her tears.

His body relaxed. He drew one long, sighing breath and fell asleep.

"See, what did I tell you?" said Jordy. "Is this a great tree, or what?"

"It looks a little bit smushed on this side," said William. Traveler gave him a worshipful look as though in complete agreement, then wandered over and dropped heavily into the little evergreen's triangular shade. The morning haze had burned off early, and in sunny, protected places like this it already felt too warm for a coat.

Jordy elbowed William in the ribs. "Shut up, that's just on the bottom. It's perfect. Isn't it, Mom?"

"Well," said Carolyn, "it is a nice tree . . ." She walked up to it, measuring it against her own height. "Don't you think maybe it's a little bit too big for us?"

"Don't cut it off clear at the bottom," Jordy said with her extra patient, boy-are-grownups-dumb look. "Look — we cut it off right here, see? From here up it's perfect."

Carolyn looked down at the small curved saw in her hand, then back at the tree. She thought there was something valiant about the little evergreen, standing all alone there on that sunny slope surrounded by the towering and haughty trunks of leafless hardwoods. It seemed to have a personality of its own, the kind of tree someone would write a classic allegorical fable about. Which she was almost certain someone had already done — Hans Christian Andersen or Shel Silverstein, she couldn't remember which.

She sighed. "Oh Jordy, I don't know if I can do this."

"Cuttin' down trees is a man's job," William agreed, puffing out his chest. "I'll do it for you."

Jordy's hoot of laughter sent a foraging squirrel skittering up the closest tree trunk.

"I'm *strong*," William insisted, looking hurt.

Carolyn put her hand on the back of his neck and squeezed it reassuringly. After a moment he swiveled his head and looked up at her with one eye closed against the sun's glare. "Why don't you ask *him* to do it?"

"Him who?" Carolyn murmured, though she knew very well.

"That guy that was here last night," said William. "You know, that big tall guy." A dimple appeared in his cheek. "He'd cut that little ol' tree down in two seconds — just like *that.*" He made exaggerated sawing motions with his arm, accompanied by the appropriate sound effects, then suddenly clutched his chest, rolled his eyes upward, and toppled to the ground with a cry of "Timm . . . berrr!"

"Oh, good grief," said Jordy.

Traveler, finding his master's face conveniently within range, began earnestly to wash it. William covered his face with both arms and giggled.

Carolyn was laughing too as she bent down to pick up the squirming child and set him on his feet, but there was a painful squeezing feeling around her heart. The resilience — and the vulnerability — of children . . .

"That would be Mr. Traynor," she said as she busily flicked dried leaves off William's back, making her tone brisk and bright. "He's our neighbor. And I'm sure he's —"

"He's not mad at us, is he?" William's thin shoulders writhed beneath her hands as he craned to look up at her with wide, worried eyes. "About takin' the food? Me and Traveler didn't mean —"

"Of course he isn't," Carolyn said, gently plucking a pine needle from his hair. "Nobody's mad at you."

"Is he going to turn us in to the cops?"

Oh God, Carolyn thought, I hope not. She took a deep breath. "William, we don't want to do that. But you know we can't let you go on like you have been, on your own, don't you? Something bad could happen to you — or to Traveler," she added with a touch of inspiration. "It's getting colder — you don't want Traveler to freeze to death, do you?"

William shook his head earnestly. "Nothin'll happen — Traveler and me, we take care of each other. And it won't be cold when we get to Florida. It's going to be warm. I know, 'cause —" He stopped and looked at his feet.

"Is that where you're going?" Carolyn prompted softly. "To Florida?"

He shrugged, and was stubbornly silent.

Carolyn kissed him on the cheek and stood up, leaving him with a startled look on his face, touching the place where she'd kissed him with a small, furtive gesture.

"So, are you going to cut it down, or what?" Jordy asked moodily, stabbing at the ground with the toe of her sneaker.

"Oh dear," Carolyn said with a sigh, "I just

don't know. It doesn't seem right."

"We need a Christmas tree," Jordy pointed out.

"You could ask Mr. Traynor to cut it for you," William said again, his mind apparently stuck on that track.

"It's not that," Carolyn said, dropping a hand to his shoulder. "It's not that I can't cut it down — I just don't know if I want to. Besides, I'm sure Mr. Traynor is busy working now. I'm not going to ask him —"

"No he's not," said William.

"How do *you* know?" Jordy asked, with more belligerence than Carolyn thought the circumstances warranted.

" 'Cause he's comin'," William replied triumphantly. "Right there."

Chapter 5

William pointed, and they all turned to watch the tall figure make his way toward them across the slope.

Carolyn's heart gave an unexpected bump and then settled down to a normal, if slightly accelerated, rhythm. But why didn't I expect this? she thought. Especially after last night, after the way she'd left him. She didn't normally go around kissing strange men out of gratitude, after baring her life's sordid secrets.

Traveler hauled himself to his feet and went pacing out to meet Clay, head down and tail wagging. Clay paused briefly to fondle the dog's droopy, black-tipped ears, then came on through tree trunks and dead leaves, moving with that distinctive, loose-jointed stride that always made Carolyn think of strong, silent cowboys strolling into Technicolor sunsets.

As he drew near he glanced at the two children in turn, nodded a greeting at Carolyn, and said a general " 'Mornin' " to everyone.

"Good morning," Carolyn murmured politely. Beside her Jordy's silence was almost palpable, an acute reminder of the need to keep her tone cool and her expression guarded.

"We're cuttin' down this tree," William announced, squinting up at Clay with one eye closed.

Clay's gaze shifted to the saw in Carolyn's hand, then to the tree and back again, seeking her eyes this time. "You short of firewood?"

Jordy gave a much put-upon sigh, rolled her eyes upward and muttered, "Oh, for heaven's sake, it's for a Christmas tree."

"We were thinking about it," Carolyn corrected quickly. His eyes, like chips of the wintry sky, held a bright gleam of amusement . . . and something else. She waved the saw nervously. "I'm just not sure . . ."

"It's our tree," said Jordy. "We can cut it down if we want to, can't we? It's not against the law."

"No," Clay said slowly, still looking at Carolyn, "it's not against the law to cut down your own tree. Not so far as I know."

"You could cut it down," suggested William. "I was gonna, but you could do it faster 'cause you're bigger."

"You want me to?" Clay asked Carolyn. His voice was soft and oddly personal — almost intimate. She wondered if it was her imagination.

As she hesitated, a gust of wind skirled down

across the slope. Oak leaves fell with a rustle and patter like rain, and the little evergreen shivered, as if in fear.

Carolyn looked up at Clay and let out the breath she'd been holding. "It's just that we do need a tree," she said. "And there wasn't much left at Wal-Mart. But it seems so . . ." She let it trail off. They all stood there looking at the tree in silence. Even William looked doleful, so that Traveler came to bump him with his muzzle in mute sympathy.

Clay folded his arms and rubbed thoughtfully at his chin. "Well, you know, when I was a kid we always used to cut our own Christmas tree. I mean, everybody'd go, the whole bunch of us, somebody'd be carrying the littlest on his shoulders. My sisters and I'd argue over which was the best tree, Mom would settle it, and Dad would cut it down with his axe — always Dad, nobody else was allowed to do that. Then we'd take turns dragging the thing home, and we'd all wind up sticky with pitch all over us . . ." He paused and looked over at Carolyn. There was a smile in his eyes.

"Then one year Mom got it into her head that it was wasteful to cut down a living tree and throw it away a week or two later, so she had Dad go dig one up with the backhoe and plant it in the yard, where you could see it from the front room windows. And we decorated it right there — put outdoor lights on it, ran an extension cord out the front door and clear across the porch."

"Wow . . ." breathed William.

Clay chuckled and looked down at three pairs of wide, intent eyes — William's, Traveler's, and even Jordy's. Carolyn wondered guiltily if her own gaze had been as fascinated, and hastily composed her features.

"Yeah," Clay went on, grinning at the children, "that was quite a tree. The wind blew off half the ornaments the first night, and about the second day the blue jays and squirrels ate up the popcorn strings. At first we tried to stop it — every five minutes one of us kids would run out and chase 'em off. And the minute we'd go back in the house, back they'd come. Pretty soon we decided it was more fun to watch the fighting and squabbling. We'd watch from the front room windows, it seemed like for hours, and when those strings were all gone, we made some more."

He looked over the children's heads at Carolyn again, with the gleam of sunlight in his eyes, a fan of creases at their corners, the smile-lines deepening in his cheeks, and she forgot to worry about the expression on her face.

"Well, my dad stood it up until the day

before Christmas. Then he got in his pickup and drove to town and bought what must have been the last Christmas tree in the whole county. Ugliest damn — excuse me — tree you ever saw. And of course we didn't have much in the way of decorations to put on it, most of 'em being already on the tree outside. Just some lights and tinsel, and some paper chains we made in a hurry. I mean, it was one ugly tree."

The children giggled — even, incredibly, Jordy. Clay turned his attention back to them, leaving Carolyn free to breathe again. "Well, after that we always bought a tree in town, but we decorated the outside tree, too. Miss Leona always helped us. We put on popcorn and cranberry strings, and we tied apples and slices of dried bread to the branches. Miss Leona showed us how to take pine cones and smear 'em with peanut butter and then roll 'em in birdseed, and we hung those on the branches, too. And then we'd stand in the windows and watch the birds and squirrels fight over everything. It got to be one of the best things about Christmas." He stopped, and in a different voice altogether added, "When I was a kid."

"We could do that!" William was hopping up and down with eagerness.

"Could we, Mom?" Jordy asked with more

reserve, pointedly addressing the question to her mother rather than Clay.

"I guess so," Carolyn said. "I don't see why not."

"Could you help us?" William asked Clay, trying his best to look winsome.

"Nah . . ." Clay squatted down, balanced on the ball of one foot so he was closer to William's height. "Miss Leona's the one you need to talk to about that." When he reached out and hitched up the neck of the borrowed sweatshirt which had been threatening to slip over William's skinny shoulder, Carolyn's heart gave a queer little lurch. "That's the dog food lady, in case you're wonderin'. I'll bet if you guys go over there right now, she'd be glad to get you started."

"We have popcorn at our house," said Jordy, in a snooty tone of voice.

Clay glanced over at her. "Plain?"

"Butter-flavored."

"No good," said Clay. "It needs to be plain."

"Clay's right," said Carolyn, catching on belatedly to what he was trying to do. "It should be plain. And I don't think I have big needles and heavy thread to string it on, either."

"Dental floss," said Clay. "That works best. Go see Miss Leona — she'll fix you right up." He turned William around and gave the sweatshirt a swat in the approximate vicinity of his bottom.

William looked at Carolyn over his shoulder. "You comin'?"

"Well, I . . ." She hesitated, knowing Clay was trying to get her alone so he could talk to her, presumably about William, but not wanting to be too obvious about it.

"Why don't you come along with me in my truck?" Clay suggested smoothly. He was looking up at her, one eye squinted against the sun. Something about the changed perspective made him seem younger, almost boyish. And incredibly appealing.

As if in full agreement with her feelings, Traveler pushed in under Clay's arm and began to wash his face with great enthusiasm. Clay tried his best to defend himself, but precariously balanced as he was, it was pretty much a lost cause. He went over backward, one arm covering his face, yelling, "Stupid mutt. Hey kid — call off your damn dog!"

Jordy put her hand over her mouth to cover a giggle. William slapped his leg and called obligingly, "Come on, Traveler, come on, old boy." Traveler gave Clay's chin one last swipe and trotted off to join the children.

"I know a shortcut," Carolyn heard William confide as they set off up the hill. "Come on — I'll show you."

"I know the way," Jordy informed him loft-ily.

"You want to race?"

"Don't be juvenile."

Their voices became lost in the rustle of leaves and the sighing of the wind.

"Traveler's the sweetest old dog," Carolyn murmured, hoping laughter would cover the effects on her vital signs produced by the un-expectedly delightful vision Clay made, sprawled in the leaves at her feet.

"He's not old," Clay muttered, then raised himself on his elbows to stare thoughtfully after the departing trio. "His fur's too soft, and he's got too much of it." He frowned. "And for a dog that's been on the lam for weeks, he sure seems well fed. You know something —"

"William's sweet, too," Carolyn said. "Don't you think?"

Clay swiveled his frown back to her and held out a hand for her to help him up. "Come on," he grunted, "I know what you're thinking."

Carolyn doubted that very much. At least, she hoped he didn't. As she took his big, warm hand in both of hers and braced her body against the pull of his weight, she prayed de-voutly that he'd never find out. Because from the moment she'd set eyes on him this morning all she'd been able to think about was the way she'd left him the night before. Funny — at the time she'd hardly noticed how his mouth felt. Now she remembered that it had been firm, satiny, and warm, with the faintest prickle of whiskers. Something about *seeing* him — and it was all she could do not to stare — and she could feel it all over again . . . feel his lips against hers. She could almost taste him . . .

"Look," Clay said impatiently, brushing himself off, "I got rid of the kids so I could talk to you about —"

"And it was masterfully done," Carolyn cooed. "Did you really trim a Christmas tree just for the birds?"

"Thank you. Yes, we did. And don't try to change the subject. You know damn good and well what we need to talk about. The fact is, I've just come from town, where I dropped in on some friends of mine at the sheriff's station. I stopped by here on my way home because I thought you'd want to know what I found out."

"Of course I want to know." Obviously out of sorts with her, Clay had started walking back to the summer house, and she almost had to run to keep up with his long legs. "So," she panted, "what did you find out?"

Clay snorted and kept walking. "Nothing."

"Nothing?"

"Not a damn thing. No reports of any missing kid matching William's description. *Nada.*"

"Well . . . okay . . . so . . ." Carolyn's forehead knotted as she focused on the uneven ground ahead of her. "What does that mean? What do we do now?"

"What that *means*," Clay said, enunciating carefully, "is that we do what we should have done in the first place. We turn the kid over to the proper authorities, who will see that he's taken care of while the pros try to find out who he belongs to. That's it. End of story."

Carolyn plodded on, not saying anything because suddenly there was a lump in her chest the size of a tennis ball.

Clay glanced over at her and his voice softened. "Carolyn, look, you asked me for one day —"

"I asked you to find out about him! And you haven't."

"Okay, as it happens, there's nothing to find out. That's not my fault. Now it's time to turn this thing —"

"William is not a 'thing'! He's a little boy!"

Clay turned around and Carolyn stopped abruptly, and they stood there facing each other. Carolyn was breathing hard. Clay was trying to look patient.

"That's right," he said softly and carefully, as if addressing a not very bright child, "and if we're ever going to find out whose little boy he is, we're going to have to let the people who know how in on it, so they can do their job. Y'understand?"

Carolyn wanted very much to strangle him, but she held on to her temper, breathing through her nose for self-control. After a moment she said reasonably, "What about you? You're a cop — couldn't you find out who he is just as well?"

Clay smiled thinly. "I'm not a cop anymore — as you so sweetly pointed out to me last night. Remember?"

Oh, did she ever remember. And she could see by the glitter in his eyes that he did, too — every word, every gesture. Her cheeks began to burn with the mutual awareness, but she didn't let go of the eye contact. She leaned stubbornly against it, openly challenging him.

"I remember," she said evenly. "What I meant was, you've been a cop. You have the knowledge and the skills. You must know how to go about finding someone."

For a few seconds their eyes remained locked in a battle of wills. It was Clay who broke the tension first, letting his breath out in a hiss of frustration and looking up at the sky as if for divine guidance.

"I have the knowledge and the skills — maybe. What I don't have is the resources. I don't have access to FBI records and computer files, I don't have the manpower — Dammit, police work is ninety percent tedium and ten percent luck. To tell you the truth, the only way I can think of right now to find out who that kid is, is if he tells us. And he's not talking!"

"Oh, but he will," Carolyn assured him, her words tumbling eagerly, "once he learns to trust us. He's already starting to — just a little while ago he was talking about Florida. He said he was going there, and when I asked him what was in Florida he clammed up, which made me think it was for some specific reason, not just because he might have heard Florida was a nice place. Maybe he has somebody there."

"Maybe so," said Clay dryly. "Which certainly does narrow it right down, doesn't it? From the whole damn South to one little ol' state."

Carolyn gave him a reproachful look. "I never suggested it was enough to find him with, Clay. I just thought you should know."

She jammed her hands into her jacket pockets and set off again. After a moment Clay fell into step beside her, and she noticed that this time he shortened his stride to accommodate hers.

For a while neither of them said anything more, just walked along, dodging brambles, listening to the sound of their footsteps crunching in the dry leaves. And — Carolyn thought it very strange — with every step she took she felt her anger with Clay drain away, and a strange kind of contentment creep in to take its place. It began to feel very good to be there, walking through the winter woods with him beside her, smelling moist earth, and the distant hint of wood smoke, watching sunlit water come into view through the trees. It felt . . . comfortable. Familiar, even. As if it were something she'd done many, many times before.

They stopped on the hill looking down on the summer house and the lake beyond, and Clay's tan Chevy pickup parked in the lane beside Carolyn's maroon Toyota. For a while they still didn't say anything. Then Clay glanced briefly at Carolyn, then away toward the shimmering water and said casually, "What about the kid's backpack — the one I brought in last night. You have a chance to look through it yet? Maybe there's something there."

Carolyn looked up at him. "I didn't think I should. I mean — going through his things . . ."

He reached for her hand and jerked his head toward the house. "Come on — no time like the present, while the kids are gone."

"I don't know . . . I don't feel right about doing that."

"Ma'am," Clay said, "you'd never make a cop."

"Well, now I'm really crushed," Carolyn retorted jerkily, as they half ran, half slid down the slope. Clay laughed. She would have joined him, but a slip in the treacherous leaves made it a soft squawk of dismay instead. Instantly, his hands caught and held her, saving her from a fall.

"I can't help noticin', ma'am," he drawled as he steadied her on her feet, "that you seem to have kind of an ambiguous attitude toward cops."

"Ambiguous?" Carolyn murmured, looking up at him. "What do you mean?"

He had a smile on his lips and twin commas etched in his cheeks, but there was a wicked gleam in his eyes. Her heart began to beat faster. "I mean, you don't seem to think much of 'em, except when you happen to be in need of their services."

Carolyn started to say something, then bit down on her lower lip, catching back both the retort and a smile. He didn't know it, but he'd just pretty accurately summed up the way she felt, not just about cops, but about men in general.

"Well," Carolyn said, "that seems to be it." She turned the backpack upside down and gave it a shake, and a little rain of dirt and bits of dried leaves spattered down onto the assortment of items spread out on the bed.

Clay sat down on the edge of the bed and let his hand travel slowly over the pitiful collection, lightly touching here and there, pausing to rearrange, turn something over. There wasn't much — a pair of light blue shorts; a long-sleeved T-shirt with the Atlanta Braves logo on it, a short-sleeved black one with a picture of Batman on the front — both worn, wrinkled, and very dirty; three stiffened and crusty mismatched socks; two pairs of what had originally been white cotton undershorts from JC Penney's; a cellophane wrapper that had once held Twinkies, an empty potato chip bag, and a crumpled, grease-stained brown paper lunch sack, empty except for a few unidentifiable crumbs; a green toothbrush with a handle shaped like a Teenage Mutant Ninja Turtle; seventeen cents in change, and a handful of rocks.

"Not very much to go on, is it?"

Clay didn't say anything. He picked up the toothbrush and looked closely at it, then carefully plucked a hair from its bristles. He was thinking that, with this much evidence, a good forensics lab would probably have the kid ID'd by now.

"I don't think that's seen much use," Carolyn said, trying her best to laugh.

He grunted and put the toothbrush back on the bed. "Forgot to pack toothpaste. Seems like a pretty normal kid." He stirred the change with a forefinger and muttered half to himself, "Left home with money and provisions. The kid had a plan."

"I told you," Carolyn said. "He was going to Florida. It must have turned out to be farther than he thought." The last word broke off too soon.

Clay glanced up at her, but she ducked her head quickly so that her hair swung forward and hid her face from him. She gathered up the pile of rocks in her two cupped hands and said with another of those suspiciously uneven laughs, "What on earth do you suppose he kept these for?"

"Just to have them, I imagine," said Clay, watching her warily. "Didn't you ever collect rocks?"

She raised her too-bright eyes to his and shook her head. The movement of her throat caught his gaze and drew it, forcing him to notice the softness of her skin there, the vulnerable drape of her collarbones, just visible above the neck of her sweatshirt . . .

"Huh," he said, giving himself a mental shake, "that's funny. I guess it must be one of those Y-chromosome things." He saw a smile flick at the corners of her mouth and went on talking to give her more time to pull herself together. Or maybe, a small inner voice suggested, it was he who needed the time.

"I'll never forget the time my sister Addie threw away my rock collection in a fit of spring house-cleaning. My mom took her side and my dad sided with me — it was almost civil war, there for a while."

"Your family had fights?" Carolyn asked in a wondering voice.

"Hah," said Clay. "Like cats and dogs."

"But I always thought — you seemed so close."

"Sure we were — still are. Doesn't mean we never fought."

"But . . . over a bunch of *rocks?*"

"Hey," said Clay dangerously. "Now you sound like my sister. Anyway, it wasn't even about rocks."

"It wasn't?"

"Hell no — it was about individual rights, personal privacy — things you have to fight for a lot when you come from a large family. Besides," he added in a wounded tone, "those weren't just ordinary rocks. They were treasure. I'll bet these are, too. Here, look — let me show you."

He reached for her hands and pulled them closer to him, over the tumbled pile of William's belongings. Steadying her cupped hands in one of his, he selected one rock, looked at it closely, then held it up to the light so she could see it too. "There," he said, "see that? What does that look like to you?"

"Well," said Carolyn doubtfully, "I suppose it looks a little like gold."

"Fool's gold." *Fool's gold . . .* A pretty good description of those eyes of hers, he thought. Tearing himself away from their enchantment, he picked up another stone. "He probably found this one in a creek somewhere — see how smooth it is? I'll bet it's pretty when it's wet." He moistened a fingertip with his tongue, then rubbed it on the pebble. She leaned closer, and together they watched the dull gray stone turn a dusky pink.

"See?" he murmured, watching her cheeks turn the same soft shade, feeling the warm weight of her hands in his, the moist brush of her breath on his fingers, the tickle of her hair falling across his wrist. "Pretty, isn't it?" But his voice was suddenly filled with gravel. Something seemed to be amiss inside his chest, something out of place, getting in the way of his breathing. He wondered if she was having the same problem.

A moment later, when she suddenly dropped the handful of stones onto the chenille bedspread and stood up, dusting herself off with quick, clumsy movements, he was pretty sure that she had been.

"Well," she said in a breathless, too-bright voice, "I know one thing. He is going to have to have some *clothes*." She picked up one stiff sock with a thumb and forefinger. "These are ready for a decent burial. I wonder — does Wal-Mart have children's clothing? Maybe this afternoon —"

"Ah, hell, don't do that," Clay said moodily. "I've probably got whatever you need."

He knew it was a capitulation, of sorts, not pointing out to her that the kid wasn't going to be her responsibility long enough to need new clothes. But for some reason right at the moment the argument, in fact the whole damn subject, seemed like an intrusion on more important things. He didn't want to think about William. He wanted to think about the way Carolyn Robards' skin felt, and the way her hair smelled, and the way she made his blood heat up when she looked at him. He hadn't felt like this in a long time, and he wanted to enjoy it without the complications of a mixed-up teenager and an unidentified runaway kid.

Carolyn was looking at him with her eyebrows up. "You?"

"Mom always kept a trunkful of clothes in various sizes in case one of the grandkids needed a change," Clay explained. "Which on a farm you can almost count on. Somebody's always getting wet or muddy or worse. I imagine it's still there, unless Miss Leona gave it away; her church is always scrounging stuff for the poor baskets. We can take a look right now, if you want to. Let's get this stuff put back —"

"Leave the clothes out," Carolyn said. "They need to go in the washing machine." She picked up the pair of shorts and gave them a shake, then paused and stuck her hand into one of the pockets. He heard her breath catch; her eyes widened and flew to his face.

"Find something?" he asked with some chagrin, thinking he was surely slipping for not having thought of going through those pockets first thing. Where would a boy keep anything that was important to him? Where had *he* kept his treasures?

Carolyn slowly withdrew her hand from the pocket, bringing William's "treasure" with it, and after a moment's hesitation, passed it over to Clay.

"What is it?" she asked, her voice tense and

breathless, as if it really were a treasure they'd found.

Clay frowned, turning it over in his hands — just a small plastic box about the size of a pack of cigarettes, heavily and ornately decorated with seashells. "They sell these by the millions in the seaside tourist traps — see?" He held it so she could read the label on the bottom. "This one's a souvenir of Myrtle Beach." He lifted the lid.

"What?" she asked suspensefully, watching his face, then came to look over his shoulder so she could see better.

His first impulse was to move it so she couldn't. She was already too damned emotional about this whole thing, and he didn't like to think about what she might do when she saw what was written on the inside of the lid. He didn't try to stop her, though, when she took the box from his fingers.

" 'World's Best Mom' . . ." she read, in a tight, puzzled voice, and threw him a quick, almost angry look.

"Kind of blows your theory, doesn't it?" he said gently.

"What do you mean?"

"'World's Best Mom'? That doesn't sound like the sentiments of a mistreated kid to me."

"You couldn't be more wrong. Even abused children love their parents," Carolyn said softly, with a sad little half-smile. She gazed at the box, caressing it with her fingers, turning it over and over. Then all at once she went very still. "Clay — why does he have this?"

"What?" said Clay. "I don't follow you."

She held out her two hands, the little box cradled protectively between them. "If he gave this to his mother, why does he have it with him now?"

Her voice was beginning to show signs of a tremble, and his mind sent up a silent *Uh-oh.* "Maybe he stole it," he said frivolously, hoping to head her off at the pass.

"I don't think so. And it's not new. Look — there are some shells missing, see?" She pointed out a dimple in the hardened glue on the lid, then wrapped the box back up in her hands as if she feared he'd steal it from her. "Dammit, *think* about it, Clay. If his mother was in the home when he left it, why would he take her box — something he presumably gave her as a gift? And if she wasn't there, why didn't she take it with her when *she* left?"

"Ah, geez, Carolyn, there are so many possibilities it isn't even funny. Maybe he ran away from a foster home, did you ever think of that?"

"Then why didn't they report him missing? Clay, I think his mother must be dead. It's the only explanation."

Clay threw up his hands in frustration, something he'd seen his dad do a thousand times during arguments with his mom. Now he knew why. "For crissakes, Carolyn, it's not either the only explanation. How do you know it's even his? Maybe he just found it somewhere. Maybe he just kept it because it's pretty, and he likes it — like those rocks."

"No — no, I don't think so." Oh Lord, she was on a roll now, those eyes of hers shining like headlamps on an eighteen-wheeler. "I think this is something very precious to him. You know what I think? After what he said, I think he must be going to Florida to find someone. His father, maybe. Or maybe . . . oh dear. Clay, maybe he was *kidnapped!*"

"Oh Lord," Clay groaned, and put his head in his hands.

"One of those custody things," Carolyn rushed on, getting up and beginning to pace. "We see that kind of thing more and more. You know, where one parent steals the child and the other searches desperately for years and years? It would explain why nobody has reported him missing. Think about it, Clay. One parent wouldn't even know, and the other would be afraid to tell anyone. It makes perfect sense!"

"Where do you get this stuff?" Clay said

wonderingly. "Paperback novels? What kind of book did you say you were writing? Maybe you ought to think about writing fiction!"

"And maybe," she said, pausing in her pacing to give him a frigid glare, "you ought to keep a more open mind. These are all real possibilities. These things really do happen. If you'd just consider —"

"Open mind! Open mind?" Clay yelled, which was something else he remembered his father doing a lot of. "My mind *is* open. You're the one who's refusing to see reality here. What is it with you? Why do you want to get involved in this? Why are you so determined to make this kid your problem?"

She had her arms folded on her chest, and was breathing hard through her nose, a sure sign that she was as close to losing her temper as he was. "Maybe," she said in her cold, snooty California voice, "a better question would be, why are you so determined *not* to get involved? What are you afraid of, Mr. Traynor?"

"Dammit," he said through his teeth, holding a warning finger up in front of her nose, "you're not my shrink. So don't try to analyze me."

He couldn't remember standing up, but he was. Close to Carolyn, towering over her — a blatant power play. Only she didn't seem to be the least bit impressed — certainly not intimidated. She never flinched, just stood there toe to toe with him, head tipped back, eyes shooting sparks.

And as they stood there like that, breathing hard and out-of-sync and not saying anything, not in words, anyway, Clay began to notice strange things happening to him. First it was a sort of all-over tingle, as if every nerve-ending in his body were snapping to attention. Every breath he took felt like an infusion of a potent drug. Pulses began to run through his veins like messages from distant drummers. He realized that he didn't feel angry anymore, or even frustrated. What he felt was exhilarated, excited — God, there was no other word for it — *turned on*. What he felt like doing more than anything was grabbing Carolyn Robards and kissing her until she caught whatever it was he had, then throwing her down on that bed — hell, even the floor would do! — and making wild, mind-blowing love to her until neither of them could walk straight.

Plainly, he was losing his mind.

Chapter 6

"Lord," Clay muttered, "this is weird."

"What is?" Carolyn mumbled, after first unsticking her tongue from the roof of her mouth. She felt a strange need herself, a need to hold on to something — like Clay, for instance — and even reached out with her hand, trying instinctively to restore her lost equilibrium. But Clay had suddenly turned away from her, raking a hand through his hair, and she touched only the air.

"We better get on over to my place," he said indistinctly, his Southern accent a lot more noticeable than usual. "Before the kids start to wonderin' where we've got to."

"What's weird?"

Clay said "Hmm?" and turned from scooping William's belongings into his backpack to frown at her as if he couldn't figure out where in the world she'd come from.

Carolyn took a deep breath. "You said something was weird." She let the breath out again in a rush. "What did you mean?"

"Oh," said Clay. "That." His glance flicked over her, then away. He straightened, letting the backpack drop onto the rug where they'd found it. When he looked at her again there was an odd expression in his eyes — puzzled, but with a bright, almost angry gleam. "I've known you . . . what — two days?"

It wasn't what she'd expected him to say. Her heart beat a syncopated cadence against her ribs as she corrected, "One and a half."

"One and a half. And every time I see you we seem to fight."

She'd noticed that, but couldn't think of an intelligent comment to make about it. He made a small exasperated sound and started out of the room, then paused in the bedroom doorway, one hand braced on the frame, to inquire abstractly, "Why is that?"

"We're dealing with a . . . sensitive issue," Carolyn ventured, though it had obviously been a rhetorical question since Clay was already halfway across the living room. She made an effort to pull herself together and followed.

"California, I got news for you," he said irritably as he held the front door for her. "Strangers don't fight. Brothers and sisters fight. Married people fight. Strangers are polite to each other. Well, okay, except for places like Chicago, and New York. . . ."

"And L.A."

"The point is, I don't generally fight with

people I've just met and I bet a dollar you don't either."

"Well, no," said Carolyn, "I don't." They were almost to Clay's pickup before she added thoughtfully, "Actually, I don't really remember fighting with anyone before."

He stopped and looked at her in disbelief. "You're kidding."

She shrugged. "I don't have any brothers or sisters, and . . ." She let it trail off, remembering she'd vowed not to discuss either his marriage or hers.

"You and your husband never fought?" His eyes were keen and curious.

She shook her head and said cautiously, "He didn't care enough to fight, and I guess I was too intimidated."

"Intimidated? *You?*" He gave a soundless whistle of mocking disbelief as he opened the pickup's passenger door for her. She threw him a quick, surprised look and he grinned. She smiled back, and the tension between them dissipated like mist in the sunshine.

"Did you and your wife fight?" she asked as she slipped past him to climb into the cab, awareness like soft breath on the nape of her neck. Seated and breathless, she gazed at him, waiting for his answer.

"No, we didn't, actually." She'd expected the question to put him on guard again, but he was leaning relaxed and easy against the door. "We were both too busy with our careers to fight. Hardly ever saw each other." The smile lines were there in his cheeks, the fan of creases at the corners of his eyes, closer than she'd ever seen them. She had to fight an urge to touch them with her fingertips. "My mom and dad were the ones who fought — like cats and dogs. Sometimes I'm surprised they've managed to live together for forty-odd years without killing each other."

Carolyn nodded gravely and said in her professional voice, "It's probably why they have. Fighting is very healthy, if it's done right."

Clay scratched his head. "I don't know if it was right, but it could sure get loud. When Mom got good and mad, she used to throw things. Once she threw a teapot — missed Dad's head by this much and put a dent in the door that's still there to this day." He paused thoughtfully. "It was Grandma Traynor's teapot. Mom never did get along with her mother-in-law, so I always thought it wasn't a coincidence she picked that particular one to throw. Sort of like killin' two birds with one stone, so to speak."

Carolyn knew the story was meant to be funny, but violence had always frightened her and it was hard to respond to it that way. She forced a smile and then asked seriously,

"Didn't it upset you? The children, I mean. Didn't it worry you, to see your parents fight like that?"

Clay shrugged. "Well, I guess it probably would have, except we were just as apt to catch 'em half an hour later snuggling and kissing out in the barn. Hell, I always figured that to them, fightin' was just a kind of foreplay."

Carolyn's little gulp of startled laughter was lost in the slamming of the pickup's door. For just a moment Clay's eyes gazed back at her through the rolled-up window, bland and blue as a clear sky. Then he went around to the driver's side and got in.

She studied him openly as he settled into his seat and turned on the ignition. Her cheeks were warm, her nerves quivering, questions and comments teetering on the tip of her tongue. To all of which *he* seemed oblivious, his profile innocent, absolutely devoid of all expression, so that there was no way in the world she could tell what he was thinking.

Foreplay. Had the sexual reference been casual or deliberate? And why on earth had it jolted her so? Jolted? No — scared to death would be more like it. The fact was, Clay Traynor was the most attractive man she'd run into in a long time, and maybe the only one who had ever generated such a powerful physical response in her. Living next door to him could prove to be hard enough on her peace of mind without him playing silly, adolescent games with her emotions. She didn't need the distraction, and absolutely could not afford the complication of a man in her life. Not right now. Jordy needed her. She had to concentrate on getting settled, starting over, making a home for them both. She had to find a way to make Christmas happy for a little girl whose father had abandoned her and her mother for a woman barely out of her teens. And now there was William to think about as well.

She began to feel very peeved with Clay. Since she was the kind of person who had trouble keeping anything she felt to herself, it frustrated and annoyed her when someone deliberately kept her guessing. Of course, it was her job to get people to open up about their innermost thoughts and deepest feelings, and she never liked being stymied. But the people who came to see her in her office were usually afraid and in pain; they held back naturally, in self-defense. She had nothing but compassion for them.

This was different. Clay was playing games with her, and she didn't like that one bit.

"Too loud for you?" he asked politely as the radio blared forth country music, and reached to turn the volume down before putting the truck in gear.

Carolyn hated playing games, but she hated making a fool of herself even more. If she had to, she could play games, too. So she gritted her teeth behind a sunny smile and replied, "Oh no, it's fine." What she was thinking was that she could easily appreciate the impulse that had inspired Clay's mother to hurl a teapot at her husband's head.

He backed the truck around and they headed for the paved road. As they jounced down the rutted and overgrown gravel lane, Clay looked over at her and said conversationally, "You like country music?"

She kept her smile in place and countered sweetly, "Oh, anything, so long as it's not rock."

"You don't like rock?"

The smile was slipping, so she turned her head to look out the window. "I told you, my father worked for a record company. About ninety percent rock . . . a little rhythm and blues. I've had enough of rock music and musicians to last a lifetime. Several, in fact."

"Well," said Clay in a country-boy drawl, "it's just as well. Here it's pretty much country or nothing." He began to tap his fingers on the steering wheel and hum softly along with a song about finding new love and leaving an old one behind.

The lyrics made Carolyn feel vaguely edgy. When that one finished and another one started in about two lonely strangers finding comfort in each other's arms, she squirmed and said irritably, "Shouldn't they be playing Christmas songs?"

Clay stopped singing. "They will," he said in an entirely different, much darker tone of voice. "Soon enough."

Intrigued, Carolyn glanced at him in time to see a tiny muscle tense in the side of his jaw. Oh Lord, she thought, suddenly remembering what he'd told her, that his wife had been killed just before Christmas. Compassion flooded her. Christmas was such a terrible, complicated, difficult time, especially for someone still grieving. She forgot all about being peeved, and instead felt sad for him, and for some reason, a little depressed on her own account.

A cloud of gloom seemed to settle over them both, and it stayed there until they came in sight of the Traynors' farm. Then, for Carolyn, at least, it was as if the sun had peeked from behind the cloud and touched her soul with warmth and joy.

"Oh," she breathed, "it looks just the same."

It didn't, of course. It had always been summer before. Now the rolling sweep of pasture was yellow-brown instead of green, the morning glories and goldenrod that usually tumbled over the fences in glorious profusion had given way to dry grasses and buckwheat, and there were rows of round hay bales along the edge of the pasture near the winter-bare woods. Carolyn had always been fascinated by the hay bales here; in California hay bales were the shape of shoeboxes, and were stored in stacks the size of moving vans.

What hadn't changed was the house, and the way it made her feel. It wasn't anything special, just a big white farmhouse with a red shingle roof, sitting on a little knoll surrounded by pasture and woods, guarded by towering, ancient oaks. With its one peaked attic window high above the sweep of front and side porches it had always reminded Carolyn of a nesting hen, wings spread protectively over her brood. It had always seemed to her the symbol of everything a house should be, and oh, how she had envied those fortunate enough to live and grow up in its warm and nurturing embrace.

"Well," Clay said dryly, glancing over at her, "what did you expect?"

Carolyn was busy swallowing the lump in her throat and didn't reply.

The two children had been waiting for

them, apparently, sitting on the wide front steps, in opposite corners, as far away from each other as they could possibly get. William looked antsy, as if he had something he couldn't wait to tell. Jordy, as usual, looked out of sorts.

"What took you guys so long?" she said loudly before Carolyn even had the car door open.

Carolyn was immediately awash in guilt.

Traveler hauled himself up off the grass at William's feet and ambled out to meet them, head lowered and tail wagging, begging to be petted. Clay paused to oblige while Carolyn continued on up the walk, only with great effort tearing her gaze from the enchanting vision of a large, rawboned hand gently fondling the dog's silky ears.

William was hopping up and down, holding on to the newel post at the bottom of the steps, obviously bursting to say something. He got as far as "Can we —" before Jordy interrupted with "Moth—err . . ." delivered out of the side of her mouth and with a warning lilt.

The slamming of the front screen door silenced them both, and Miss Leona appeared on the top step, pulling on her gloves. I don't believe it, Carolyn thought. How can she still look the same?

"Good mornin', Miz Robards," Miss Leona

said in a rich, warm voice that showed barely a trace of her advanced age. "It's so nice to see you again. Chul'ren, are you ready to go?"

Clay took the steps in two strides and grabbed her arm just in the nick of time. "Going somewhere?" he inquired as he maneuvered her skillfully down the steps. Which seemed like a silly question, since in addition to the gloves Miss Leona was wearing a long gray coat and a tidy little blue hat, and there was a car just coming up the lane trailing a plume of red-brown dust.

"I am going to the church, John Clayton," Miss Leona informed him, pausing on the bottom step to set herself to rights. "We're putting the Christmas charity baskets together today. If it's all right with you, the chul'ren can come along and help." Her tone made it clear she considered their permission only a formality.

"Can we?" said William, hopping on one foot.

Jordy was rolling her eyes and making mumbling noises without moving her lips, her standard signal for a negative response which Carolyn decided for once to ignore. As a matter of fact, she thought that doing something for someone less fortunate than she was might be a good experience for her daughter. Especially now. Especially at Christmas time.

"Of course it's all right with me," she said, beaming at Jordy, adding over her disappointed snort, "I think it's a wonderful idea. They'll be a big help . . . *won't* you, honey?" Jordy, who knew better than to argue at that juncture, muttered a reluctant, "Okay . . ."

Carolyn focused on William, standing there in his tattered tennis shoes, rolled-up sweatpants, and a shirt that came almost to his knees. "Oh dear," she said. "What about William? His clothes — he's not really dressed for . . ."

"William's just fine." Miss Leona's frail, clawlike hand rested briefly on the little boy's shoulder. "Jesus loves him like he is."

"Can Traveler come too?" asked William.

"Traveler be happier here in the sunshine," Miss Leona told him firmly. She stepped off the bottom step and went briskly down the walk to the waiting car, scorning any further help from Clay and calling imperiously over her shoulder, "Come along, chul'ren."

William went skipping delightedly after her and Jordy slouched sullenly along in their wake. Clay scooted on ahead of them to open the car door and leaned down to speak briefly to its occupants, inquiring after their health and kin, commenting about the long dry spell they were having, and urging them finally to

"Take care, now, y'hear?"

Miss Leona was installed in the front passenger seat while the children piled into the back with the several others that were already there. Doors slammed. The car started up and slowly pulled around in a semicircle and headed off down the lane. Silence settled down like a blanket.

Oh Lord, Carolyn thought, what have I done?

Clay watched the car and its diminishing dust cloud until they reached the road, then turned and went back up the walk. Carolyn was waiting for him with her hands tucked into the pockets of her jeans, shoulders hunched inside the baggy sweater she was wearing. She was backed up against the old wooden newel post as if it were a wall blocking her escape, and he wondered what he'd said or done to make her think she'd just been left alone with the Hillside Strangler. The look in her eyes was pure panic.

"Would you like to come inside?" he said kindly. "I think those clothes are probably upstairs in the attic."

"Yes, sure," she said, straightening up in a businesslike way, as if she'd just remembered why she was there in the first place. Anyway, she didn't look panic-stricken anymore, for which he was grateful. He really didn't like the idea that she might be afraid of him. Just thinking about it made him feel moody and cross, like a bad storm brewing.

He held the screen door for her, and as she went by him up the steps she gave him a brief, almost puzzled look that for some reason had a disruptive effect on his breathing. Those eyes of hers were so damned expressive; he just wished he knew what it was they were trying to say to him.

Instead of going around to the side porch and through the kitchen like he always did, he took her through the front door, which nobody ever used. Something about that, plus her obvious nervousness, made the whole thing feel awkward and vaguely illicit. There was a clumsy little shuffle just inside the door, him trying to shut it and her trying to get out of his way, and another minuet of uncertainty at the foot of the stairs while he debated whether to bring the stuff down for her or invite her up to look for herself. *Come into my parlor* . . . He found himself bending over backward trying to be friendly and cordial and nonthreatening, and probably only succeeded in acting like an idiot. He'd smuggled girls into his dorm room at college with more aplomb.

"It looks just the same," Carolyn said softly as she followed him up the stairs, trailing her fingers along the oak banister that had been polished to a satiny luster by the numerous blue-jeaned bottoms — one of them his.

"That's right," he said, "I keep forgetting you've been here before."

"Oh yes — many times." Her eyes had a warm, wistful glow.

At the top of the stairs Clay turned right and headed back along the landing toward the back of the house, where the door to the attic was, but Carolyn just kept going straight ahead, as if following her own enchantment. Backtracking, he found her in the doorway to his parents' room, gazing raptly at the sunshine streaming through the dormer windows.

"Hannah Lee's sewing machine," she whispered. "It's still here." She wandered on into the room, moving dreamily, with no apparent awareness that she might have been trespassing, speaking to him more as if she were talking to herself. "I used to sit here with her while she sewed — she was always sewing. Sometimes I'd help her with the handwork — basting . . . buttons. Jordy was just a baby — I'd put her in the middle of the bed and she'd take her nap while we visited and talked. When she got older, your little sisters used to play with her to keep her occupied, right there on that rug. And then later, when she was old enough, they'd take her outside and push her in the swing. We could see them from here . . ." She leaned over to look out the window. "Oh God, the swing's still there. I wonder if Jordy remembers. . . ."

"Sounds like you spent some time here," Clay mumbled gruffly from the doorway. "I didn't realize you knew my folks so well."

He hadn't followed her in, and he wasn't about to. It was hard enough for him to stand there and watch her, with the sun striking sparks off the gold in her hair and backlighting her body through the sweater so that for the first time he had a hint of what she might look like without it. The sight of her there, in his parents' bedroom, did something to him he couldn't explain or define. He did know it wasn't at all like the lust that had hit him like a ton of bricks right in the middle of their quarrel, down there at her place; this was something a whole lot more complicated. Because he wasn't just seeing a sexy and beautiful woman standing there; he was seeing Carolyn, in all the stages of her life, from abused child, desperate runaway, disillusioned bride, and lonely young mother, to compassionate counselor and now, to a courageous woman determined to start all over again. And in each of the stages it was her eyes that haunted him, that same look of wistfulness, and hope. He didn't know what it meant, and he didn't want

165

to think about the possibilities.

Carolyn glanced at him and smiled. "I adored your mother," she said simply. "I came over as often as I could. Some of the best times of my life were spent in this room." She looked around as if fully taking in her surroundings for the first time. "It's exactly the same — so this isn't . . . your room?"

Clay shook his head. "My folks were still living here when I first came back, so I took my old room. After they moved out I didn't see any reason to change. Besides, I always liked the view from my room better — the pasture, the woods. You can see deer, sometimes . . . wild turkeys, foxes."

The spell was broken. He moved on down the landing and she followed him, pausing only briefly to glance into his room when he showed it to her.

"Hmm," she said, and moved on to the narrow door next to his. "Is this the attic?"

"That's it." He opened the door and tried the light switch just inside. "Damn," he muttered, "the bulb must be burned out. Stay here — there's another one up there with a string pull. I'll get it." He went hand over hand up the ladder, explaining over his shoulder about his dad taking out the windows and putting in louvered vents instead, along with a fan to blow the heat out of the attic in the summertime. It had been a damn good idea, and sure made the house easier to cool, but it did make it dark, and stuffy, too, when the fan wasn't on.

He made his way through boxes and piles of miscellaneous junk, banging his shins and stubbing his toes and swearing a lot, groped for the dangling string, found it and gave it a yank.

"Okay, you can come on up," he called, and turned to find Carolyn's face hovering above the top of the ladder like a disembodied mask in the ghostly light of the single bare bulb.

"Are you all right?" Her voice sounded anxious.

Clay frowned. "Of course I'm all right. Why wouldn't I be?"

"Your claustrophobia." She hauled herself over the edge of the dusty floor and stood up, brushing her hands on her jeans. "I thought —" She stopped and looked at him, her expression both puzzled and accusing.

"Ah, my claustrophobia," Clay heard himself say in a dry voice. "Yes, well it comes and goes. Sort of depends on the circumstances, more than the place."

"Circumstances?"

He almost told her. And what surprised him more than anything was the fact that he actually wanted to, when he hadn't told anyone close to him, not even his family. He had an idea that someday maybe he would tell her, but not yet. He just wasn't ready for that. Not yet.

So he just shrugged and said, "Yeah, you know — circumstances. Sometimes it gets to me, sometimes it doesn't." He knew he sounded glib and evasive as hell, and that it wasn't going to fool a trained psychologist like Carolyn for a minute, but he also knew she was too well trained to try to drag something out of him he wasn't ready to discuss.

It was easy to change the subject; all he had to do was remind her what they were in the attic for in the first place. "I think . . . those clothes are probably in one of these trunks over here," he muttered, maneuvering through boxes labeled "Kids' School Stuff" and "Extra Quilts," pausing to kick a tricycle out of the way.

"Oh my, what a lovely antique," Carolyn murmured, pausing to run a hand over a white-painted iron bedstead that was leaning against the sloping ceiling.

"That was Grandma and Grampa Traynor's. Mom banished it up here first chance she got." He grabbed at a floor lamp in time to keep it from toppling across Carolyn's path.

She had to do a little dance to avoid tripping

over the lamp anyway, and in doing so un-balanced a toboggan that was propped against a chest of drawers. She clutched wildly at it, tripped over a doll buggy, and just did manage to avoid disaster by catching Clay's arm and holding on to it for dear life.

"Easy does it," he murmured, when she seemed to be stable again.

"I'm sorry," she said breathlessly, brushing a hand over her face and leaving a dusty smear across one cheek. ". . . Clumsy."

"Hold still . . ." She turned questioning eyes upward, eyes that continued to gaze at him while he wiped the smudge off her cheek with the ball of his thumb. Eyes the color of straight whiskey, and every bit as potent. Dangerous and intoxicating eyes. "You, uh . . . had some dirt . . ." He didn't recognize the croak that came from his own throat.

"I do?" Her fingers flew to verify the fact and accidentally brushed against his on the way.

What could he do? Entirely of their own volition his fingers intercepted and captured hers. His breathing stumbled and his heart began to pound. He felt a tremendous sense of awe, as if quite by accident he'd caught something elusive and wonderful, like a but-terfly, or a moonbeam.

She didn't pull away, at least not then. For

a few moments she seemed as thunderstruck as he, her luminous eyes reflecting back everything he felt — surprise, exhilaration, terror, and desire. The atmosphere in the attic was heavy and humid and alive with tension, like the air just before a summer storm. His world darkened and began to revolve in slow motion. He felt his thumb stroking the warm, moist pocket of her palm; that, and her eyes, were his entire universe.

For a few moments. Then, with the suddenness and violence of a thunderclap they both moved at the same time — but in opposite directions. Clay let go of her hand, and the broken contact left him shaken and clammy with adrenaline.

"Hot in here," he mumbled distractedly. "I'll turn on the fan. . . ."

The whole experience had taught him something, anyway. It wasn't fighting with Carolyn Robards that turned him on. It was just Carolyn. Period.

Chapter 7

The louvered vents creaked open and a stiff breeze blew through the attic, stirring the hair on Carolyn's damp forehead.

"That feels good," she said in a light, controlled voice. But her eyes were closed, and she was glad Clay was behind her and some distance away, giving her time to regain her balance. She needed it. Badly.

I can't let this happen. I can't.

He'd wanted to kiss her — she knew it. And she'd wanted him to. Oh, how she'd wanted him to. She could still feel his touch, an exquisite tingle in the palm of her hand, and she could feel the kiss, too . . . the way it would have been . . . the heat of his body, the taste of his mouth. Nothing at all like the way she'd kissed him on her own front porch — dear Lord, had it only been last night? — briefly and thoughtlessly as a child. There was nothing childlike about the emotions churning and twisting inside her now — elemental hungers and powerful needs as impossible to deny as a gathering storm. And it would not have been brief. Oh no. Kisses like that had a way of becoming unending. It had all been up to her — she knew that, too. If she had moved toward him, rather than away . . . Her stomach knotted; the hunger became a physical pain.

Why not? I have needs too! Why can't I have this? Oh God, it's been so long.

She couldn't do it. She didn't dare. Bad enough that the attraction was there and seemed to be mutual. Bad enough he happened to be her nearest neighbor. But kissing Clay — not to mention what that would almost certainly lead to — would make for an uncomfortable situation at best, and at worst, emotional disaster. She couldn't let it happen, for Jordy's sake and her own.

"That should clear it out," Clay said, coming close again — but not too close. There was a telltale awkwardness in the way he sidestepped around her, a certain too-bright note in his voice, the slightly stretched quality of his smile. "Gets stuffy in here sometimes. Well — want to take a look at those clothes?"

It took all the strength she had to reply just as coolly, and as falsely, "Sure — lead the way."

He opened the trunk lid and stood back, making sure there was plenty of room between them, even in that cramped space. She supposed she should have been glad he seemed as eager as she was to avoid a repeat of what had just happened, but all she felt was a sharp sense of loss, as if something she'd wished for had been shown to her and then cruelly snatched away.

"What's on top is probably the bigger stuff," said Clay, looking down over her shoulder from his great height, somewhere up near the sloping attic ceiling. "They get smaller as you go down, if I remember right. Baby clothes on the bottom."

Carolyn was already lifting the first item from the trunk. She held it up, a high school letterman's jacket, wrapped in dry cleaner's plastic and reeking of mothballs. "Is this yours?"

He took it from her with a soft hiss of surprise. "Geez, my old jacket. I wondered what became of it. Do you know — I worked all fall, weekends and evenings, odd jobs — whatever I could get — to pay for this thing? It was my junior year, and I had hopes of being able to get it in time or the start of the regular basketball season, which was right after Christmas vacation. Only it didn't look like I was going to make it. And then Christmas morning, there it was. Mom and Dad had bought it for me, but they didn't tell me, just went ahead and let me work my butt off anyway. *Damn.*" His voice was soft, and curiously husky. Still shaking his head, he handed the jacket back to Carolyn.

She laid it carefully aside and dove once more into the trunk, into the past, into a well of memories that she'd had no part in. Wistfulness and envy settled over her like a thick fog, and the deeper she went, the heavier it became. Winter coats and bathing suits, cotton school dresses and patched blue jeans, faded T-shirts and itchy hand-knitted sweaters that looked seldom worn, little boys' Jockey shorts, and little girls' panties with pink and blue flowers, everything clean and well worn, smelling of mothballs, of soap and sunshine . . . relics from the childhoods of seven children growing up with two terrific parents in a big old farmhouse full of laughter and love.

"What's the matter?" Clay asked her, when she was forced by circumstances to give a loud, unmistakable sniff.

"Nothing," she lied. "I think I'm allergic to mothballs. What do you think of these? Think they'll fit William?" She held up two pairs of jeans and some T-shirts.

"Looks about right. What about that jacket there — the corduroy one?"

"It'll come to his knees."

"It'll keep him warm," Clay pointed out. "What about shorts?"

"Shorts?"

"Underwear."

"Oh — check." Carolyn added several pairs

to the pile in Clay's arms and went back to digging. After a moment she looked up, frowning. "No socks?"

Clay rubbed his chin doubtfully. "Maybe none survived. We were pretty hard on socks."

"That's okay," said Carolyn. "He can wear some of Jordy's. What about shoes?"

"That's . . . another box. This one over here, I think."

While Clay rummaged through a cardboard box filled with a varied assortment of shoes, Carolyn repacked the trunk. The last thing to go in was the letterman's jacket. She laid it carefully, almost reverently on top of the pile and closed the lid, and the fan blew away the last, lingering traces of camphor.

She rose stiffly, brushing dust from her knees, and stood for a moment gazing down at Clay, at the back of his neck, the wide sweep of his shoulders under his plaid flannel shirt, the way his hair grew, crisp and dark and short — cut the old-fashioned way, not styled. She thought about the way he must have looked at seventeen, wearing a basketball jersey, a layer of sweat, and a look of wild-eyed intensity . . . body long and strong but rawboned yet, and still unformed. Seventeen . . .

She turned away abruptly, picked up the pile of clothes and began to make her way back through the piles of boxes to the ladder. Just beyond the hole in the attic floor, tucked in under the sloping eaves, she noticed several large boxes marked "Christmas." She was still standing there a few moments later when Clay came up, dangling a pair of sneakers by their knotted laces.

He glanced at her, went to turn off the fan, then gave her another look and said, "What?"

She nodded toward the boxes. "Don't you want to take those down while we're at it? It's less than a week till Christmas."

"Oh." For a second or two he seemed a little surprised, as if the fact really hadn't occurred to him. Then he shrugged and said in a neutral voice, "I guess we can do that, yeah."

"Don't you decorate for Christmas?" Carolyn asked curiously when they'd wrestled the boxes down the ladder and onto the landing.

Clay pulled the attic door shut and turned to her with a hard, narrow look that banished all remaining thoughts of the gangly seventeen-year-old from her mind. "Mom likes to do that stuff. I'll leave it for her." His keen blue eyes rested unnervingly on her face for a long moment before he finally nodded toward the bedroom that had been his parents' and said gently, "There's a bathroom in there. You might want to wash up. Why don't I meet you downstairs?"

"Oh," said Carolyn. "Sure. Thanks."

The first thing she saw when she looked in the bathroom mirror was that she had another dust smudge on her cheek.

After she'd washed her hands and face and done what she could to spruce up her hair, she went downstairs to find Clay. Following the sounds of clanking dishes and mild swearing, she located him in the kitchen, rummaging through the refrigerator. He'd taken off the plaid flannel shirt and was now wearing only a formfitting plain white T-shirt with his jeans.

When he saw her he looked up and said "Oh, hi —" almost guiltily, then just stood there looking at her, hefting a large head of cabbage in one hand as if he couldn't decide whether to dribble it or go for the slam dunk. "I, uh . . . was thinking maybe we could have some lunch." He lobbed the cabbage into the sink and closed the refrigerator door. "You hungry?"

"Don't go to any trouble," Carolyn murmured, finding any speech at all difficult.

"No trouble. I found some fried chicken that looks pretty good. You like cole slaw?"

Carolyn lifted her hands, shrugged, and stuck them into her pockets. "Sure."

"Want the chicken microwaved or cold?"

"Cold's fine."

"Okay . . . I like cold chicken, too. We'll save the nuker for Miss Leona's scones. They're not too bad warmed up, with loads of butter." He paused to frown at her. "You're not on a diet or anything, are you?"

She smiled slightly and shook her head. She'd lost quite a bit of weight going through the divorce — not that she'd minded — and was only just beginning to gain some of it back. She wasn't at the point where she was worrying about her weight again, though, as she'd done most of her adult life. Russell, of course, had wanted her thin and girlish, and in that as in all other ways she'd tried her best to please him. She'd always thought it was kind of ironic that the only time she'd ever managed to be as thin as he wanted her to be was after he'd left her.

"Actually," she said, recovering her equilibrium enough to wander over to the counter, "I like Miss Leona's scones. They're good — warm or cold."

"Well . . . I guess I'm just . . . a country boy," Clay drawled with little grunts and pauses as he prowled through the cupboards, dragging out a shredder, a cutting board, and a plastic bowl the size of a bushel basket. "It's kind of hard to adjust to something tastin'

178

sweet when you're used to eatin' it with chicken-fried steak and country *gravy*." The last word was punctuated by a *thunk* as he halved the cabbage with one stroke of a meat cleaver.

"Wow," said Carolyn with admiration as the bowl began to fill with mountains of shredded cabbage. "You do that very well."

Clay looked over at her and grinned. "I'm a damn good cook. The only thing I can't figure out how to do is make small amounts, since it's usually pretty much just me. Miss Leona eats like a bird."

"You do the cooking?" Carolyn said in surprise. "I thought Miss Leona —"

Clay snorted. "Miss Leona cooks when it pleases her. She's not my servant. Miss Leona's probably one of the wealthiest people in the county — used to own half of it. Inherited it from her mother." He stopped suddenly and pointed the cabbage core at Carolyn. "Now there's a story for you, if you want to write a book. The hell with this pop psychology stuff. For instance — did you know she used to be the midwife around these parts?"

"No," Carolyn murmured, fascinated. She'd already discovered she loved to hear Clay talk, whatever the subject. He had a real gift for anecdotes.

"Yep — like her mother before her. Never had any children of her own, but she still calls most of the black people around *her* kids."

"I didn't think she'd ever been married."

"Oh yeah, she was married. Her man — Thomas, his name was — was killed in World War II. I imagine originally it was *Miz* Leona, but since most people alive now can't remember a time when she wasn't single, it just sort of became 'Miss' all by itself after a while." He went to get a jar of mayonnaise out of the refrigerator and came back with it, shaking his head. "Either way, she's probably the nearest thing to a saint walking this earth — proud and stubborn as they come, though. Insists on paying me rent for that room of hers." He gave a short, dry laugh. "With that and what I make teaching, I can just about afford to farm this place."

"Teaching!" Carolyn paused in the middle of helping herself to a wad of shredded cabbage from the bowl. "You *teach?* What? Where?" Somehow it was the last thing she'd ever imagined Clay Traynor doing.

"Criminology. City College. I'm on winter break right now. Hey — quit that. By the way, how do you like your cole slaw? Besides plain."

"I'm not fussy." She tilted her head to one side. "Except I don't like it sweet."

"Like me and biscuits," Clay said, grinning at her.

She grinned back, thinking she hadn't been as happy in years as she was right this minute, leaning up against the counter in the Traynors' big old kitchen, munching shredded cabbage and soaking up sunshine from the windows above the sink while she watched Clay's wonderful, work-worn hands turn the cabbage into cole slaw. How nice it would be if she could stay here just like this, this sheltering nest of a house, and pretend there was no one else in the world to be considered! How nice it would have been if she could have forgotten her responsibilities and listened to the demands of her own body and the yearnings of her own heart, and kissed Clay in the attic as she'd so desperately wanted to. Oh God . . . how nice. If she didn't have Jordy to think about . . .

I didn't mean it, God. Please, I didn't mean it! Oh yes, she had that superstitious streak in her, the one every parent has, the one that whispers, *If I don't appreciate my child enough she'll be taken away from me.*

But of course she really didn't mean it. Jordy was the most precious thing in the world to her, the most important person in her life. And Jordy needed her. She needed her patience and love, her time and undivided attention. What Jordy didn't need was to have her mother going starry-eyed and air-headed over a man who didn't even seem to like her.

Nor, a small voice whispered, does she need to have her mother's attention taken up by a homeless runaway waif she found in the basement.

Guilt flooded her, making her feel cold and a little sick. She inquired brightly and briskly what she could do to help and was quickly put to work setting the table and microwaving scones. It was a relief to have something to do to keep her mind off the hollow feeling in her stomach . . . a curious feeling, since she was no longer the least bit hungry.

While they were eating, she brought the conversation back to Clay's teaching, which had been a surprising revelation, and certainly a new facet to the man's character. It occurred to her that it might even account for the rather cavalier way in which he'd dealt with Jordy; it would be a relief not to think he really disliked her daughter. Though she didn't like to think about why she should care if he liked Jordy or not. Bad enough that she did.

One thing, however, became very clear to her — that whether or not Clay liked kids or teaching, he dearly loved criminology. When he talked about investigating crime scenes, searching for evidence, unraveling mysteries, and solving crimes, his face lit up and he forgot to eat while his hands drew pictures — sometimes much too vividly — in the air. She wondered what had happened to make him leave behind a career he'd obviously found so fascinating and rewarding.

So, after he'd finished telling her about a particularly complex and difficult case he'd worked on in Chicago and had turned his attention back to his neglected plate, she laced her fingers together over her empty one and asked him point-blank, "Clay, why did you leave?"

He looked up, then snorted. "Hah — a better question would be, Why does anybody stay in that place?"

"I didn't mean, why did you leave Chicago. I meant, why did you leave law enforcement altogether? Heavens, if it was Chicago you didn't like, you could have been a cop somewhere else, couldn't you? You could be a cop here."

He shrugged. "I suppose so."

"Why didn't you? You obviously like it, or you wouldn't be teaching it."

He thought about that for a moment, toying with a drumstick, making patterns in his cole slaw. Then he said slowly, still looking down at his plate, "What I like is the detective work

183

— the problem solving. Lots of other things I didn't like."

"Such as?"

He looked up and straight at her, his eyes glittering cold and bright. The lines around his mouth seemed deep and frozen, as if they'd been etched in stone. "Like the ugliness, the filth, the corruption — you wallow in that long enough, sooner or later it starts to rub off on you." His gaze dropped once more to his plate and his voice became hollow . . . strangely remote, as if he'd distanced himself from the subject. "I'd seen it happen too many times. Decided I'd better leave before it happened to me."

Carolyn knew he meant to drop it there, but for some reason she couldn't. After a pause she persisted softly, "Does it have anything to do with what happened to your wife?"

He leaned back in his chair, tilting it a little, letting his breath out in a long, slow hiss. "Maybe. Partly." A wry smile tugged at one side of his mouth. "Hey, you tryin' to psycho-analyze me again, doc?"

"I'm not a doctor," Carolyn said quietly. "And you're not my patient. I'm just asking — as a friend. Why are you so paranoid about the subject?" It was her turn to try that wry half-smile. "Speaking as a friend, of course."

He chuckled, a soft, intimate sound without

much humor in it. The glitter of his eyes seemed to gentle as the silence lengthened, and then abruptly he shook his head and his gaze slid past her and away . . . far away. "I just don't like to talk about it — nothing paranoid about it." He took a deep breath. "Those weren't good times for me, California."

"I understand," Carolyn whispered. But it wasn't true, really. What she didn't understand was why she should feel so fragile, so shaken, so delicately balanced, almost the way she'd felt in the attic, when they'd come so close to physical intimacy . . . and backed away from it.

After an awkward pause she rose and carefully gathered up her plate and Clay's and carried them to the sink. With her back to him, and with the sound of running water to mask the unevenness of her voice, she said lightly, "Detective work . . . problem solving. Well. It sounds to me like this little job should be right up your alley."

"What job is that?" He was there behind her, too close to her again, reaching past her with the glasses and silverware. His tone was ominous.

Carolyn gave him a look of surprised innocence. "Why, finding out about Will —"

"Dammit, don't start." His hand came

down on the edge of the counter with controlled force, emphasizing each word. "You — can't — keep — the — kid. He's not a a *puppy,* or something. You're an adult, a professional — dammit, when are you going to start acting like it?"

"Are we fighting again?" Carolyn asked dangerously.

"*Hell* no!" Clay exploded. His breath burst from him in a hiss of exasperation as he reached around her to turn off the faucet. "Listen," he said in a gentler tone, taking both her wet hands in his, "I know how you feel, I really do. But we have to turn that boy over to someone who knows how to deal with his problem —"

"You mean the police, don't you?"

"— and he has to go today. This afternoon. Carolyn, the deputies, most of 'em, are friends of mine. All they're going to do is turn him over to social services, and the social services people around here are the best people in the world. This isn't L.A. or Chicago, where there's so much of this all the time and everybody's so overworked and stretched so thin kids sometimes do fall through the cracks. This is a small town. They'll take good care of him, find him a nice foster home —"

"What about me?" Carolyn interrupted in

a low voice, staring down at their joined hands.

"What?"

She looked up defiantly, trying desperately to keep her voice steady. "Why can't I be his foster home?"

Clay hesitated, then shook his head emphatically. "You have to be licensed."

"I could get licensed. You said you knew people. You have friends. You could pull strings —"

"Geez, Carolyn, I would if I could, but you can't just bypass the regulations, you know that! Not even in South Carolina. There has to be a background check, they'd have to come and inspect your house — and I'm sorry, but I don't think you'd ever get approval on that house of yours."

"What's wrong with my house?"

He made a disgusted noise. "What isn't? Wait until you try to spend a winter in it. It's not insulated, it's got outdated wiring, inadequate heating, unreliable plumbing, not enough bedrooms —"

"He could have his own room! Jordy and I can share —"

"Carolyn."

She bit down on her lip and swallowed the rest of it, knowing how childish she was being, and how patient he was. Here he was, holding her hands pressed together between his two big strong ones as if he were trying to press his words and his strength into them. But she took no comfort from that. All she could think about was William's face when she told him, and whether they'd let him keep his dog. It was all very well for Clay to say he understood, but he didn't. Of course he didn't. How could he, when he'd grown up loved and secure in this big, wonderful house . . .

This house.

". . . If you were a relative, maybe. But even then it would take time —" Clay got that far before he realized he'd lost her. Her lips were slightly parted and were looking as sweet and lush and appealing as it's possible for a mouth to look. He thought he probably would have lost his head and kissed her right then and there, if it hadn't been for the fact that her eyes were focused somewhere between the barn and the south pasture. He doubted she even knew he was there.

Her lips moved, and he leaned closer to catch her whispered words. "This house . . ."

This house?

Panic seized him. He gripped her hands and gave them a shake to bring her back from whatever fantasyland she'd been in and yelled, "No — don't even think it!"

"What? But Clay, I —"

"It's out of the question!"

"But I didn't —" Her whiskey eyes were focused on him now, all right, and he felt like he'd just swallowed two straight shots of the stuff, neat. He felt like he was drowning in it.

"You're nuts!" He let go of her hands and started waving his arms around in his dad's grandest style. "I'm not even going to talk about it anymore!"

He was just about to start contradicting himself when another commotion interrupted him. The front door slammed, rattling the windows. "What the hell?" he muttered. Footsteps thundered down the hallway accompanied by loud, contentious voices. Children's voices. "Wonderful," he said sourly, giving Carolyn a meaningful look. They were both halfway across the kitchen when Jordy and William burst in together, jostling for position and arguing at the tops of their lungs.

Clay put out his hand like a traffic cop and bellowed, *"Quiet!"*

A startled silence fell. Two pairs of round eyes stared up . . . and up . . . at him. He planted his feet wide apart and folded his arms across his chest, put on his sternest scowl and in a dangerous whisper said, "Thank you. That's better." He raised his voice a couple of notches. "Number one: this is a house, not a gymnasium. You want to run and holler, you got all the room you need outdoors. Got that?"

"Yes sir!" William said smartly. Jordy mumbled something similar to the toes of her shoes.

Clay bent toward them, which caused both children to take a simultaneous involuntary step backward. "Number two. The two of you turn around and march back out there and help Miss Leona up the steps. What's the matter with you? Where are your manners?"

The two children looked at each other and bolted for the door.

"Walk!" Clay yelled after them, fighting an impulse to laugh. Then he turned to look at Carolyn, standing there with one hand clamped over her mouth. Her eyes were suspiciously bright, but he had a feeling it wasn't laughter she was holding back. He raised his eyebrows and said, "What — you don't approve?"

It wasn't that. What she didn't approve of was her daughter's behavior, but having someone else — especially Clay — call attention to it was humiliating. And just as she had when the same thing had happened in her own kitchen, her shame made her defensive. And angry.

"Did you have to shout?" she said in a furious whisper. "You frightened them!"

"Those two?" Clay snorted. "Trust me, they'll recover. Look, it doesn't hurt kids to learn a few manners. Gives 'em self-confidence. As a matter of fact —"

"Confidence?" Carolyn felt her temperature rising. She threw back her head and glared at him. "Since when are you an expert? Shouting at children doesn't build confidence, it damages self-esteem. You don't seem to realize —"

"Ah, for crissake. If you'd —"

"Ssh!" Carolyn hissed as footsteps sounded once more down the hallway. "They're coming!"

The kitchen door swung open and William entered, wearing a precariously grave expression. With solemn ceremony he pushed the door wide and held it. Carolyn watched in awed silence as Miss Leona walked sedately into the kitchen with one gloved hand tucked in the crook of Jordy's elbow. Jordy's expression was undecipherable, even to her mother.

Clay gave Carolyn a smug look, then jumped forward to pull out a chair.

"Thank you, John Clayton," said Miss Leona with a regal nod. "And thank you, chul'ren. Afternoon, Miz Robards. Jordan, honey, did you tell your mama what you and

191

William get to do tomorrow night over at the church?"

Jordy shook her head and dutifully opened her mouth to do so.

"We get to be in a pageant!" William piped up, beating her to it. "Some kids got the chicken pox and they don't have enough kings, so I get to be one, but Jordy can't because she's a girl, so she hasta be a shepherd."

"I can *so* be a king," said Jordy, giving him a dirty look. "Mom, it's just so stupid. I mean, the stupid kings wear these turban-things anyway, so who can even tell if you're a girl or not? I just don't think it's fair. Mom, they were going to make me be in the angel chorus, and you *know* I can't sing."

"Chile, that's not true," said Miss Leona, looking deeply affronted. "*All* God's chul'ren can sing."

"Well, I can't," said Jordy flatly, the borderline rudeness making Carolyn wince. "Anyway, they let one of the shepherds be the other wise man, and they said I could use his costume and be a shepherd. How come I can be a shepherd and not a king? It's not fair!"

"Girls can't be kings," said William stoutly. "Kings are boys."

"My brothers and I were the Three Kings three years running," said Clay.

"No kiddin'?" said William, looking at Clay as if he'd just turned into Michael Jackson. Jordy looked as if that was enough to change her mind about wanting to be a wise man right there.

"Yep," said Clay. "Up until eighth grade. That's when my voice started to change, and I couldn't sing on the same key as my brothers. I kept squeaking on the 'field and fountain, moor and mountain' part and the whole angel chorus kept busting up with the giggles, so they made me give it up."

"You mean I get to sing too?" William was hopping delightedly up and down. "Oh boy!"

"Well, I guess that settles that," Jordy muttered, propping her chin on one hand. "I'm stuck being a dumb old shepherd. At least I won't have to sing."

Miss Leona beamed at her. "Honey, *everybody* sings for Baby Jesus. I know you're gonna do just *fine*." She leaned forward and levered herself upright without assistance, announcing, "I'm gonna go change out of my hat and gloves. John Clayton, the chul'ren need to be at the church for practice tomorrow afternoon, and Sunday right after the mornin' service. You see to it they're there on time, now."

William ran smartly to open the door for her. "Thank you, William," Miss Leona said softly, then placed a tiny gloved hand on

193

his shoulder, turned to Carolyn and added sedately, "William's robe could use some hemmin' up before the performance Sunday evening. Just so he won't trip over it comin' down the aisle."

"I'll take care of it," said Carolyn breathlessly. She was trying not to grin from ear to ear. Even out of the corner of her eye she could see that Clay was looking as if he could spit nails. "And I'll make sure everybody's there on time with bells on."

Miss Leona nodded and made her queenly exit. William tugged at Carolyn's elbow and whispered excitedly, "And guess what else — I get to be first, because I'm the littlest, and I get to carry a present, and it's *gold*."

"It's not real, dummy."

"So what if it's just pretend? That doesn't matter!"

"Then don't say —"

"Knock it off!" yelled Clay. Both children stopped in mid-syllable to look at him. He pointed to the porch. "Out! Now!" Without another word they trooped to the door, William hopping with eagerness, Jordy grumbling under her breath. "There's a bucket out there," Clay called after them. "Gather the eggs while you're at it."

"Oh boy!" said William.

"Oh brother," said Jordy.

The screen door had barely had time to slam behind them before Clay turned to Carolyn and growled, "I know what you're up to, and it's not going to work."

"Up to? What could I possibly be up to?" But try as she might, she couldn't keep the exuberance out of her voice. She couldn't keep from smiling, either. "Come on, Clay, how could I? Even a cop couldn't be that paranoid."

"Paranoid? Listen, I know a conspiracy when I see it."

"Are you accusing Miss *Leona?* Clay, how could you?"

"Because," he said darkly, "I know Miss Leona. And I'm beginning to think you're as bad as she is. Worse, because you're a professional, and you ought to know better. Carolyn, I meant what I said. That kid has to be turned over to Social Services today. Now. Tonight."

"Clay," she said, softly pleading, "it's only for the weekend."

Clay threw up his arms. His face looked as if he were in great pain. "Ah, geez, Carolyn, are we going to fight about this again?"

Carolyn smiled sweetly up at him. "Not at all. I'll just leave it to you to go and tell Miss Leona her church's Christmas pageant is going to be one wise man short this year."

Clay glared at her for a moment or two as if he'd dearly love to strangle her, then whirled and slammed out of the kitchen.

Standing at the window, Carolyn watched him stride furiously across the yard toward the barn, waving his arms and talking to himself. She was hugging herself against shivers of laughter, effervescent as a vat full of champagne, fragile and giddy as soap bubbles. And although she didn't really believe in such things, she whispered a fervent "Thank you . . ." to anyone who might be listening.

Chapter 8

Since it was Friday night and he was in a dangerous mood, Clay thought he ought to try a change of scenery, maybe even find a little excitement. So after the chores were done he took a shower and shaved for the second time that day and put on his best pair of Levi's and a clean shirt and topped it off with his favorite bomber jacket, the one somebody once long ago had told him made him look sexy.

"Goin' out tom-cattin', are you?" said Miss Leona when he stopped by the parlor to tell her he was going into town for a while. She had her feet up and her Bible in her lap and the TV tuned to *Jeopardy*, and a wicked look in her eye which he was in no mood for.

"I might stop by Bucky's for a beer," he told her defensively, scowling at his reflection in the mirror above the piano. "Where's that movie I rented for you the other day? Might as well take that back while I'm at it. Did you ever watch it?"

Miss Leona sniffed. "Didn't care for it. Too much bad language. Give me a good love story any day."

"Well," said Clay, "I guess I'll be off, then. Don't wait up for me."

"Hah!" said Miss Leona. Whatever that meant.

He drove around the lake the long way, telling himself it was because it was a nice moonlit night and he was just enjoying the drive, and that it had nothing to do with avoiding having to pass by the Robards place.

He turned his radio up loud and sang along with it to keep from thinking about Carolyn Robards and all the trouble she was getting him into, which was about as effective as telling yourself not to think about a toothache. Then he switched the station to rock 'n' roll, which he figured ought to numb both his brain and his senses, but all it did was make him remember what Carolyn had said about hating rock music, and why. And of course that started him thinking about everything she'd said about her childhood including the part about being a runaway herself. Which made him think of William, which was exactly what he didn't want to think about. Finally he gave up and tuned the radio to a gospel preacher raving about hellfire and damnation and left it there all the way into town.

After he dropped off the movie at the video rental place and paid the late charges, he went across the street to Bucky's Bar and Grill. He figured his chances of running into at least a couple of his old buddies in Bucky's were pretty good. Things hadn't changed much since they were all in high school; it was still the only game in town.

The grill half of the place was mostly full of teenagers laughing and talking loud, plus a few families with crying babies. Next door in the bar it was quieter, since it was early yet. Later on there'd be live music, but right now there was a basketball game going on the TV above the bar and a Reba McIntyre song on the jukebox, turned low enough so you could still hear the clack of balls from the pool table up front by the window.

Clay exchanged greetings with the bartender, whose name was Hank and who'd gone to school with Clay's youngest brother, and most of the other people in the room, all of whom he knew. Then, since there didn't seem to be anybody there he wanted to get involved in a conversation with, he settled down to watch the ballgame.

"Seen Farley lately?" he asked Hank after a while. It was halftime, plus the score was lopsided and he was losing interest in the game anyway.

Hank shook his head. "Baby's due any minute. Old Farley stays pretty close to home these days."

"Ah," said Clay. "Right. What about Joe? Heard he was getting divorced again."

"Callahan?" Hank made a disgusted noise and shook his head again. "Last I heard ol' Joe was tryin' his best to bed everything in Augusta with legs. That wife of his really took him to the cleaners this time."

"Poor Joe."

"Yep," said Hank, still wagging his head in sympathy. "Poor ol' Joe. You'd think he'd learn. Can I get you another beer?"

Clay shook his head. "Maybe later."

"Hey," said Hank, leaning closer, "you know those two girls over there playin' pool? I think they're cousins or something of Brenda Watson's, from Columbia, up for the holidays. Been in here the last couple nights. They been watchin' you like a hawk."

"Yeah?"

"Yeah, and the blond one's not bad. Kinda reminds me of that singer, what's her name, the one used to have her own TV show?"

Clay picked up his beer and swiveled around on his stool to get a better look.

"You sure you don't want some more milk?" Carolyn asked, hovering. "You kids don't seem very hungry tonight."

"Probably because we had an enormous lunch," said Jordy with a sigh. "Oh Mom —

they had *pecan pie*. It was *fabulous*. I had *two pieces*."

"Ugh," said Carolyn. "No wonder you're not hungry." Pecan pie was Jordy's favorite dessert; it had also been her father's, which was probably why Carolyn wasn't fond of it. "What about you? Did you eat too much pecan pie too?" She paused beside William, who had his head propped on one hand and was stirring scrambled eggs around on his plate in a desultory fashion.

He swiveled his head upward and gave her a sleepy and utterly irresistible smile. "No, ma'am, I had chocolate cake. I get kinda tired of pecans after a while."

"How can you get tired of pecans?" Jordy asked in disbelief.

William yawned and shrugged. "If you have to pick enough of 'em you do."

"Really?" said Carolyn, trying hard to keep her voice light, only casually interested. "You picked pecans?"

"Yes, ma'am," William mumbled.

"Where was that? Somewhere around here?"

Another shrug. "Lots of places."

"They grow pecans all around here," Jordy informed her. "Lots of them. Clay even has pecan trees in his yard, did you know that? Two great big ones. Oh — and *Mom* — guess

201

what else Clay has?" Her tone became reverent. "*Horses.* And he even said we could ride one sometime. One of them — the brown one — he says is too frisky for kids, but the other one's old and gentle. He's white, and his nose is so soft — just like velvet. His name's Silver. Clay let me feed him some oats, right out of my hand. Oh, Mom, can we ride tomorrow? If Clay says we can? Please? He promised he'd teach us."

When in the world, Carolyn asked herself as she gazed at her daughter's eager, beseeching face, had this happened? *Clay let me . . . Clay says . . .* Strange feelings were coming over her . . . tender, fragile, wondering feelings. *Clay promised . . .* She felt like a baby discovering soap bubbles.

"I suppose so," she murmured bemusedly, "if the weather's nice."

"It will be," Jordy declared, shoving back her chair and hop-skipping to the sink with her dishes. "They're having a drought here, can you believe it? Just because it hasn't rained in two whole weeks. Everybody at church was talking about it. They should come to California if they want to know about droughts, huh, Mom?"

"What about you, William?" Carolyn asked, dropping her hand to the back of his neck. "You like to ride horses?"

"Yes . . . ma'am," William mumbled through a huge, unfettered yawn.

Carolyn chuckled and gave his neck a gentle waggle. "Hey, kiddo, would you like to go to bed?"

"Yes, ma'am, I guess I'm pretty tired," said William with a sweet, sheepish smile, then added earnestly, "I think I'm too tired for a bath."

She laughed and leaned down impulsively to kiss his cheek, and to her surprise, two scrawny little arms crept up and wrapped themselves around her neck. "Okay, no bath tonight," she said huskily. "Go on, get into bed, and I'll come tuck you in."

"You will?" He looked a little wistful, as if he didn't really believe she would.

Carolyn's heart turned over. It was all she could do to murmur, "Of course I will — now scoot," as she started him on his way with a gentle swat to the seat of his pants. Traveler hauled himself to his feet with a groan and padded after him.

There was a lump in her throat and her chest was full to bursting with warm maternal feelings as she watched the bedroom door close softly, just missing the dog's waving tail. Then she turned to find Jordy leaning against the sink with her arms folded on her chest, staring moodily at the toes of her Nikes, and just like that those fierce maternal fires became the cold gray sludge of guilt.

"How much longer is he going to be here?" Jordy asked in a hard, belligerent voice. Her chin came up and her face settled into the look Carolyn had seen so much of in the past year — hurt, defensive, and full of reproach.

"I don't know," Carolyn said carefully. "You know we're trying to find his parents."

"Aren't the cops supposed to do that?"

Carolyn opened her mouth, but couldn't seem to think of a reply. After a moment she let her breath out and said, "Honey, that's true. But then in the meantime William would have to go to a foster home, and Traveler would probably go to the pound. I just thought . . . Well, I thought that would be a lousy way for a little boy to spend Christmas. And, I thought maybe if Clay could find out who he belongs to, maybe we wouldn't have to get the police involved at all. That would certainly be better for William, don't you think?"

"I guess so." Jordy looked as if she wasn't sure she believed it, and after listening to a replay of her own words, Carolyn didn't blame her. She was crazy to be doing this. *Crazy.* Clay was right — there was no justification for her behavior, especially for someone with her professional background, no justification at all.

Well . . . maybe that wasn't true. As far as Carolyn was concerned there were two very big justifications — one irrepressible little boy with a dimpled, urchin grin; and one big sweet, shaggy dog.

"I guess I don't mind," Jordy said reluctantly, then added with more spirit, "I just don't think it's fair for Harriet to have to be shut up in my room all the time, that's all." Right on cue, as if she'd heard her name mentioned, Harriet began to make loud and querulous complaints about her ill-treatment from behind Jordy's bedroom door.

"You can let her out now," Carolyn suggested.

Jordy went to do so, soothing the cat's ruffled feathers and commiserating in baby talk. Unmollified, Harriet stalked into the middle of the room, paused for a long moment to stare fixedly at the other closed bedroom door, then sat down to show her contempt for everyone involved by giving herself a good washing.

"How long do you think it'll be before you find William's parents?" Jordy asked, a precarious look to her mouth and chin.

Carolyn sighed deeply and murmured, "I don't know. Clay's working on it."

She devoutly hoped it was true.

Clay could smell the fudge clear out in the yard. He went up the back steps two at a time, through the porch and into the kitchen, where he found Miss Leona sitting at the table shelling pecans. The fudge kettle was on the counter, propped up and dripping sluggishly into a glass bowl.

"Miss Leona," he scolded, taking off his jacket and going to feel the sides of the bowl, "what in the world are you doing cookin' up a batch of fudge when I told you I wasn't gonna be here? Who were you going to get to stir it for you? You know you can't beat it by yourself."

Miss Leona grunted without looking up. "You're here, aren't you?"

"Yeah, but you didn't know I would be. You knew I was going out for the evening —"

"Tom-cattin'," said Miss Leona, and chuckled. "I knew you'd be back early."

"You did no such thing." Clay was beginning to get irritated with her, which was something he almost never did. "What would you have done with all that fudge if I'd found some action in town? You'd have to dump it down the sink, that's what."

"Did you?"

"Did I what?"

"Find you some 'action'?"

Clay shifted his shoulders, feeling a little bit like he used to as a kid when his mom had him cornered after he'd been smoking out behind the barn. "I had a couple beers at Bucky's. Played a little pool with some girls up visiting from Columbia. Nice ladies, too. Could have spent more time in their company if I'd wanted to." He shrugged. "I just didn't feel like it, that's all."

"Of course you didn't," said Miss Leona soothingly.

"Now, what in the — what's that supposed to mean?"

"What it means" — she whisked pecan shells into a basket and set it down on the table with a smack — "is those young ladies from Columbia might very well have been nice ladies, they just wasn't the *right* lady."

Clay threw up his arms. "Miss Leona, what in the he— what are you talking about?"

"John Clayton, you know what I'm talking about. I'm talking about why I knew you'd be home early to stir my fudge, that's what."

"And why's that?" asked Clay in a soft and dangerous voice.

Miss Leona just poked her chin out at its most stubborn and infuriating angle and stabbed at him with her finger. "Because *I* know it's not a *woman* you're wantin' so much as it is one particular woman, and I know she don't live in town, that's why."

"Oh for Chri— for heaven's sake," said Clay, trying his best to look as if he were amused by the whole idea. "Where do you get this stuff?"

Miss Leona didn't say a word, just went on breaking up pecans and dropping them into a bowl.

Clay chuckled, but it didn't sound any more convincing to him now than it had when he was thirteen. "I suppose it's that new neighbor of ours you're talking about?" Still no reply. So he chuckled some more. "Miss Leona, how in the he— how in the world could I have something going on with Carolyn Robards? I've only known her for a couple of days."

"Never said you had somethin' goin' on," said Miss Leona stubbornly. "Said you *wanted* to. And it only takes a minute to want to."

"Dammit, Leona —"

"John Clayton, you watch your language!"

"Miss Leona," said Clay, trying hard to hold on to his temper, "Carolyn's a nice lady, and maybe you think it'd be nice if she and I got together, but the truth is, she's got baggage I just don't want to take on. I got enough of my own to carry. Listen, maybe you want me to feel something more than neighborliness for her, but all your wishful thinking isn't gonna make it so."

Miss Leona nodded sagely and pressed her palms down on the tabletop. "Fudge is ready for stirrin'," she announced as she pushed herself upright and shuffled toward the door. "I'm goin' to bed."

But as she passed Clay she put her hand for a moment on his arm and said gently, "And all your wishful thinkin', John Clayton, isn't gonna make it *not* so."

"Wishful thinking . . ." Clay muttered angrily, and followed it up with a derisive snort. But of course there wasn't anybody around to hear it.

He'd have been willing to bet no double batch of chocolate pecan fudge ever got beaten with more energy and enthusiasm.

Carolyn woke up Saturday morning to the sounds of William helping himself and Traveler to a breakfast of Cheerios and milk.

"I've *got* to buy dogfood," she muttered, peering cross-eyed at her watch.

The first words out of Jordy's mouth, issuing from underneath her pillow, were, "Can we go ride horses today?"

Harriet, who had been performing her morning ablutions on the foot of the bed, came padding up through the comforters to investigate the signs of life, chirruping hopefully.

"Oh no — go away," Carolyn groaned, but she knew it was hopeless. The cat was, as far as she was concerned, the worst disadvantage to sharing a room with Jordy.

It wasn't that she disliked the cat. Well . . . not really. Harriet had belonged to her mother-in-law, and had been inherited on her passing along with a houseful of antiques, a vintage Chrysler, and the summer house. Russell, who hadn't a sentimental bone in his body, had promptly sold everything of value, which had left the cat and the summer house. It was probable that he'd have found a way to dispose of Harriet, except that Jordy, who was six years old at the time, had promptly fallen in love with her. Carolyn had never understood why; a less lovable feline had never been born. In those days she had been a prolific hunter and shameless street brawler, quickly driving off all the other cats in the neighborhood and staking claim to it as her own private hunting preserve. As the years went by the trophies gradually became fewer and farther between, and Harriet grew more and more neurotic, jealous, greedy, and ill-tempered — not unlike her original mistress, Carolyn had always secretly thought.

Now suddenly here she was, seventeen years old — eighty-seven in cat years — and having trouble just getting up and down off the bed.

She snored when she was asleep, and when she was awake her only purpose in life seemed to be to complain, beg for food, and get under people's feet. And it gave Carolyn a queer feeling in her stomach to think about what it would be like not having her around anymore, and to realize that she was going to miss her when she was gone.

"Hold on to the cat," she said resignedly to Jordy as she swung her feet to the floor and reached for her bathrobe. "I'm opening the door."

Aged Harriet might be and probably senile besides, but Carolyn figured it would take the cat about ten seconds to rip poor gentle Traveler to shreds.

It was another cold, frosty morning, with a silvery haze that promised to clear after sunup to another warm, lovely day. The children wanted to be off to Traynor's for their first horseback-riding lesson right after breakfast, but Carolyn informed them that farmers have chores to do first thing in the morning, and so did they. Before they could go anywhere, they would have to wash and dry the dishes, make their beds, and straighten their rooms.

Upon hearing the news, Jordy as usual began to argue and complain and try to negotiate her way out of it.

William jumped up and ran to the sink, shouting, "Oh boy, can I wash? Can I, huh?"

Jordy gave him a dirty look and muttered, "Oh good *grief.*"

With all the arguing and bickering the chores took twice as long as they should have, which Carolyn had been counting on. That made it at least a relatively civilized hour by the time she was forced to call Clay and ask if the children could go over and ride his horse. But it still wasn't something she was looking forward to. In fact, whenever she thought about picking up the phone her stomach knotted up, her heart began to pound, and her palms got sweaty.

I don't have to tell him, she argued with herself. Not now, at least. When there's so much else going on.

Bad enough she was asking him if she might inflict two kids on him for an entire morning, one of whom he considered rude and obnoxious, and the other . . . well, at the very least, someone else's problem. Of course, according to Jordy he'd *offered,* and it really would make her own plans for the morning a lot less complicated. On the other hand, she really did hate to impose on him again. She was beginning to look to Clay Traynor far too often, and to depend on him much too much.

I don't have to tell him about William and

the pecans right now. I'll tell him later. I promise.

She dialed Clay's number with unsteady fingers.

"Send 'em on over," said Clay without hesitation. "I'll put 'em to work — no problem."

Carolyn took a deep breath and pressed a hand against her stomach where the guilt-butterflies were still kicking up as strong a fuss as ever. "Jordy said something about um . . . a horse. Did you really offer to teach her to ride?"

"Sure, why not?"

"Are you sure —"

"Hey, don't worry, old Silver's gentle as a lamb. They'll be fine. He's used to havin' kids climb all over him."

"It's not the kids I'm worried about," Carolyn said under her breath.

"What was that?"

"Nothing. I was just . . ."

"Hey, listen," Clay said, "tell you what — they're supposed to be at the church for pageant practice right after lunch anyway, and since Miss Leona's decided I'm the one responsible for getting 'em there, why don't you just let 'em eat here and then they'll be here and I won't have to worry about picking them up. How's that?"

"F-fine," Carolyn said. "If you're sure you don't mind."

"Why would I mind? Send 'em on over."

She said thank you and hung up feeling a little weak and wobbly, as if she'd survived a brush with disaster. "But . . ." she murmured with a frown, "why does he sound as if he's angry?"

"*What,* Mom?" asked Jordy, waiting on pins and needles at her elbow. "Did he say we can go?"

"Yes, you can go."

This time it was Jordy who shouted "Oh boy!" and took off out the door as if she had springs on her feet. Though William wasn't far behind, running as hard as he could to catch up, clumsy in a coat that came to his knees and shoes a size or two too large. He seemed so excited that he forgot to call to Traveler, who was napping on the rug in front of the heater and didn't seem to mind at all being left behind.

With the children out of the house Carolyn indulged herself in a nice hot bath, washed her hair and dressed up in gray wool slacks and one of her favorite sweaters, a soft blue with snowflakes embroidered on it. Then she drove into town to do some shopping. She did need groceries, of course, particularly dog-food and Cheerios, not to mention hot dogs and milk, and more popcorn and cranberries to string for the outdoor Christmas tree. But

Bi-Lo could wait. What she was really looking forward to — and the reason she'd been happy to have the children occupied for the day — was some Christmas shopping.

Ordinarily Carolyn was the sort of person who had her Christmas shopping all taken care of by the week after Halloween. Jordy's presents, for instance, had all been bought and wrapped weeks ago, including the ones from her father, and had made the trip East disguised as a suitcase full of clothes. They were now safely hidden under her bed — or what had been her bed until it had been taken over by Traveler and William. She did that for a reason. For one thing, it left her with more energy to spare for the seasonal pressures of her job. And for another, it insured that she would have time to enjoy all the other things the season had to offer. For the truth was, Carolyn loved Christmas.

She'd never spent a Christmas anywhere except in a big city, and she loved it all, everything the song said, the city streets and busy sidewalks dressed up in holiday style in tinsel wreaths and Styrofoam candy canes. She loved the tawdry Santas on street corners — both the legitimate ones and the copycat panhandlers — as well as the opulently bearded Santas holding court for long lines of dumbstruck children in the shopping malls. She loved the millions of strings of colored lights that every year turned even Southern California's sun-baked suburbs into Christmas wonderlands. She never missed *Miracle on 34th Street* when it came on television, or the Grinch, Frosty, Rudolph, and the Peanuts gang, whether Jordy wanted to watch them with her or not.

She wasn't sure why her love for the season had managed to survive so many disappointing childhood Christmases, including a few that could only be described as nightmarish. She didn't know how she'd managed to keep it intact through the years of helping people for whom the season of joy meant only depression, loneliness, and pain. Sheer stubbornness, perhaps.

But this year, though she hadn't wanted to admit it, for all her brave talk for Jordy's sake about picking holly and putting up decorations, she'd been having a hard time getting in the Christmas spirit. Jordy was right — without the glitz and hype of the shopping malls and television, there didn't seem to be anything to make it seem like Christmas for her.

But now . . . now there was William. William, with his dimpled grin and that twinkle in his eyes and enthusiastic shout of "Oh boy!" reminding her so much of Jordy before the clouds of disillusionment had overshadowed

her naturally sunny nature. Carolyn had for-
given Russ Robards many things, given his
own barren childhood, but she didn't know
whether she could ever forgive him for rob-
bing his little girl of a sense of wonder.

Soon, Carolyn knew, she was going to have
to tell Clay about the pecans. And he would
come to the same conclusion she had. Soon
the pageant would be over and he would take
William and turn him over to the authorities
along with what he knew. But even if that
happened, Carolyn vowed, she was going to
see to it that William had Christmas presents.
No matter where he was. Or with whom. Her
stomach knotted and twisted, but she refused
to be depressed about it. Maybe . . . just
maybe, something would happen. A miracle.
It was Christmas time, after all.

As before, she found Christmas in Wal-
Mart. There were Santas handing out candy
canes, carols blaring from the loudspeaker,
tinsel garlands festooning the displays, and
hordes of frantic shoppers crowding the aisles.
Carolyn didn't mind the crowds; even the
most distracted seemed able to muster smiles
of apology for their cart collisions and crying
children. Anyway, it was all familiar music
to her ears.

She bought William a Christmas stocking
and some Ninja Turtles to go in it; also some

Ninja Turtle socks and a Ninja Turtle flashlight and some bubblebath in a green plastic bottle shaped like a Ninja Turtle. She debated long and hard whether to buy him a pair of fantastically expensive running shoes advertised as being like the ones Michael Jordan wears. *Could* she afford it? No, she really could not. So she settled for a sweatshirt with Michael Jordan's picture on it instead.

For Traveler she bought a nice big rawhide chew toy, and a collar with a nametag on it. After a great deal of thought she picked out a pretty apron for Miss Leona and a nice pair of gloves for Clay. Even if he already had gloves, she reasoned, he could always use another pair.

She bought a Christmas tree, too, not as pitiful as Charlie Brown's, but close. She bought a couple of strings of lights, which she hoped wouldn't weigh it down too much, and some red ribbon, construction paper, and glue for the kids to make ornaments out of. At the last minute she decided on some tinsel garland — what was Christmas without tinsel? — and a cassette tape of Christmas carols sung by various country music stars.

After a stop at Bi-Lo, where she remembered to pick up wrapping paper and Scotch tape, she felt broke but positively drunk with Christmas spirit. She put the tape in the car stereo and sang out loud with it all the way home, tapping her fingers on the steering wheel.

She'd intended to call Clay as soon as she got home to see how the children were getting along, but by the time she got there it was nearly one o'clock, which meant they were probably already on the way to pageant practice. It also meant she had only a couple of hours left to play Santa Claus, so she got the groceries unloaded and put away as fast as she could, made herself a hot dog in the microwave, and sat down to wrap packages. When all her new purchases had been safely tucked away under the bed along with Jordy's presents, she carried in the Christmas tree and stood it in front of the window. She didn't decorate it, though, since that was something she knew the children would enjoy doing. Instead she dug a stapler out of her box of office supplies and set about hanging the tinsel garland.

Somewhere along the line she decided that since she was decking her halls, so to speak, it would be nice to have the appropriate musical accompaniment. She wanted to play her new Christmas tape and was very disappointed to recall that her stereo was still in California, in storage. Then she thought of Jordy's Walkman.

★ ★ ★

Clay didn't know what to do, which wasn't a situation in which he often found himself. He was standing on Carolyn's front porch, having just knocked twice on the door and gotten no answer. He knew she was home, because he could hear singing coming from inside the house and because he could see someone moving around when he looked in the front window. The trouble was, he couldn't see clearly because there was a tree in the way, and he couldn't figure out a good reason why she wasn't answering her door.

Now, normally he'd just open the door, stick his head in, and holler, which was the way things were done around here and always had been. On the other hand, people from places like Chicago and L.A. had different ideas about locked doors and neighbors walking in unannounced. But on the *other* hand, what he had to tell her was important and he knew she'd want to know about it. What in the hell was he supposed to do?

What he did was knock one more time, then ease the door open a crack and call tentatively through it, "Carolyn? You in there?"

The singing continued uninterrupted, and he could tell for sure now that it was Carolyn, and that she was managing a pretty fair imitation of Brenda Lee doing "Rockin' Around the Christmas Tree." Fascinated, he pushed the door wider and stepped inside. Then for a while all he could do was stand and stare.

He could see now why she hadn't been able to hear his knock. She was wearing headphones. And she still didn't know he was there, because she had her back to him. She was standing on the back of the couch stapling tinsel garland high on the wall, except that *standing* didn't begin to describe what she was doing. She had her hair tied up on top of her head with some kind of puffy material — kind of an *I Dream of Jeannie* effect that was enhanced by the six-inch gap between the bottom of her sweater and the top of her slacks that was caused by her upraised arms. Her feet, bare except for nylons, were performing some kind of jitterbug dance step along the back of the couch, and her bottom was . . . well, moving with the beat of the song she was singing. Except that "moving" didn't come close to describing what her bottom was doing.

"*Deck* the halls with *boughs* of *ha*-ah-ly . . ."

With the word "deck" her bottom went *bump* in one direction, and with "boughs" it went *bump* in the other, and on the hiccupping syllables of "holly" it executed a back-and-forth wiggle that just about stopped his heart. He didn't think he'd ever seen anything so adorable and sexy before in his life. Part of what made it so sexy, of course, was the fact that she was absolutely oblivious to his presence, as free of self-consciousness and inhibition as a very small child, as joyous and unfettered as a butterfly. In fact he was beginning to feel guilty as hell about standing there watching her like that, but he couldn't for the life of him think what to do about it. Probably the decent thing to do would be to just turn around and walk out and pretend he'd never been there, except he still had something to tell her that she really did need to know.

Trouble was, no matter how he got her attention it was almost certain to scare the living daylights out of her, which, considering the precariousness of her position, might even be dangerous. On the other hand he knew he'd better do something right quick, because if she turned around and caught him staring at her with his mouth open she was going to be embarrassed for sure, and probably ticked at him besides.

The song was wrapping up, and he knew if she was ever going to notice him it would most likely be during the silence between songs. It was now or never. With his heart thumping and his pulse rate soaring he crossed the living room and lightly touched her on the small of her back.

She squawked like a frightened hen and whirled around, catching him alongside the head with the stapler. The next thing he knew he was flat on his back on the sofa with Carolyn on top of him and the world spinning around like a carousel gone crazy.

Chapter 9

"Clay! Oh Lord, I'm so sorry. Did I hurt you? I didn't mean —"

With a tremendous exercise of will Clay managed to make the room stand still. "No," he muttered thickly, "you didn't."

"Yes I did. I clobbered you with the — oh God, I knew it. You're *bleeding!*"

"I'm fine. S'only a scratch."

"How do you know? You can't see it. Here, let me —"

Clay groaned. He couldn't help it, not with her wriggling around on top of him. "Carolyn."

"What?"

"Lie still."

"Oh no — you are hurt, aren't you? Somewhere else . . . I knew it. When you — when we —"

"Carolyn, for God's sake, *hold still.*"

"But I want to see —"

"Hush."

Then for a while he just lay there listening to the sounds they made breathing together, feeling their hearts knocking against each other in offset rhythms, bellies touching, pressing, withdrawing and touching again. Feeling the tender weight of her fingers on his cheek, the humid warmth of her breath. Trying to think whether he'd ever felt like this before in his life. Trying to *think* — period.

He opened his eyes, then began to laugh softly. With the headphones looped over one eyebrow, lips parted, and cheeks softly flushed, she looked like a tipsy angel.

"What?" she said breathlessly.

He reached up and slowly pushed the headphones back where they belonged. And felt her fingers curl against his cheek in involuntary response.

"What —"

"Ssh . . ." He touched her lips with his forefinger. "Don't move." He was the one who felt drunk . . . drowning in her whiskey eyes.

He couldn't kiss her — he knew that. If he kissed her he wouldn't be able to stop, and the consequences of that were not something he wanted to face. He knew he'd never wanted anyone the way he wanted her at this moment; the pain and pressure of it were excruciating. But the confusion and fear that went with the wanting were a whole lot worse.

He heard the soft, vulnerable sound of her swallow, as loud in that charged silence as a cry in the night. Contrition and tenderness filled him.

"California," he said softly, "what are we going to do about this?"

A tiny frown appeared between her eyes. She cleared her throat delicately and murmured, "Well, I suppose I should get off of you."

"Yes," he said on a long exhalation, letting it go at that, "I suppose you should."

"Is it . . . is it okay if I move now?"

"What? Oh —" He began to laugh again, silently, then put his head back and closed his eyes, steeling himself. "Yeah," he whispered, "it's okay." But she still wasn't moving. He lifted his head and looked at her. "What now?"

"I can't get up." Her cheeks were pink, her eyes distressed.

"Why not?"

"You're, um . . . holding me. Your hands are on my . . ."

His hands were on her waist, that's where they were, the part of it that had been so charmingly exposed while she was dancing on the back of the couch. They were underneath her sweater, his fingers touching satin skin, supple muscle, the enchanting undulations of her spine.

"Oh," he said in an airless voice, and peeled

his hands away from her. "There."

"Thank you."

The moments that followed were difficult for both of them, but in the end Carolyn was standing up tugging at her clothes and Clay was sitting on the edge of the couch feeling as if someone had pulled all his covers off on a cold night.

Carolyn fidgeted, pulling off the headphones and looking distractedly around her for a place to put them, finally dropping them onto the arm of the couch. She lifted her arms to restore order to her hair, but dropped them hurriedly when she felt cold air on her bare skin and saw Clay glance quickly up, then even more quickly away.

"Well," she said, clearing her throat. "What did you . . . uh. Would you like some . . . coffee?"

"Oh, no thanks, I just . . ." He stopped suddenly. "You know," he said, frowning at the Christmas tree, "that's not quite as ugly as the one my dad bought, but it's close."

"Thank you," Carolyn said sweetly. "It's going to look wonderful when it's decorated."

Clay shook his head morosely. "It'll only get worse. Trust me — this is the voice of experience talking." He stood up, stretched his back in a testing sort of way, then gingerly touched the cut on his cheekbone, making

Carolyn cringe with guilt. She really had caught him a good one with that stapler. Although it served him right, sneaking up on her like that. She hated to think how long he might have been standing there . . . watching her. Oh Lord — and she'd been dancing. And singing. And . . .

"Well, I guess I'll be going," he said absently, frowning at his fingers. He started for the door.

"Clay?" *Tell him. You have to, you know you do.*

He turned, one hand on the doorknob, the other braced against the frame. "Hmm?"

And then it suddenly occurred to her to wonder just why he'd stopped by. Her heart began to pound again, in a much less pleasurable way than before. "Is everything okay? With the kids, I mean. Is it — have you found out something?"

"Found out something? Oh — you mean about . . ."

"William — yes. Have you? Or did you — you didn't —"

"No, I didn't. I haven't." He studied her for a moment, his expression grim. Then he made a soft ironic sound and smiled wryly. "I just stopped to tell you the kids have a ride home from practice. You don't need to pick 'em up."

"Oh," she murmured, weak-kneed with relief — and another tidal wave of guilt. "Thank
you."

But he went on standing there in the doorway, an arm's length away, and she didn't
know what she wanted more — for him to
go away or stay. She felt battered and shaken
and badly in need of a chance to pull herself
together, and having him there was only making things worse. But the idea of ending this,
of his leaving . . .

"What this door needs," he said suddenly,
frowning at the door panels, "is a wreath."

"I know." Carolyn sucked in air, which always seemed to be in short supply when he
was near. "They had some nice but expensive
ones at Wal-Mart."

Clay snorted. "You don't buy a wreath, you
make one. All you need is some evergreen,
a little holly, a few pine cones . . ."

"I thought about it," Carolyn said distractedly, gazing up at him. "But I don't
know . . ." There was such an air of unreality
about standing there discussing Christmas
wreaths face to face with him when she
could still feel the imprint of his body
stamped on the front of hers, and when her
body still trembled inside from the effects
of it.

"I'll make you one," Clay said, sounding

as if he needed to clear his throat.

"Right now?"

"Sure, why not? You got a pair of pruning clippers around here?"

"In the basement, I think . . ."

"Well, okay then." Scowling fiercely, he turned and stomped across the porch.

"Hey," Carolyn panted, skipping down the steps and running to catch up with him, "I thought you didn't like Christmas."

"Got nothing against Christmas." He looked down at her and his expression softened, deepening the creases at the corners of his eyes in the way she was beginning to find so terribly appealing. "Just a few bad memories and associations, that's all." He tweaked her ponytail in a big-brotherly sort of way. "I'll tell you about it someday."

"Is that a promise?"

"Hah!" He grinned wryly and shook his head. "No promises, doc."

And then they were at the basement door, and she was remembering the last time they'd been there, and knew that he was remembering it, too. For a few moments the world seemed to darken and the air fill with tension, the way it does just before a storm.

I wonder, Carolyn thought. I wonder . . .

But once they were out in the woods, tramping up and down hills and crunching through drifts of dry, dead leaves, it seemed to Carolyn as though the storm had already passed, leaving the world bright and glorious, full of sunshine and singing birds. Clay pointed out birds to her she'd never seen before, and told her their names. He showed her the muskrat's burrow under the roots of a tree on the edge of the lake, and the tiny ferns growing among the rocks in the gulley that fed into it. He pointed out a massive oak tree he said was over a hundred and fifty years old. "Think of it — this tree was alive during the War Between The States. Imagine the stories it could tell." "Were there battles fought around here?" Carolyn wanted to know. "No," said Clay, "but if there had been, this tree would've seen 'em."

He showed her how to identify the dogwood by the lacy pattern of its bark. "Have you ever seen the dogwood in bloom?" he asked her. And in his words she saw the woods in April, with clouds of white petals drifting down like snow.

They talked and laughed, their voices floating like birdsong on the champagne air. Carolyn pricked her fingers on the holly and didn't feel it; somewhere she lost her ponytail holder — snagged by a twig, perhaps — and didn't care. She forgot *everything* in the sheer joy of being with Clay — forgot Jordy's emo-

231

tional problems and the matter of William, forgot the book she was supposed to write and how she was going to earn a living when her settlement money ran out. Sitting on the summer house steps watching Clay's big strong hands bend pine and holly boughs into the shape of a wreath, watching his fingers deftly weave twine and wire and pinecones, she knew only that she'd never been happier in all her life than she was right then.

Happy. What am I afraid of? she thought. Am I afraid of happiness?

Because at the moment she couldn't think of any reasons compelling enough to make her back off from this thing that had been staring her in the face for a while now. Problems and responsibilities seemed inconsequential. Right now nothing seemed as important as being *happy*. And happiness was being with Clay.

Oh, I do want to be happy . . .

Next time, she promised, gazing at his rugged face, focused in rapt concentration on the job his hands were doing. The face that suddenly, miraculously had become the focus of her own existence. *Next time I won't back away*.

Who am I kidding? Clay thought, feeling her gaze like a physical touch. *It isn't going to go away. She's here and so am I and neither of us is going anywhere. It's inevitable. Why am I fighting it?*

He looked at her and smiled, and was instantly swallowed up in her marvelous golden eyes.

"You have twigs in your hair," he said in a voice that didn't belong to him, that seemed instead only a part of that enchanted golden haze. "Here, hold still. . . ."

He removed the twigs but his fingers stayed, weaving themselves through the sun-shot strands of her hair. *Who am I kidding?* He found himself gazing at her mouth, thinking that the undefined upper lip gave it a crushed-blossom look, as if she'd just been thoroughly kissed. *Why am I fighting this?*

He couldn't remember why. He forgot that he hadn't wanted to get involved with a divorced woman with problems; forgot she even had a smart-mouthed teenaged daughter; forgot that she wanted him to help her keep a ten-year-old runaway she'd found in her basement. There was only the intoxicating glow of those eyes . . . the soft sweet sigh of her breath . . . the silken warmth of her hair slipping like melted butter through his fingers . . .

The slamming of a car door shattered the enchantment like a rock hurled through a plate-glass window, letting in the sound of running footsteps and — children's voices:

"Ha, ha, I beat you, I beat you!"

"Yeah? Well, I wasn't even racing, dummy."

"Yes you were, you were running."

"Was not."

"Were too. Hey — what are you guys makin', huh? Can I help?"

"All done," said Clay softly, and stood up, dropping the wreath into Carolyn's lap. "Chore time," he muttered. "Gotta go. See you all later."

When he got to his pickup he opened the door and climbed in, then sat there for a minute or two, just trying to decide what he was most — relieved, or sorry.

"Mom," said Jordy, "do you believe in angels?"

Carolyn looked up from the bowl of cranberries she was sorting. "What in the world brought this on?"

The question took her by surprise. Something had obviously been bothering Jordy ever since the children had gotten home from pageant practice. She'd been unusually quiet and seemed to spend a lot of time staring at William in a troubled, measuring sort of way. They'd had another fight or argument of some kind, Carolyn assumed. She'd figured Jordy would talk about it sooner or later, but she definitely hadn't expected to be asked about angels.

Jordy was pretending to concentrate on poking a needle through a cranberry and pulling the berry all the way to the end of the string. She shrugged and said, "Nothing." Then, in the supercasual way that meant she really wanted to know, asked, "Do you?"

"Well, uh," Carolyn floundered. Her childhood had been a little short on religious education, and the fact was, she wasn't sure what she believed. "If you mean the kind that wear white robes and golden halos and fly around with feathery wings," she said, thinking about it, "I guess the answer is no. If you mean, do I believe people's spirits go somewhere when they die . . ." Actually, she'd never been quite sure about that. She'd always thought it was something a person had to take on faith, faith being something you either felt or you didn't — like love.

"Miss Leona does," said Jordy, still carefully stringing cranberries. "She says angels come to visit us all the time, and sometimes Jesus does too, and we don't even know it. She says an angel could be anybody — a homeless person, or somebody who doesn't have enough food to eat or warm clothes to wear, or even somebody who's just lonely and needs a friend. She says that's why we should always be kind and help people when they come to us, because we never know when it might be an angel."

Carolyn nodded. "I think I've heard that story."

"It's in the Bible," said Jordy. "Miss Leona said so."

"Well," Carolyn said, tiptoeing carefully through unfamiliar territory, "I'm sure she knows. I think what it means is just that, um . . ."

"Mom, could I ask you something?"

"Honey, of course you can."

She dropped her gaze to her hands and squirmed in her chair as if there were rocks in it. "Uh, uh . . . it's silly."

"Jordy, whatever it is, it's not silly, especially if it's bothering you. Come on — spit it out."

"You'll laugh."

"I will not."

"Yes you will. It's pretty wild, Mom."

"I promise I won't laugh. But I may kill you if you don't —"

"Okay, okay. But you promised." She glanced over her shoulder at William's bedroom door. William had nodded off over his supper an hour ago and was sound asleep with Traveler curled up beside him, but she lowered her voice to a hoarse whisper anyway.

"Mom . . . what if—" She took a deep breath. "Do you think William could be an angel?"

"Oh, Jordy."

"Mom, you *promised*."

"Clay? I'm sorry to bother you . . ."

"California," Clay mumbled, "is that you?" He'd dozed off at his desk, something he couldn't remember ever having done before. He hadn't been sleeping well; lately his bed seemed lonely and cold.

"I shouldn't have called so late."

He squinted at his watch, then sat upright. "That's okay. What's wrong?"

"Nothing's wrong. I just . . . There's something I have to tell you. About William."

"Shoot."

He could hear her take a breath. "I think he might be from a migrant family. He told me . . . they picked pecans."

"Huh," said Clay, trying to rub the sleep out of his eyes. "I don't know too much about migrants. Seems to me there's a special agency deals with them. I'll have to look into it first thing Monday."

There was a long pause. Then: "Clay. . . ."

"What?"

"Nothing." The phone clicked softly in his ear.

He hung it up and sat back in his chair with

a sigh, but it was a long time before he went upstairs to bed.

Clay spent most of Sunday in the barn, mending stalls. He'd come to the conclusion sometime in the middle of the previous night that the only way he was going to survive his current predicament was if he saw as little of Carolyn Robards as possible. He probably would've spent the whole day in the barn — maybe even the rest of his life — if Miss Leona hadn't come looking for him about the middle of the afternoon.

"John Clayton," she called, rapping on the barn door with the cane he'd bought her, to get his attention. "What are you doin' out here so long?"

"Getting ready for the lambing," Clay mumbled around a mouthful of nails.

"Lambing isn't going to start until February."

He took the nails out of his mouth and stuck them in his shirt pocket. "Yeah, but the goats are due to kid in January. Never hurts to get things done ahead of time."

"Did you eat?"

"Yes, ma'am, I did."

"You goin' to the church tonight?"

"Didn't plan on it."

"John Clayton," said Miss Leona sternly,

"you haven't been inside a church since you got home from up North. You mean to tell me you're not going to church on Christmas Sunday?"

Clay picked up a board and scowled at it. "If I haven't been before, why should I go now?"

"The chul'ren's pageant's tonight, you know that."

"Miss Leona, I reckon I've seen enough Christmas pageants. Got no reason to see another one."

"You got three good reasons," snapped Miss Leona, whumping the floor with her cane.

Even with his back to her he could tell she was good and ticked at him, but he was feeling too stubborn to answer. Instead he fitted the board into place, took a nail out of his pocket, and started banging away at it with his hammer.

"Those chul'ren will be heartbroken if you don't come see 'em sing."

Clay doubted that, but he didn't say anything — just hammered in another nail.

"Be nicer for Miss Carolyn if she didn't have to sit alone."

"She'll have you," Clay said, gritting his teeth as he hit the nail a glancing blow and bent it double.

"Not the same thing, and you know it."

He yanked the nail out of the board and threw it into the bucket at his feet.

"John Clayton," Miss Leona said while he was reaching for another nail. He turned and looked at her; he knew implacability when he heard it. "I need you to drive the chul'ren and me to the church tonight. You can sit out in the car and sulk all evening if you want to."

"How am I gonna take everybody in my pickup?" he argued as he pounded in another nail. But even to his own ears it sounded whiny and futile.

"We'll be taking my car," declared Miss Leona, stumping toward the door. Clay groaned. "So you better stop all that bangin' and go see to it the car's in working order. Been a while since it was driven last."

Clay just stood there and muttered help-lessly under his breath.

"What's that you say, John Clayton?"

Because it was inappropriate for both Sunday and Christmas, he didn't tell her.

"My goodness," said Carolyn softly. "I'm impressed."

"It's Miss Leona's," Clay muttered, casting a glum look over his shoulder to where a shiny black car the approximate size and configuration of a small ocean liner sat idling lustily in the driveway. "I think it used to belong to a Mafia don in Philadelphia."

"That's impressive, too," she murmured, patting his shirtfront as she moved past him through the doorway. "But I was talking about the tie."

She hadn't thought it possible for Clay to be any more attractive than he was in the hip-hugging Levi's and macho plaid shirts he always wore. Certainly he could never look sexier than in the T-shirt he'd stripped down to in the kitchen the day he'd fixed lunch for her. She knew now she'd been wrong. Clay in a suit and tie was enough to make her forget all the resolutions she'd made to herself during the course of a long, sleepless night.

"You look nice too," he growled, as if it pained him to say it. "Is that your coat? Here, let me get that for you . . ."

"Thank you," Carolyn murmured as he settled the coat over her shoulders, closing her eyes while her stomach did flipflops. She'd chosen a long-sleeved cream-colored wool dress with beading around the neckline, over the shoulders and in a vee down the front. She'd worried that it might be too dressy for the occasion, but now, seeing Clay, she was glad she'd worn it.

"I'm going to throw up," Jordy announced as she joined them on the porch. "*Where* is

William? He's just a kid, and it takes him longer to get ready than anyone. *Will-yum!* Will you hurry *up!* Mom, how's my hair? I can't find my red ponytail holder *anywhere.*"

"You're going to be wearing a towel on your head anyway," said Carolyn distractedly. "What does it matter? William? What are you doing, honey? We have to go."

"Just sayin' good-bye to Traveler." William's voice was a bit muffled by the fact that he was lying on his stomach on the rug with his face buried in the dog's thick fur.

"That dog's too fat and too lazy," Clay commented, watching with a thoughtful frown as Traveler thumped his tail twice and then laid his head back down with a groan. "Sure doesn't act like a young, healthy animal should. Probably ought to take him to the vet."

Carolyn's breath caught and she glanced up quickly, wondering if he was even aware of what that remark implied. But then William came charging headlong out the door and she had to snag him and see that he was brushed off and buttoned up, and that the lights were turned off and the doors shut, and everybody herded down the steps and into the car.

"I can't believe this thing," she murmured as Clay held the door for her. "What is it, a Lincoln? It's as big as a boat. How did she ever drive a thing like this?"

"Like the *Queen Mary*," Clay muttered out of one side of his mouth, bending his head close to hers. Carolyn's heart jumped and they both laughed softly together.

"John Clayton, I heard that," said Miss Leona from the back seat.

The church, like so many southern rural churches, stood alone at a crossroads, set back from the road a bit on its own little hill, surrounded by its own tidy cemetery and beyond that, woods and fields and great, spreading oaks. It was well cared for and sturdily built of red brick and white clapboard and had a tall white steeple that was floodlit for the occasion like a lighthouse beacon against a wintry, indigo sky. Carolyn thought it looked exactly like a Christmas card.

The church yard was already crowded with cars. Clay parked the Lincoln along the driveway and got out to open the door for Miss Leona.

"I'm going to throw up," Jordy said again, emerging from the car. "I know I am. The minute I open my mouth."

"What's the matter?" asked Clay. "You sick?"

"Nah, she's not sick," said William. "She's nervous. So am I. I got bugs in my stomach."

"Butterflies, dummy," said Jordy automatically. "I'm not either nervous. It's just that I *can't sing*. I'm going to make the biggest fool of myself, I just know it."

"Nah, you won't," said Clay as they started up the driveway, he and Carolyn with Miss Leona between them and the children skipping all around. "What you do is, you pretend you're wearing headphones. Like you're listening to your Walkman, you know what I mean? Listening to the music and just singin' and rockin' along — Carolyn, you okay?"

"Hold your arms up, honey-chile," said Miss Leona. "That always helps me when I get somethin' down the wrong way."

"I'm fine," Carolyn wheezed. "Just . . . choked on a breath mint."

Clay reached across Miss Leona to thump her helpfully on the back. Carolyn turned to glare at him and caught an unmistakable light in his eyes, even through the glaze of tears in hers. Her heart was already pounding, but it went on doing so long after the coughing fit had passed.

"Run on, chul'ren," said Miss Leona. "They'll be waitin' on you in the Sunday school room."

Jordy groaned dramatically. "Okay — don't do anything dorky, Mom, *please?* Promise me you're not going to wave or anything like that?"

"You can wave at me," said William, showing his dimples.

Carolyn bent down to give him an impulsive kiss, then turned him with a swat to his backside. "Go on — sing pretty, now, you two."

The children went running off, and Carolyn, Clay, and Miss Leona went to find seats in the sanctuary, which turned out not to be difficult even though the church was already crowded. Miss Leona seemed to have her regular spot down near the front. Everyone stood up to let them in, greeting Miss Leona with affection, Clay with pleased surprise, and Carolyn with cordial curiosity. Clay ushered Miss Leona into the pew first and then followed himself, so Carolyn wound up sitting between him and a heavyset lady wearing a navy blue and white polka-dot dress and white gloves. It was a tight squeeze. Clay's thigh was pressed all along the length of hers, and he had to turn a little bit sideways to accommodate the breadth of his shoulders. His body heat seemed to envelop her; she began to be very glad they'd left their coats in the front entry.

To distract herself from the sensations produced by the nearness of Clay's body, which she was guiltily certain were inappropriate for church, she began to notice the people around her. A nice mix of black and white, which surprised her a little; ladies in hats and gloves fanning themselves with their programs, antsy children in bright new Christmas clothes, stoic farmers in ill-fitting, seldom-worn suits, all turning to talk to one another, clasping hands, waving to people they knew across the room. It wasn't what she'd expected — certainly nothing like the church in town she'd attended with Russell on a few tedious occasions early in their marriage, or the one in Beverly Hills she'd been married in. This church was noisy and warm and filled with something she couldn't define at first, a kind of *lightness* she realized at last must be joy.

The lightness was everywhere — in the white-painted walls and pews hung with pine garlands and big red bows; in the towering Christmas tree beside the pulpit and the brightly colored homemade banners hanging from the choir loft; the candles and crèche on the altar, and the empty manger on the chancel steps, overflowing with fresh, sweet-smelling hay. But it was especially noticeable in the faces of the people around her.

As she sat there with the warm press of Clay's body against hers, looking at the faces and listening to the babble of joyful voices, Carolyn felt herself filling up with emotions she couldn't name, feelings she couldn't explain or understand. She felt . . . tremulous inside. Fluttery, almost as if it were she who had butterflies. But there was a strange weight inside her, too, as if her chest didn't quite have enough room in it. She drew a deep breath and stole a puzzled glance at Clay, but he was staring straight ahead with set jaw and narrowed eyes, seemingly the only face in the place — other than hers — not touched by joy.

A door at the back of the chancel opened and the minister came in and took his place in the pulpit. The noise gradually subsided and the minister began to speak, welcoming everyone and praising the opportunity to get together for the celebration of the Christmas Story. As he spoke, the congregation answered him with nods and murmured phrases that had a rhythm all their own, almost like a counterpoint to the melody of a song.

The minister concluded his remarks to a chorus of "Hallelujah!"s. The lights went out, except for the candles on the altar, and in the near darkness, to the accompaniment of shuffles and nervous coughs, the choir loft began to fill with children wearing white cotton robes and cardboard wings and wire halos with tinsel wrapped around them. Then a light came on above the pulpit, revealing a little girl with her hair in stiff pigtails, wearing a red choir robe, holding a big open book in her hands. In a slow, solemn voice she began to read: " 'A decree went out from Caesar Augustus. . . .' "

The angel choir began to hum, and then to sing "O Little Town of Bethlehem," but with a new rhythm and a few gospel riffs Carolyn hadn't ever heard before. At the same time, a spotlight was trained on the door at the back of the church, and Joseph appeared pulling a wagon with cardboard cutouts of a donkey fastened to its sides. In the wagon sat Mary, eyes demurely downcast, wearing a white scarf over her head and a blue bathrobe over an enormously bulging middle.

". . . are met in thee tonight . . ." sang the angel choir. Then there was silence in the church, except for the creaking sound of the wagon making its way slowly up the center aisle.

While Mary and Joseph took their places at opposite ends of the manger, the angels began to hum once more. And then, from a side door came a line of tiny angels — cherubs — who marched smartly in and arranged themselves on the bottom step of the chancel, in front of the manger. (Except for one cherub who seemed to be so enthralled by the spectacle that he wandered out of line and stood with his back to the congregation and his fingers in his mouth, watching his brother and sister cherubs in absolute awe.)

The crowded feeling in Carolyn's chest grew worse. It rose into her throat, causing congestion there, too. She put her hand over her mouth, but the feeling moved on anyway, stinging her nose and eyes. And when the cherubs began to sing "Mary Had a Baby" in their sweet baby voices, she knew with certainty and dismay that she was going to cry.

Something nudged her elbow. "Here," Clay growled in her ear, "take my hand."

"What?" she whispered, not understanding.

"Just . . . give me your hand."

The next thing she knew, her hand was being enveloped in Clay's, and she was holding onto it for dear life.

Chapter 10

It was something he'd seen his father do in church more times than he could remember — just reach over without saying anything and take his mother's hand. Now for the first time he understood why.

His mother was a strong woman he'd never seen shed a tear when the going was tough. But weddings, baptisms, certain old hymns, and *especially* small children singing always, *always* made her cry. Which he'd always thought must have made it tough on her husband, because like Clay, his dad never could stand a weeping woman. He'd wondered how his dad could do it, just sit there and hold his wife's hand while the tears ran down her face, and never say a word.

Now, with Carolyn's hand clasped tightly in his, he knew that what his dad had been saying to his mom was all the things he probably never could put into words. That he understood, and loved her enough to put up with the waterworks. That he was there if she needed someone to hold on to, and always would be.

The revelation gave him a few moments of

panic; he felt as if his heart had grown too big for his chest. But then he looked down at his big rough hand wrapped around her small, soft one, and he began to think that maybe there was a kind of *rightness* about it, a certain continuity, like the turning of the seasons. He began to feel . . . peaceful. As if his life had come full circle and finally brought him back to where he belonged.

" *'There were in the same country, shepherds abiding in the fields, keeping watch over their flocks. . . .' "*

"Look," Clay said softly as the shepherds began to file in wearing dishtowels on their heads and carrying their long, crooked staves. The "flocks" consisted of stuffed toy lambs, Clay noticed, which made him smile a little, remembering the year they'd tried to use real sheep, with disastrous results.

"Look," Carolyn whispered, squeezing his hand, "there's Jordy. Oh my — I don't believe it — she's *waving.*" She looked up at him with swimming eyes, her free hand over her mouth, silently laughing. "Do I dare wave back?"

"By all means," Clay whispered. "It's expected."

"When do they sing?"

"Not yet. Not until the end. The wise men are up next. Look — here they come."

As the girl with the book was finishing up

the part about the wise men from afar, a star was illuminated high above the altar. The angels began humming the chorus of "We Three Kings," and the spotlight shone once again on the door at the back of the church. Clay heard Carolyn suck in her breath and wondered if she was holding hers, too, as he was.

Some things never change, Clay thought as he watched William come through the door, somber as a judge, resplendent in his purple turban, carrying his gift of gold as if it were the real thing. The littlest one was always first. It almost put a lump in *his* throat, remembering the times he'd followed his brothers through that same door, always the last, since he was the oldest and tallest.

"We three kings of Orient are. . . ."

"Oh my goodness," Carolyn whispered through her fingers. "I didn't know he could sing."

"All God's children can sing, don't you know that?" Clay whispered back, bending his head close to hers.

She looked at him, half-laughing, half sobbing, and whispered, "Oh God — you know what? Jordy's afraid he might be an angel."

"Hush up, you two," whispered Miss Leona, jabbing him in the ribs with her elbow.

So they had to sit there laughing together and trying to do it silently like misbehaving children, Clay feeling like it wasn't enough to just be holding Carolyn's hand. He wanted to wrap his arms around her and hold her close so she'd know he was feeling the same things she was, plus a lot of things she didn't know about, a lot more than he could ever tell her just by holding her hand.

The tableau was complete. There they all were — Joseph and Mary with the Baby Jesus doll, which had appeared miraculously in the manger, the shepherds and the wise men with their heads reverently bowed, and all the choirs of angels, including the cherubs who had come back in, hippy-hopping with excitement. A hush fell upon the congregation. Clay tightened his hold on Carolyn's hand.

Now the spotlight zeroed in on the angel choir — on one angel in particular, a black girl about high school age. In a deep, rich gospel voice she began to sing a capella . . . slowly, emotionally,

"Go tell it on the mountain . . ."

First the chorus, then the first verse. The shepherds all straightened up, getting ready. So did most of the congregation. When it came around to the chorus again the shepherds joined in lustily:

". . . over the hills and everywhere . . ."

He heard Carolyn's soft gasp as she grabbed for his arm.

All the shepherds were singing — every last one of them. Including Jordy, the smart-mouthed kid. She had her eyes closed and her hands up to her ears as if she were wearing headphones, and her lips were moving and she was rocking and swaying to the beat.

So, by this time, was everyone else in the building. Down the chancel steps came the shepherds, leading the way, clapping their hands and dancing, singing at the tops of their lungs. The congregation was on its feet, clapping and dancing and singing too. The wise men and angels, Mary and Joseph, the girl with the book, the minister and finally all the congregation followed the shepherds up the aisle and out into the crystal, starry night. Once outside the church, the song sort of broke up into shouts of "Hallelujah!" and "Amen!" And then everybody was laughing, crying, and hugging everybody else and wishing everybody within shouting distance a Merry Christmas.

In all the confusion, and trying to get Miss Leona safely through the crowd, Clay lost track of Carolyn. When he finally had Miss Leona safely outside and busy with all her friends and relations wanting to say "Merry Christmas," he went looking and found her over by the Sunday school rooms, sandwiched by excited children, both talking at once.

"Did you see me?" William yelled as soon as he spotted Clay. "I get to keep the present — isn't it *great?*"

Clay never got a chance to answer that. Before he knew what was happening, Jordy had thrown her arms around his neck, pulled his head down and given him a big, noisy kiss on his cheek.

"It *worked,*" she said in an elated whisper. "I pretended I was listening to my Walkman, and it worked! Can you believe it? I was singing — really *singing.*"

"Well . . . humph . . . ah," muttered Clay, or words to that effect. He really wasn't certain what he said, because while he was saying it he was looking over Jordy's head at Carolyn, who was kind of hunkered down on one knee with William's arms wrapped around *her* neck. And she was looking back at him, those big golden eyes of hers pleading with him, asking him to give her the moon.

God knows, the way he was feeling right then, if he could have thought of a way to give it to her he would have. But he knew he couldn't, and the knowledge filled him with a despair unlike anything he'd ever felt before. Since he was still feeling everything she did, he knew that what Carolyn felt for that little boy had gone way beyond her ability to control it. It had been a mistake to let her keep the rascal even for one day, but he'd done it, and she'd fallen for him in a big way. What he was dealing with now was Maternal Love, pure and simple; he'd experienced a whole lot of it himself, firsthand, and he knew the real thing when he saw it, and he knew it was a natural force all its own. He knew that Carolyn loved the boy now as much as she loved her own child, and that it was going to break her heart to give him up.

Please, her eyes begged him. *Please let me keep him.*

Bleak with despair, aching for her, he shook his head slightly. *You know you can't. It's impossible.*

Her head came up, her arms tightened around the child, and her eyes burned fiercely, like candle flames. *Until Christmas, then. Wait until after Christmas. That's all I ask.*

After a long moment Clay closed his eyes and slowly nodded. If he couldn't give her the moon, at least he could give her Christmas.

When Carolyn went to tuck William in and kiss him good night she found him wide awake for a change, instead of snuggled up with Traveler and already half-asleep. This time Traveler was snoring on the rug and William was sitting cross-legged in the middle of the bed with the contents of his backpack arranged before him on the spread. His newest treasure, the Magi's gift, a shoebox wrapped in gold foil, was balanced on one knobby knee.

"What's the matter, honey?" she asked softly, sitting down beside him and ruffling his hair. "Too excited to sleep?"

"Yes, ma'am," said William, gazing down at the gold-wrapped present. But he didn't sound excited. He sounded thoughtful, even a little dejected.

It wasn't surprising, Carolyn thought, gazing at him tenderly. After such an emotional high there was bound to be a letdown. She put her arm around his shoulders and gave them a squeeze. "Hey, you were great tonight, you know that? I was really proud of you."

A ghost of his dimpled grin appeared and he muttered with uncharacteristic shyness, "Yeah, I was proud of me, too." But there was clearly something else on his mind, and after a moment, still looking down at the Magi's gift and idly teetering it back and forth, he said slowly, "Miss Leona says that's the reason we give presents on Christmas — because the wise men brought presents to the Baby Jesus. Do you reckon that's true?"

Carolyn thought about it for a second or two, theology not being one of her strong points, then laughed. "If Miss Leona says it's true, then it must be. It does make sense, doesn't it?"

William looked sideways at her and grinned ruefully. "A lot more sense than dumb ol' Santa Claus, that's for sure."

"What?" said Carolyn, rearing back in mock surprise. "You mean to tell me you don't believe in Santa Claus?"

"Do you?" asked William, looking wary.

"Well, of course I do," said Carolyn, on much firmer ground now. "Santa was a real person, you know. His real name was Saint Nicholas, and he lived a long, long time ago. He was a kind and wealthy man who went around giving away money and presents to the poor. That's not so different from the wise men, is it?"

"So," said William carefully, "we're supposed to give presents to poor people?"

"Well, yes . . . and to people who are close to us."

"I gave somebody a present one time," said William. And he uncurled his fingers to show her the tiny, tacky shell-covered box.

She took the box from his outstretched hand and slowly lifted the lid. "Did you give this to your mother, William?" she asked softly. He nodded, still looking down, and something twisted painfully inside her chest. "Where is your mother now?"

He shrugged, and in a barely audible voice said, "I don't know. She went away one time and she didn't come back."

"Do you miss her?" Carolyn whispered, unable to speak through the ache in her throat.

"Yes, ma'am," William mumbled, and came into her arms in a blind little rush.

"It's okay, it's okay," she murmured as she held him and rubbed his thin little back. "I know you do." She looked up at the ceiling, then closed her eyes on her tears. "Would you like to tell me about your mother?"

He nodded, but no words came. She stroked his hair and felt him tremble.

"Well then," she said gently, with the tears running down her cheeks, "why don't you tell me her name?"

"His mother's name is Susan," Carolyn said. "Susan Potts."

She was standing in the barn doorway, a silhouette with the cold winter light behind her, hands jammed deep in her pockets, hair caught in her coat collar and spilling out onto her shoulders.

Clay straightened up slowly, easing the stiffness out of his back, and leaned his pitchfork against the stall. "He tell you that?" he asked quietly, pulling off his gloves.

She nodded and came toward him. "The

last time he saw her was in Florida. He was going there to find her."

He watched her warily, as if he thought she might self-destruct at a moment's notice, but as she moved away from the doorway and into the overhead electric light he could see that he didn't need to worry. She had a hunched-up, drawn-in look, as if her coat wasn't warm enough, but her face seemed calm. He took a deep breath. "You think he's telling the truth?"

She shrugged. "As he knows it, yes. He doesn't remember very much." She stopped a few feet away from him, her lips forming a small, sad smile. Her voice was faint. "He says they picked oranges."

"Migrants," Clay said on an exhalation. "You were right."

"I thought —" She stopped for a quick breath, and his heart gave a lurch. But again, though her eyes were dark and soft with pain, both her voice and features remained under perfect control. Just like his mother, he thought; when her heart was truly breaking she'd never shed a tear. "I thought it might be enough information for you . . . to find her. Maybe —"

"Carolyn —"

She finished it in a rush. "Maybe you could find her in time for Christmas." Her eyes were huge, her face unbearably transparent.

He raked a hand despairingly through his hair. "Carolyn, I just don't know. It would be — my God, it's only three days. It would take a miracle."

"It's Christmas, isn't it? The time for miracles?" Her laugh was precarious. The sheen in her eyes made him think of dewdrops quivering on the petals of a flower; a breath, a whisper would turn it to tears.

Very softly he said, "Are you sure you want to do this?"

Her answer was a whisper. "Yes. Just . . . find her. As soon as possible." For an instant her eyes seemed to glow even brighter, and then she turned away.

"Carolyn." He touched her shoulder. She hesitated, then raised her head and looked at him for what seemed like a lifetime. His fingers curved around her shoulder, compelling her gently, bringing her slowly back to face him. Then he closed his eyes, let go a soft, sighing breath and simply gathered her in.

She came without resistance, her arms going naturally around his waist, her head finding the warm hollow beneath his chin as if it were custom made for the purpose. He held her for a long time, not saying anything, standing perfectly still, giving her all he could of his warmth and strength and understanding. And she held him tightly, without trembling or sobs, not even silent, surreptitious tears, just soaking up everything he had to give her.

Finally, after what may have been a very long or a very short time, he did feel a small quiver pass through her body. She moved her head languidly against his chest as if reluctant to give up the place she'd found there, then lifted it so she could look into his eyes and said in a soft, slurred voice, "Clay, what's happening here?"

He brought one hand to her cheek, brushing it with the backs of his fingers. "Don't you know?"

She shook her head slightly, frowning at him in a puzzled, wondering way. "I don't know if I'm ready for this."

He gave a shaken laugh. "I don't think we have a choice."

"It won't work," she said, still shaking her head, the hunger in her eyes begging him to contradict her.

He cupped her cheek in his palm, fanning his fingers over her ear and into her hair. "What won't?"

"This . . . us." But even as she said the words her eyes were closing.

"Why not?"

She rubbed her cheek against his hand. "I have a child."

He sighed. "I know."

Her frown was like a watermark in the center of her forehead; her mouth looked like her voice sounded — soft and blurry. "You don't like her . . ."

"That's not true."

Her eyes opened and flew to his face. "It isn't?"

He drew an exasperated breath and dropped his hand to her neck. "Of course it isn't. I don't dislike your kid. Oh, I'll admit she was a little hard to take right at first, but once we got to understand each other we got along fine." He smiled and nudged the underside of her chin with his thumb. "Hadn't you noticed?"

"I did," she said, not smiling back, "and that's what worries me. She's starting to warm up to you, Clay. I'm afraid she might start to get . . . attached to you."

Her eyes dropped, but his thumb prevented her from averting her face as well. He studied the faint pattern of freckles across her nose, wondering when they had acquired the ability to make him ache with tenderness. "Why is that bad?"

"I don't want her hurt," she whispered, so faintly he had to bend closer to hear. "She's been hurt enough. I don't — I *won't* have her hurt anymore."

His breath caught; his heartbeat became a hollow pounding he could feel in his belly. "Carolyn," he said slowly, in a voice as low as hers, "why would you think I would ever hurt your child?"

"Not intentionally." Her head moved against his hand in quick denial. "I don't mean that. But . . ." And suddenly he could see the dreaded tears beneath the brown sweep of her lashes. "Clay, you don't . . . like children. If Jordy starts thinking of you —"

"What in the hell makes you say that?" His voice rose several notches. He'd have thrown his arms up in the air, too, except that he felt as if he were trying to hold on to something precious, and if he let go of her he'd lose it. "Why do you think I don't like kids?"

"Do you?" she asked, zeroing in on him with those eyes of hers.

"Of course I like kids!"

"Because," she went on, "you don't seem to, most of the time. And since you didn't have any . . ."

"My not having any kids doesn't have anything to do with not liking 'em. Actually —" Actually it had been Gillian who'd said it was wrong to bring more children into an overcrowded, starving, unhealthful world, when there were so many unwanted children, so many people to feed and so much that needed doing to make the planet safe for future generations. And since every day on the job he saw brutal evidence of the truth in that, he'd come to agree with her. Lately, though, he'd begun to notice a change in his thinking. He thought maybe being back home had a lot to do with it; when you lived on a farm it was hard to escape the natural cycles of life and death. And birth. Especially birth. Procreation abounded on a farm. It was everywhere, in a variety of forms — in the blossoming trees and ripening fruit, in the new grass poking up through the ground every spring and the birds building nests in the rafters of the barn, and always, in every season of the year, there were babies . . .

"It wouldn't be surprising if you didn't want children," Carolyn was saying, in that solemn, annoyingly professional tone she lapsed into every now and then. "Children who grow up in big families generally either want the same experience for their children or they reject it totally. If you felt —"

"My childhood was happy, dammit! I've got nothing against big families or small ones either, for that matter. I might even —"

"You're shouting," said Carolyn in a wondering tone. "Are we fighting again?"

"No!" Clay yelled. "Yes — hell, I don't know. Growing up in a big family's got nothing to do with why my wife and I chose not to have kids."

Someday he'd tell her all about Gillian, and Chicago, but this wasn't the time. He felt a sense of urgency, afraid that maybe this was a moment that might not come again, afraid she'd manage to sidetrack him before he got a chance to say what he wanted to say. He took her face between his hands and drew a deep, calming breath. "Look . . . Carolyn. You have a kid, I have a few scars, maybe — that's the way it is with people. You pick up baggage as you go along — that's life. It's not important. What's important —"

"But it *is* important," Carolyn said in a low, tense voice. "You can't ignore the baggage — it just won't work."

"I'll tell you what won't work." His voice was so harsh it hurt his throat. "Pretending this doesn't exist."

"What?" she whispered.

"*This,*" he growled, pushing his fingers through her hair, pressing her head gently between his hands as if that way he could imprint her with his own certainty. Her eyes stared back at him, bright with fear and yearning. "This . . ." he whispered, and finally . . . *finally* kissed her.

266

Chapter 11

She'd expected it, whether with hope or dread she wasn't sure. It didn't matter. The first sweet touch was a shock to her anyway, pleasure so exquisite it made her ache. A tiny indrawn breath whispered between her lips; tears squeezed through her lashes. She uttered a single soft whimper that was instantly lost in his mouth.

She couldn't believe how hungry she was. The depth of her need terrified her. She was so afraid of humiliating herself, of losing sanity and control, that she began to tremble.

"Please," Clay whispered hoarsely, brushing her cheeks with his thumbs, his lips taking hers in tender sips. "Please don't cry."

Her trembling became laughter, the tears purest joy. Her smile caressed his lips. She lifted her face, reaching for him, tasting and exploring his mouth with soft, wondering kisses.

"See what I mean?" His fingers were gently stroking her hair, in devastating contrast with the guttural urgency of his voice. "This isn't gonna go away, even if we want it to. Dammit, we're neighbors. And around here that means —"

"I don't want it to."

It was the barest whisper. Clay held himself very still and said, "What?"

"I said I don't want it to go away."

He stared into her eyes until she thought her heart would burst, then claimed her mouth again, sinking into it like a man coming home. Simultaneous gasps merged and melded into one soft sigh of mutual hunger. Carolyn forgot to worry about humiliation and staying in control. Her body grew heavy and hot, her legs weak and rubbery; her head fell back and the world began to spin . . .

"What are we gonna do about this?" Clay murmured after a while, pressing the words to the top of her head.

"Light-headed . . . weak in the knees . . ." said Carolyn groggily, frowning at her failed attempt to focus on the front of his plaid wool shirt. She closed her eyes and sighed. "God, how awful. All the clichés."

He laughed deep in his throat and wrapped his arms around her, holding her as close as he could. She put her arms around him, too, inside his unbuttoned flannel shirt, marveling that anything could feel so good as that lean, hard-muscled back, the body heat soaking through the thin cotton undershirt and into her hands . . . her arms. The only thing better, she thought, would be if there were nothing at all between them, to be able to touch and taste his body, to feel his skin against hers . . . Desire all but overwhelmed her.

Oh God, she thought wildly, pressing her face into his chest. I can't help it — it's been so long!

So long. She held herself very still, listening to the pounding of his heart, and her own. So very, very long. For him, too. Probably.

The thunder of their combined pulses seemed to grow more distant, and she could hear other sounds again, sounds of the world outside the barn — the creak of a shutter, shrieks and shouts from the children horse-back riding in the pasture, the slam of a car door. A measure of sanity returned.

She lifted her head and said thoughtfully, "You know, it's very understandable. Really."

"What is?" Clay asked with an indulgent chuckle.

"That we'd both be . . ." She hesitated, passed up the vulgarism and substituted somewhat primly, "Sex-starved. It's been a very long time for me, and I assume it might have been a while for you, too. It's actually quite natural that we'd —"

"Doc," he growled, shifting his arms and tightening them around her, pressing the lower part of her body hard against his. "Quit trying to analyze this."

"I'm not. I just —"

"Some things you've just got to accept and enjoy as they happen, you know what I mean?"

"No, but listen — oh!" She gave a whoop of surprise as he suddenly hooked an arm under her thighs and swung her into his arms.

"Hush up," he murmured in her ear, "or by God, California, I swear I'll take you down and make love to you right now, right *here*."

"Right here? Oh no!" She threw her head back dramatically. "A roll in the hay — that's the worst one of all. Oh, help!" She clung to his neck, laughing helplessly as he swung her around.

"Sounds like a good idea, though, doesn't it?" His voice was a delicious, lascivious murmur in her ear. His breath sent showers of shivers racing through her body, raising goosebumps and other predictable involuntary responses.

"Mmm," she mumbled, trying to focus her eyes on his face. But her eyelids, like the rest of her, had grown languid and heavy once more. She smiled, waiting for his mouth . . .

A breath away from kissing her he suddenly froze.

"What —" she began.

"Hush!" And then she heard it, too.

A woman's voice, bright and clear as

sleighbells on a frosty morning. "Hel-lo-oh . . . Well, mah goodness, where is everybody? And who are those adorable children ridin' on old Silver? John Clayton, are you out there in the barn? Come out here and say hello to your mama and daddy, you hear me?"

"Oh Lord," said Clay.

"Your parents?" Carolyn hissed.

He nodded.

"Oh God — Clay — put me down."

"This isn't over, dammit." He lowered her feet carefully to the ground and then straightened, still holding her. "You understand?" For a moment his eyes flared down at her with a fierce, frustrated light. "I'm not finished with you," he growled. Then, with one quick, hard kiss, he left her.

Carolyn stayed where she was, trembling fingers pressed against her lips, watching him move into the light, becoming a long silhouette with a distinctive, slightly bowlegged cowboy's walk, a walk already so dear and familiar to her she would know it a mile away and in a crowd.

"Carolyn!" Clay bellowed from the doorway. "Come on out here and say hello to my folks."

"Coming . . ." She took a deep breath and went forward on trembling legs to greet the Traynor family.

With the arrival of Clay's parents, John and Hannah Lee, and his two younger sisters, Dinah and Kelly Jean, Christmas descended in a flurry. It struck the Traynor household like a blizzard, slamming doors and rattling windows. The walls vibrated with pop Christmas songs played at maximum decibel level on the girls' boomboxes; footsteps echoed down the hallways; laughter drifted up the stairs. Mouth-watering smells of pumpkin, cinnamon, mince, and apples filled the kitchen, wafted through the house and out into the yard.

A Christmas tree was erected in the front room — a splendid tree, cut at a tree farm in New Mexico and carried east on top of the Traynors' new RV.

"Well, we knew sure as shootin' John Clayton wouldn't have one," said his father. "And there sure as hell — pardon me — *heck* wouldn't be a decent one left around here." And he went on to recite the story Clay had already told about the year they'd planted the tree outside the living room window and the birds had eaten the decorations, and he'd gone to town to try and buy a Christmas tree for inside the house at the last minute.

The boxes of decorations were carried down from upstairs, and all the Traynor family ornaments from years past were unpacked and exclaimed and laughed over. Stories were told about many of them, and arguments started over a few. Every last one of them, even the rumpled, battered, and faded ones, were lovingly hung on the tree's branches.

Jordy and William helped, of course. They seemed to Carolyn to be spending most of their time at the Traynors' these days. She feared they might be making nuisances of themselves until John Traynor took her aside, put a fatherly arm around her shoulders, and told her, "Honey, you let those young'uns stay all they want to. It worries Hannah Lee when there aren't enough kids around the place — if it wasn't for yours, I'd have to hire a few."

The farmhouse did seem to attract young people like a black suit picks up lint. A steady stream of cars drove up and down the lane kicking up dust — school friends of the girls coming to visit and staying to help cut out cookies or festoon the banisters with evergreen boughs. The telephone rang constantly with friends and neighbors wanting to say hello and wish a Merry Christmas, or one or the other of the four Traynor children who lived within close range calling to fine-tune plans for Christmas Day. And to add to the confusion there were Miss Leona's multitudes of friends and relatives dropping by with remembrances and gifts and platters of food.

Food! Carolyn had never seen so much food. The big upright freezer and spare refrigerator on the porch were crammed full to bursting with food — mince, pecan, and sweet potato pies; bread pudding, persimmon bread, and fruitcake; plastic bags filled with cut-up finger vegetables; a shimmering rainbow of molded gelatin and canned-fruit salads; two turkeys, a ham, and a leg of lamb slowly defrosting. The sideboard in the dining room groaned under the weight of platters of fudge and toffee and decorated cookies, covered tightly with plastic and draped with a tablecloth to discourage snitching.

"Who in the world is going to eat all this food?" Carolyn asked in awe as she delivered yet another plastic-wrapped offering to the kitchen.

Hannah Lee just laughed.

"Don't worry about that," said Clay's eighteen-year-old sister Dinah as she came bouncing up to take the plate from Carolyn's hands. "Everything'll be pretty much gone by Christmas night — well, except maybe the fruitcake. That kinda hangs around a while. What's this? Ooh, goody — look, Mom, it's some of Audrey Mae's fudge. She makes the *best* peanut butter fudge you *ever* tasted. Where is she? I want to go say hi to her —

haven't seen her in so long!"

"She's in the front room visiting with Miss Leona," Carolyn told her absently. "Uh . . . just how many people are you expecting for Christmas Day dinner?"

"Oh," said Hannah Lee serenely, "it's usually around fifty or sixty."

"*Fifty!*"

"Or more. Let's see . . . Kelly Jean, help me out here."

"Well," said Clay's second-youngest sister, muttering under her breath and counting up on her fingers, "there's twenty-seven of us, if Clay gets back, and there's at least that many of Miss Leona's, and then there's Aunt Clara and Aunt Yvonne, and," she added matter-of-factly, "there's you three guys, of course."

"Oh," murmured Carolyn, overwhelmed. Christmas at the Traynors' was beginning to seem every bit as noisy, crowded, and hectic as the big-city Christmases she was used to.

"Clay didn't tell you about our Christmases?" Hannah Lee asked sympathetically as Kelly Jean ran off to visit with Miss Leona's guest.

"No, not very much," Carolyn said, still feeling a bit dazed. She cleared her throat and added, "he, uh . . . doesn't talk about Christmas much."

"Well, I'm not surprised," said his mother

275

with a shrug. "It's probably just as well he had to go away on business. I'm not sure how he'd take to all this."

"I know," said Carolyn ruefully. "When it comes to Christmas he really is kind of a Scrooge."

It was the morning before Christmas. Carolyn had walked over with the children when they came for their daily horseback ride, supposedly to see if Hannah Lee needed any help. The truth was, being in the midst of his family made her feel closer to Clay, almost as if he weren't gone at all, but only outside somewhere, working, and would be in shortly for dinner. Her own house felt very empty and lonely these days.

She'd found the household enjoying what appeared to be a rare interlude of peace in the midst of the hustle and bustle. Hannah Lee was sitting at the kitchen table shelling walnuts for the stuffing while the girls chopped celery and onions at the sink. Miss Leona, until the arrival of her friend Audrey Mae, had been dozing in her recliner in the living room. John Traynor was somewhere outside with Raymond, Miss Leona's great-grandnephew, whom Clay had hired to tend to the chores while he was away "on business."

"He didn't used to be a Scrooge," Hannah Lee said forcefully. "He used to love it all

— he always had to be right in the middle of everything, just like his daddy." Her face turned soft and sad. "He's . . . different now. Ever since he came back from Chicago. Something happened up there to change him."

"Well," said Carolyn, "losing his wife the way he did . . ."

Hannah Lee shook her head. "It didn't happen then — not until later. Right before he came home for good. It's like . . . he lost his belief in himself, you know what I mean? Or at least in the rightness of what he was doing. That was always the thing about John Clayton — he was so self-confident. Not cocky — just so . . . strong."

"Yes," Carolyn said softly. "I know."

Hannah Lee sighed. "He won't ever talk about it, but I know. When it's your child, you just know when something's not right."

Through the window over the kitchen sink Carolyn could see the children crossing the yard on their way to the barn, Jordy in the lead, William lagging behind. Which was unusual, but not really surprising; it seemed to Carolyn that William had been acting a little depressed lately. He tried to hide it, forcing a grin that didn't reach his eyes, and like right now, breaking into a reluctant trot when Jordy challenged him to race. But Carolyn could tell. *When it's your child you just know.*

"I hope Clay gets here soon," she said suddenly, rubbing at her upper arms.

"Um-hmm," Hannah Lee agreed, craning to look out at the darkening sky, "I hope he gets here before that storm does."

"Storm?"

"Radio says it's on its way, just in time to mess up everybody's holiday plans. You ask me, I think it's gonna snow."

"Snow?" yelled Jordy when she heard the news. "Oh boy, far out! Hey Will, isn't that great?"

"Snow's okay," said William. "I guess."

"We're going to have a white Christmas — I don't believe it! That is just so cool."

Jordy was wired and giddy, William tense and moody; both vibrated with secrets.

They had a brief argument over when to open presents — Christmas Eve or Christmas morning. William was for opening them as soon as possible, maybe right after supper.

"But we've always opened them in the morning," Jordy insisted. "Ever since I was little, because Santa's supposed to come in the night while everybody's asleep."

"Yeah," William pointed out, "but there's no real Santa, so who cares?"

Carolyn was fairly sure neither of them would do much sleeping unless the presents were opened first, so she reminded them that they'd been invited to spend Christmas Day at Traynors', and it was apt to be a pretty full and exciting day all by itself. Jordy didn't take much persuading, even though it meant losing an argument to William. She'd been gleefully shaking and probing all her packages from the moment Carolyn had hauled them out from under the bed and placed them under the tree. William, on the other hand, was so awed and thunderstruck to discover that there were presents under the tree with his name on them that he seemed almost afraid to touch them.

It was while Carolyn was opening cans of clam chowder and making grilled cheese sandwiches for supper that William came strolling casually into the kitchen trying hard not to look as if he wanted something.

"What is it, William?" Carolyn asked gently, as usual having to resist an impulse to gather him into a hug.

He looked quickly and furtively over his shoulder at Jordy's bedroom door, and the handwritten sign on it that read: DO NOT ENTER ON PAIN OF DEATH!! "I was wondering if you have a . . . um . . . a bag."

"Sure," said Carolyn. "Paper or plastic?"

He thought about it for a moment. "Paper."

Carolyn gave him a small brown paper lunch sack and when he still hesitated, asked with a smile, "Anything else?"

"Could I have some ribbon?"

"Ribbon?"

"Like that." He pointed to the Christmas tree.

"Oh . . ." murmured Carolyn as the light finally dawned. "Of course." She couldn't believe she'd been so stupid, so insensitive. How could she, of all people, not have seen it? He'd asked her about presents — why hadn't she realized he'd want to give some himself? She should have seen to it he had a chance to earn some money doing chores. She should have taken him shopping, or helped him make something. She should have done *something*. She felt terrible.

She could possibly find excuses in the fact that she'd had one or two distractions to cope with lately, but she knew there was really no excuse at all.

Meanwhile, however, it was obvious that William had managed to come up with his own solutions to his gift problem. Carolyn couldn't help but be awed by his resourcefulness, and more than a little bit curious as she supplied him with wrapping paper and ribbon, scissors and tape and left him barricaded in his room, positively vibrating with excitement.

When he came out of his room for supper,

Carolyn's heart turned over and tears rushed to her eyes — his dimples were back in place, and the cocky swagger was back in his walk. That's all it was, she thought. That's what was bothering him.

During supper there was none of the usual arguing and squabbling; just the soft sounds of chewing and slurping, and knowing looks and secret smiles. It seemed unnaturally quiet, Carolyn thought. *Not a creature was stirring* . . . The only one stirring seemed to be Traveler, pacing restlessly from the couch to the bedroom and back again. Harriet was quiet, and so was the wind. The phone didn't ring. She hadn't heard a word from Clay.

"Wouldn't it be nice if we had some music," she said, jumping up from the table. "Jordy, maybe if we turned up your Walkman all the way —"

"We don't need any old music," said Jordy. She snatched up her plate and William's and dumped them in the sink, then turned with a comic little twist and growled, *"It's present time."* William giggled.

Carolyn gave in with a mock sigh. "Oh, all right. William, while Jordy clears the table, why don't you see if Traveler needs to go outside?"

"It's cold out there," William protested.

"Too bad," said Jordy. "If he's gotta go,

281

he's gotta go. That's what you get for having a dumb ol' dog instead of a cat."

Right on cue, Harriet began to yowl. "I swear that animal can understand us," Carolyn muttered, glancing at the closed bedroom door.

"She wants to come out, and I don't blame her," said Jordy. "It's not fair she has to stay locked up on Christmas Eve."

"I told you, she could come out any time she wants," said William. "Traveler won't hurt her. He likes cats. Come on, boy, good boy — want to go out? Huh?"

He opened the door and held it. Traveler peered out into the cold twilight and whined softly, then turned and trotted back into the bedroom. "He doesn't want to," said William with a shrug. "Now can we open presents?"

"Yeah," shouted Jordy. "Who goes first?"

"You guys go first," said Carolyn. "I'll watch." It was the part she enjoyed most anyway.

Of course the children needed no further urging.

Carolyn had worried a little about the fact that there were more presents for Jordy than William, but she needn't have. Jordy tore into her packages with the eagerness and expertise born of lots and lots of practice, exclaiming with joy and enthusiasm over everything she got, especially the fake fur jacket and purple miniskirt from her father. (Carolyn wondered briefly whether the "Strawberry Tart" had picked them out — they did seem to be her style.) Meanwhile, William treated each of his packages as a miracle, a treasure to be unearthed as slowly and painstakingly as possible, so as not to miss a single moment of discovery. While Jordy gradually disappeared in a mound of wrapping paper and ribbons, he held each package and gazed at it in awe, ran his hands over it and turned it over and over, almost as if he were afraid to open it. Only at someone's impatient urging would he finally show his dimples and slip his fingers under the tape with exquisite care. Once he had them open, though, he was as boisterously delighted as Jordy, exclaiming "Oh boy!" over his Michael Jordan T-shirt and insisting on wearing it immediately.

"Okay," cried Jordy when the last present had been opened, breathless with excitement. "Now it's your turn, Mom. Me first!" She snatched up a small, silver-wrapped package from under the tree and thrust it at Carolyn. "This is from me — I bought it with my report card money — I hope you like it."

"Of course I'll like it," Carolyn murmured, laughing as she peeled off the paper and lifted the lid. "Oh, my goodness." It was a gold heart etched with flowers on a slender gold chain. She heard a soft gasp from William as she held it up for him to see, but when she glanced at him his dimples were showing and his eyes were shining with his own delicious secrets.

"It's a locket," said Jordy. "See? You can put pictures in it. I thought you'd like it."

"I love it," Carolyn whispered. "Thank you, sweetheart."

"Now me," said William breathlessly as soon as hugs had been dispensed and sentimental tears surreptitiously disposed of. He went running into the bedroom and almost instantly returned with both hands hidden behind his back. Slowly and shyly he withdrew one and placed a ball of wrapping paper glistening with tape carefully in her lap. "This one's for you." He seemed almost to have stopped breathing entirely.

Carolyn smiled at William, and he ducked his head shyly and leaned against her arm. It took a little doing, but she got the wrapping off at last. And then she was looking down through a rainbow shimmer at the tiny, shell-encrusted box in her hands.

"Oh, William," she whispered.

"You could put the locket in it," said William, reaching eagerly to take the box from her so he could demonstrate. "See? It'll fit just perfect."

Carolyn put her arm around him, trying desperately to swallow the lump in her throat. "Honey," she said softly, "are you sure you want to give this to me? Maybe —"

But he was nodding vigorously, pulling away from her to look for the other package he'd put down somewhere in his excitement.

"Here," he said, retrieving a brown bag tied at the top with red ribbon from the couch cushions and shoving it at Jordy, "this is for you."

"What on earth — ?" Jordy breathed, clearly intrigued by the weight of the bag. She gave William a curious look and slowly untied the ribbon and opened the bag. Her breath escaped in a single soft gust of puzzled laughter.

"It's my rock collection," said William. "But you could have it. It's got some really neat stuff in it —" His hand dove into the bag. "See? This one's got gold in it — only it's not real gold, it's just fool's gold. And this one here, if you polished it up, it'd look just like a marble."

But at that moment, before Jordy could say anything, Harriet began to yowl with even more urgency than usual. Both children looked up and Jordy groaned, "Mother . . ."

Grateful for any distraction that might give her a chance to speak to Jordy in private, Carolyn said brightly, "Listen, why don't we just let her out and see what happens?"

Jordy looked at her as if she'd lost her mind.

"Honey, listen — it's been almost a week. She knows the dog is here, maybe she's used to it by now." After all, it was Christmas. Hadn't she seen Christmas cards with lions and lambs cuddled up together? Maybe the same idea applied to dogs and cats.

"I don't know . . ." Jordy shook her head slowly.

"Come on, let's try it," said Carolyn, warming to the idea. "We'll be careful. You hold Harriet and we'll hold Traveler —"

"Traveler doesn't need to be held. He won't hurt her."

"We'll just let them get acquainted a little, that's all. Honey, nothing's going to happen."

"Well . . . okay." Jordy looked doubtful, but put her presents aside and got up from the couch. "Harriet," she cooed as she opened the door to her room, "come here, sweetie, come on . . . that's a good girl . . ."

"Here, Traveler, come on, boy. That's a good dog."

Jordy emerged cautiously from the bedroom with her arms full of suspicious black cat. Harriet's front paws were on Jordy's forearm, her head was up and alert, ears erect, eyes round as marbles as she watched the dog advance slowly toward her with William's hand on his neck.

The four met in the middle of the room.

"That's right," said Carolyn, letting her breath out. So far so good. "Now — let them sniff each other."

Jordy glanced at her nervously but knelt down. Traveler whined softly.

Feline and canine noses reached, quivering . . . and touched.

Harriet hissed, baring her teeth. Traveler went "Yike!" and the cat recoiled in a ball of spitting fury. Traveler gave a frightened "Woof!"

William yelled and Jordy began to shriek as Harriet catapulted out of her arms and hit the floor with a THUMP.

"Grab her!" Carolyn shouted. But at that precise moment the front door burst open. The cat went streaking past Clay's legs and disappeared into the night.

Chapter 12

Clay had walked straight into pandemonium. He'd heard the commotion coming up the steps, and when Jordy screamed he had only one thought: *Carolyn.* Naturally he didn't stop to knock, just opened the door and barged in. He felt something brush his leg, and that's when everything went crazy.

Jordy was screaming and crying, William was yelling, "I'm sorry, I'm sorry," and trying to hold on to his dog, who was trying his best to hightail it for the bedroom. Carolyn was sort of flapping back and forth between the two, trying to calm everybody down, but when she saw him she just stopped, her shoulders slumped and she gazed at him with wide, distressed eyes.

"What the *hell*," said Clay, brushing snow-flakes from his jacket, "is going on here?"

"It's all your fault!" Jordy shrieked at everybody in general. She pushed past them and raced out into the darkness and snow after the cat.

"I'm sorry," William cried in a high, stricken voice as Traveler finally managed to break loose from him and made a beeline for the bedroom. "Traveler didn't mean to — she just scared him, that's all. We'll find her — we will. I'm gonna go look for her right now."

"You'll do no such thing," said Carolyn in a trembling voice. "It's dark, and it's snowing out there." She glanced at Clay and he nodded in confirmation. "Honey, it's not your fault. It's not Traveler's fault, either. It just —"

"She's gone," Jordy sobbed, bursting back into the house, red-nosed and dusted with snowflakes. "I can't find her anywhere. It's snowing, and she's old and she'll freeze to death. She'll *die*. And it's all your fault! You and your stupid dog! If you hadn't come, this never would have happened. I hate you!"

She picked up the brown paper bag that held William's rock collection and hurled it across the room where it struck a leg of the kitchen table and broke open, spilling out rocks in all directions.

There was a single, collective gasp. Then Jordy whirled and ran into her bedroom, sobbing. William whispered, "I'm sorry," and ran for his. The soft closing of his bedroom door made a poignant echo to the slamming of Jordy's.

Carolyn just stood there with her back to Clay, staring at nothing, until he touched her arm. Then she turned, gave him an anguished look, and walked into his arms. She didn't cry. He almost wished she would — anything would have been better than that silent trembling. All he could do was hold her and stroke her hair and rub her back and wait for it to stop.

"It'll be okay," he whispered after a while. "Cats are resourceful. Most likely she'll be back yowling at the door in a couple hours, cranky as ever."

She drew a long, uneven breath. "It's not the cat I'm worried about."

"I know," he rasped. "I know."

"Oh God, I can't believe this has happened." She pulled away from him, drove her hands through her hair, holding it away from her face, and stood like that for a few moments with her eyes closed. At last she gave herself a little shake, opened her eyes and looked at him. "I'm glad you're here," she said with a feeble smile. "Did you . . . um . . . find out anything?"

Clay took a deep breath. "Yeah, I did." He glanced at the two closed doors and growled, "Get your coat."

"What? My coat —"

"I don't want to talk about it in here. Let's go outside."

He waited for her, leaning on the porch railing, watching the snow and listening to the quiet, dreading what he had to tell her. He heard the door softly open and close, the scrape of her footsteps on the rough plank floor, and drew a deep, preparatory breath. But she spoke before he could.

"His mother *is* dead, isn't she?"

"Yeah." He let the breath out in a rush and turned around. She was standing with her hands thrust deep in her coat pockets. He reached out with both hands, one on either side of her neck, and gently lifted her hair out of her collar. Her neck felt strong and warm, and he wanted to leave his hands right there. "How did you know?" he asked softly. "Did he tell you?"

"In a way." She drew one hand from her pocket and he saw the little shell-covered box on its palm. "He gave this to me tonight. For Christmas." She gave a high, shaken laugh. "He gave us all something. The rock collection was Jordy's. I wouldn't be surprised if he has something for you, too."

"So," he said, "Florida was a fib?" He didn't dare touch her now. He had the feeling that if he did he'd upset the delicate balance of her self-control and she'd fall apart in his hands.

"A fib or a fantasy . . ." She opened the box and stared at it for a long time. "I don't think he was going to Florida. I don't think he cared where he was going. He just wanted to get away from wherever he was."

Clay nodded. "You're probably right about that, although he might have had some idea about Florida. His mother's there, all right. She's buried there — near Tallahassee. After she died, her sister took the boy in. The mother wasn't married — he probably never knew his father. The sister seems like a good sort —"

"You saw her?"

Clay nodded. "Just come from there. Seems they found winter work in the mills up near Lumberton. Anyway, the sister's husband's the problem. They've got three little ones of their own and not enough money to go around as it is, and I guess the guy was pretty hard on the kid. And when he brought home the dog, it was the last straw. Apparently he told William he either had to get rid of the dog or he'd shoot it. The next morning William and the dog were both gone."

"Oh God," whispered Carolyn. "No wonder. But why on earth didn't she report it? Somebody should have —"

"Her husband told her it was good riddance," Clay told her grimly. "And that the kid was old enough to look out for himself anyway. Poor woman's been worrying herself sick ever since, but too scared of her husband to say anything."

"He can't go back there," Carolyn said flatly.

"No." Clay took another deep breath and leaned back against the railing. He waited for a long time before he said, "I asked her if she'd be willing to sign over custody . . . to you." He heard her breathing catch. "She wasn't happy about the idea of turning her sister's child over to a stranger. I told her to think about it and give me a call."

"But . . . do you think —"

"I think she will. The court will have to approve it, of course, but —"

She interrupted him with a soft, sad laugh. "They'd never do that. You were right — look at this place. I'd have to completely renovate, add on a room — and I can't afford it right now, Clay. I just don't have the money."

"Not this place," Clay said quietly. He took another breath, waited, then said it. "Mine."

It seemed an eternity before she whispered, "Clay, what are you saying?"

"You know what I'm saying."

And then she confounded him completely by turning her face from him, holding up one arm as if to ward off a blow. "No! Don't do this. Don't —"

He caught her arm and held it tightly, forcing her to look at him. "What do you mean, 'don't do this'?" he said incredulously. "Are you trying to say you haven't thought of it? That you don't want it as much as —"

"Of course I've thought of it," she cried, then lowered her voice to a furious, broken whisper. "And yes, I *want* it. That's just it, don't you understand? *I want it too much.* And I can't do it — I just can't. I can't do that to Jordy, or William either, for that matter."

"What the hell are you talking about? It's just what both of those kids need — a stable home, a strong father figure — and I'd make a damned good one, by the way —"

She shook her head violently and wrenched her arm away from him. "Don't you think I've imagined it a thousand times? A perfect happy family, just like the one you grew up in and I always dreamed of? It was a fantasy, Clay — my beautiful, selfish fantasy. The reality is in there in the house, right now. We can't force people to love each other and get along happily together, any more than you can make a cat get along with a dog. I shouldn't have done it — I shouldn't have kept him here. It was selfish of me. I wanted —"

"Selfish!" Clay exploded. "You're probably the least selfish person I've ever met in my life!"

"If that's true," said Carolyn softly, "then why are there two heartbroken children in there crying their eyes out on Christmas Eve? Huh?"

He could only stare at her in frustration, knowing she was wrong, but unable to find the words that would convince her she was. After a moment she let her breath out and turned her face away from him. She looked down briefly at the shell-covered box in her hand, then jammed it and her hands deep in her pockets.

"I know all about selfish parents," she said in a tight, bitter voice. "I was raised, more or less, by the world champions of self-indulgence. And you know what? Right now I don't see myself as being any better than they were."

God, he felt helpless. "Carolyn, this is all going to blow over. Trust me — my brothers and sisters and I had a lot worse things —"

She wouldn't listen to him. Just stood there looking at him with that unnatural calm. "Clay, please. I know you mean well. And I'm very grateful for all you've done. But right now I think you'd better go on home to your family. I need to go in and see if I can do anything to make those children feel better."

"Dammit, Carolyn —"

"Please." Her voice was finally breaking. So, he knew, was her heart. And all he could do was stand there and look at her, at her huge, compassionate eyes, dark now with self-loathing and misdirected blame.

"Good night, Clay," she whispered, and added ironically, "Merry Christmas."

With that she turned and walked back inside, leaving him no choice but to do as she'd told him to, go down the steps and get into his truck and drive home to a house that he knew would be positively bursting at the seams with Christmas cheer.

Jordy was pretending to be asleep. Carolyn knew she was pretending but didn't have the courage to challenge her, so she just went quietly out again and closed the door.

She found William sitting cross-legged in the middle of his bed with the gold-wrapped box, his "gift of the Magi," balanced on one knee. It seemed an eerie reprise of the night of the pageant, except that Traveler, obviously still upset by his encounter with the cat, instead of snoring peacefully on the rug beside the bed kept pacing around the room poking his nose into nooks and crannies as if he were looking for something.

"Hi," said Carolyn softly, going to sit beside William on the bed. "How are you doing?"

He looked up and asked with forlorn hope, "Did you find Harriet yet?"

"No," said Carolyn. "Not yet."

His face fell. "We didn't mean to make her run away. Traveler just got scared for a minute, that's all."

"It wasn't your fault," Carolyn said, putting her arm around him and drawing him close.

"Jordy's pretty mad at me."

Carolyn laughed painfully at the understatement, then sighed. "I know. But she'll get over it. Listen — why don't you go to bed now and get some sleep, huh? Everybody will feel better in the morning."

"Yes, ma'am," William mumbled, looking down at his hands. He picked up the gold box. "I didn't get a chance to give Clay his present. Would you give it to him for me?"

"You can still give it to him," Carolyn reminded him gently. "You'll see him tomorrow."

William shook his head firmly. "No, you." He laid the box in her lap. Then, as if he were unspeakably weary — he lay back and curled up on his side with his head on his arm.

Carolyn leaned over and kissed him good night, her heart aching. "All right, honey. Don't worry about it, okay? You just go to sleep now." She rose stiffly with the box in her hands, tiptoed out and closed the door.

The house seemed unnaturally quiet after all the commotion. She found herself still tiptoeing as she set about tidying up the mess of gift wrappings, picked up what she could find of William's rocks and put them in a jar, filled the children's stockings and propped them against the back of the couch. She didn't know when she'd ever felt so alone.

When there was nothing left to do and she was ready for bed, she went out onto the porch one last time and called softly into the night. The snow was still falling, sticking to the ground, to the drifts of fallen leaves and to the branches of trees. It was cold and still, a night of almost mystical loveliness. Finally, unable to bear it any longer, she went back inside and crawled into bed beside Jordy, absolutely certain she would not sleep.

"Mom! Oh Mommy, please, *please* wake up . . ."

She was having a dream, a terrible nightmare. Jordy was crying, heartbrokenly, hysterically!

Only it wasn't a dream. She sat up, awake in an instant, shaking violently and groping for the floor with her feet. "Honey, what is it? What on earth's wrong?"

"He's gone. Oh Mommy — he's *gone*. I couldn't sleep —"

"*Who's* gone? *William?*" Her throat seemed to have locked; her voice was a croak. She lurched through the living room and threw open the door to William's room. Panic zapped through her like a bolt of electricity; she felt cold, hollow, boneless.

"See?" sobbed Jordy, coming up behind her. "I told you, he's gone — they both are. I couldn't sleep, and I wanted to tell him I was sorry. But I never got a chance, and now . . . and now he's *gone*. It's all my fault — it's because I was mean to him. He really *was* an angel, Mom, he must have been. This proves it. He was an angel, and I was mean to him, so he went awa-ay."

"Jordan Robards, pull yourself together," Carolyn snapped, taking her sobbing daughter by the arms and giving her a quick, hard shake. She wasn't sure whether she felt most like laughing or crying herself, but at least Jordy's hysterics were forcing her to control her own panic. She was beginning to think again. "Honey, William ran away because he thought he'd done something terrible, and because he thinks you don't want him around anymore. But he's not an angel, he's a little boy. And it's cold and snowing outside. We have to find him — quickly. I need you to stop crying and help me. Understand?"

Jordy nodded, valiantly gulping down a sob. "And I wanted . . . I wanted to g-give him this." She thrust a paper-wrapped bundle into Carolyn's hands.

"What's this?" She stared down at it, turning it over and over. Its shape seemed vaguely familiar.

"It's my . . . *Walk*-man," Jordy whispered, beginning to hiccup, which she always did when she cried too much. "I was . . . going to give it to hi-im for Christmas."

"Your *Walkman?*" Carolyn stared at Jordy's swollen, tear-streaked face, first in disbelief and then in absolute wonder. "Oh, sweetheart — you were going to give William your Walkman?" She folded her daughter into her arms, laughing *and* crying, both at the same time.

"*Well,*" said Jordy on an enormous hiccup, "I figured I could buy myself . . . a ne-ew one out of my . . . allowance, if I saved *up.*"

"Oh, honey — you'll have a chance to give it to him, I promise." Carolyn took a deep breath, wiped away her tears, hugged her daughter hard and gave her a push through the door. "Tell you what — you go and call Clay while I get dressed. *Hurry!*"

Clay had undressed and gotten into bed, but he wasn't asleep. Neither, it seemed, was the rest of the household. He'd been lying there for what seemed like hours, staring morosely at the ceiling of his room while he listened to floorboards creak and doors open stealthily and softly close. Santa's elves, going about their work.

When he heard the phone ring downstairs in his office he thought for a moment or two he'd let somebody else answer it. But then it occurred to him that it was the middle of the night, and nobody in his right mind was going to be calling to wish somebody a Merry Christmas. Which meant it was probably for him and probably bad. In his experience, phone calls in the night almost never had good news. So he pulled on his pants, grabbed up his boots and a pair of socks, and went downstairs in his undershirt and bare feet.

After he'd finished talking to Jordy on the phone he didn't bother to go back upstairs for a shirt. He was in the kitchen pulling on his boots when Miss Leona came shuffling in in her robe and slippers, carrying a drinking glass in her hand.

"John Clayton," she said, looking surprised to see him there, "what you doing up this time a'night?"

"I have to go out," he grunted, tugging on his boot laces. "What are you doing up?"

"My stomach's a little poor — too much rich food. I come to get myself a glass of buttermilk. What do you mean, you goin' out? It's snowin' hard out there."

"Yeah, I know." He set that boot down and pulled up the other one. "It's William — he's run away."

Miss Leona turned from the refrigerator to frown at him. "You mean that poor little boy's gone off all by himself?"

Clay nodded and stood up. "Him and the dog. Gotta go look for 'em."

"Well," said Miss Leona, reaching for the pitcher of buttermilk, "he won't get far."

Clay went to take down the pitcher for her. "What do you mean, 'he won't get far'?"

Miss Leona shrugged. "Not with that dog with him, he won't."

"Why, what's wrong with the dog?" Clay set the pitcher down on the table, trying his best to be patient.

Miss Leona looked at him in surprise. Then her eyes got sharp and wicked and she jabbed him gleefully in the ribs with a finger. "John Clayton, you mean to tell me you didn't know? Shame on you — and you a farm boy born and raised."

"Know what?" said Clay warily. He was beginning to have a bad feeling about this.

Miss Leona went back to pouring her buttermilk, shaking her head and muttering to herself. "You best go find those chul'ren quick. Take my car — be better for the dog. I'll go wake up your folks."

"Are you trying to tell me —"

"That's right," said Miss Leona as she shuffled toward the door with her glass of buttermilk. "That's what I'm tellin' you. That dog's due to whelp any minute now. Any minute . . ."

"How in the hell was I supposed to know?" Clay demanded, peering through the basketball-sized patch of windshield the wipers and defrosters had managed to clear of snow. "I didn't see that much of the damned dog to begin with. And to tell you the truth, I never even noticed." He glanced over at Carolyn and added dryly, "I've had one or two other things on my mind."

"I can't believe I didn't notice," Carolyn said, rubbing distractedly at her forehead. "He's — I mean *she's* so shaggy. I guess I just took it for granted when William said *he* . . ."

"I knew there was something strange about that dog," Clay muttered. "I knew it."

"I just hope we find him soon." Carolyn hitched herself forward on the seat, as if that would help her to see better through the swirling curtain of snow. "It's coming down even harder. The little idiot — what was he thinking of?"

Clay looked at her. "You check the basement?"

"Of course I checked the basement. It was

the first place I thought of."

He reached over and covered her hand with his. "Hey," he said gruffly, "take it easy. Dad's gone the other way with the truck — between the two of us, we'll find him. If he sticks to the roads, anyway. If he took off through the woods . . ." His voice trailed into grim silence.

"He'll be on the road."

He glanced at her. "What makes you think so?"

"Because," she said softly, "it's what I would have done. Because —" She drew a quick breath and looked out the window. "Deep down in his heart he wants to be found."

Clay didn't say anything, but she felt his hand tighten around hers, snug, warm . . . secure. Emotion surged into her throat and threatened to overflow. How can this be happening? she thought. *Why now, of all possible times?* The best and worst that life can offer, both happening at once . . . She didn't know if she could survive it.

"Hey, look," said Clay, pointing to the clock on the dash. "It's past midnight." He threw her a lopsided smile. "Merry Christmas."

She made a soft, ironic sound. "Some Christmas, huh?"

Clay gave a snort of mirthless laughter.

"Listen, compared to a couple of my recent Christmases, this one'll have to get a whole lot worse before it even comes close."

"I know your wife died right before Christmas," Carolyn said, turning her head to look at him. "Was there . . . something else besides that?"

"Oh, yeah . . ." She saw the creases beside his mouth deepen in a brief grimace of pain.

She squeezed his hand, her heart inexplicably quickening. "Want to tell me about it?"

There was a long, long silence while the big car prowled slowly through the snow, following the pathway laid down by the headlights. Clay stirred restlessly and let go of her hand, putting it on the steering wheel instead. She wished he hadn't — she wanted to be there for him as he had for her, giving him her strength and support. But she knew better than to push it. Whatever he had to tell her would have to come in his own time and at his own pace.

"I said I'd tell you," he said at last, with another of those dry little snorts of laughter. "Actually, I meant to tell you before now. *Should* have told you — it wasn't fair of me not to." But then he was silent again, and she knew he was searching for the right words, words he'd probably never uttered before.

Finally he glanced over at her and said in

wry understatement, "The year after my wife died was kinda rough. The department wanted me to take some time off, but I didn't want to do that. Working seemed like the only way I could keep my mind off what had happened — the way it happened, you know? But then . . ." He stopped, shaking his head as if it perplexed him still. "I don't know, it just all began to seem . . . different to me. When I first started out, I really thought I was going to make a difference. I *did* make a difference. I'll never forget the first time I saved somebody's life — they gave me a commendation for it, a medal, the whole bit. But the best part of it wasn't the medal — it was just the feeling I had, you know?

"But then it started to pile up — the filth, the ugliness. It was already starting to get to me, I guess, but after Gillian was killed it just seemed to me more and more like the bad guys were winning. Like I was sitting there with my finger in the dike, only there wasn't going to be anybody come and rescue me. I was angry, and I was frustrated . . . as my dad would say, I was spoilin' for a fight." He bit the last word off, briefly fighting the car as the tires slipped a little on the snowy pavement.

When the car was under control again and he still hadn't spoken, Carolyn said quietly, remembering with anguish what Jordy had said to him that morning in the kitchen, "You shot someone, didn't you?"

"Worse than that." His voice was low and gravelly. He paused again and finally said flatly, "I shot a child."

Oh God. She didn't say a word. She couldn't. Clay gave her one brief, unforgettable look, his eyes wide open, stark and unshielded, glittering with pain. Then he went back to staring through the windshield, his throat moving convulsively against the collar of his coat. She wanted so much to touch him, to move closer to him and put her arms around him and hold him . . . but she didn't dare. All she could do was sit there, aching for him, waiting for him to go on.

He did, finally, in a raspy, uneven voice, frowning hard at the swirling mass outside the windows. "He was nine — about William's age, matter of fact. Sometimes the kid reminds me of him — except he was black. Not that that had anything to do with anything — I didn't know anything until after I'd shot him. He was just a shadow . . . a shadow on the wall, behind the Christmas tree. A shadow with a gun . . ."

"He had a *gun?*"

Another snort of that terrible laughter. "A toy. He was all alone — his mother was on welfare and working a secret job at night so she wouldn't lose her payments. We'd gotten a tip on a drug deal going down — turned out we'd got the wrong information, the wrong number. Hell, we were in the wrong *building*. Anyway, the kid was scared to death, hiding in the dark with his toy gun. I could see the shadow. I kept telling him to come out, telling him we were police officers, but he just raised up that gun . . . And I was just waitin' for him. I was waiting for the moment — my finger was on the trigger, and I was thinking, *Come on . . . Come on.*"

Carolyn's heart was pounding; she could feel it in her stomach, hear it inside her head. She felt the tension, smelled the fear that must have been in that room exactly as if it were happening right now. As if she were there too.

"It's funny," Clay said softly. "It all happened so fast, and yet when I remember it it's always in slow motion. The kid stood up, my partner hit the lights — I heard him yell, 'Don't shoot, it's a kid!' But it was too late, I'd already squeezed off a round." He tilted his head sideways, as if he were hearing the echo of that shot, rebounding again and again through barren rooms.

Carolyn felt something tickling her cheek. She brushed at it and her fingers came away wet.

"It must have been just enough, my partner yelling like that," Clay said in a quiet, matter-of-fact voice. "I grew up shooting squirrels out of trees and I'm a damn good shot, but that bullet went high and wide."

"Then you didn't —" Carolyn whispered.

"No. The bullet damn near tore his arm off, but it didn't kill him."

"Oh," she gasped. "Thank God."

"Yeah," said Clay bitterly, "that's who you'd have to thank, all right — you sure as hell couldn't thank me. Internal Affairs cleared me and the department shrinks sent me home for a rest, but I never went back. I knew I didn't belong there anymore. See — I was always used to thinking of myself as one of the good guys. After that . . . well, I just couldn't see that there was that much difference between Them. . . . and me."

Once again there was silence in the car, broken only by the thump of windshield wipers and the crunch of tires on snow. Then Clay spoke without looking at her, frowning at the unbroken curtain of white. "So what do you think, doc? Think it'll make an interesting chapter in that book of yours? The one on job burnout?"

Carolyn shook her head, realized that her hand was clamped tightly over the lower part of her face and peeled it off. "I couldn't possibly," she said, her voice liquid and indistinct.

"What's that?"

"I couldn't put you in my book."

"Why not?"

"How could I be objective?" she whispered, swallowing tears. "I love you."

Clay seemed to freeze, but he never got a chance to answer. Because at that precise moment, as if even the forces of nature had been waiting for her to say the words, the snowy curtain lifted.

He gave a hoarse shout. "Look — there he is!"

He hit the brakes, the big car fishtailed, swerved, and came to a stop, its headlights trained on a small figure standing alone by the roadside, frantically waving his arms.

Chapter 13

Carolyn was out of the car and running before Clay even had the thing stopped, but he wasn't far behind her. William was slogging toward them, coming as fast as he could in the snow and the shoes that were too big for him. When they got closer they could see he had tears running down his face in rivers.

"Traveler's sick," he gasped, stumbling and all but falling into Carolyn's arms. "He's hurt real bad!" He pulled away from her, tugging frantically at her hands. "Come on — please — you gotta help him. I think he's dyin'."

Clay grabbed him by the arms and gave him a little shake, speaking calmly, trying to quiet him down. "Where's your dog, son? Where's Traveler?"

"Over th-there — come on, hurry!" He took off running, hauling on Clay's arm like a tugboat pulling an ocean liner. Carolyn followed, slipping and sliding in the snow, and they all made their way down the road, back in the direction William had come from, to the place where a dirt road angled off to the right. And there, sheltered under a nice little evergreen that looked as if it would have made

311

a perfect Christmas tree, they found Traveler.

"You take the kid," Clay shouted as the snow started to come down again, harder than before. "I'll bring the dog." He thrust William at Carolyn and knelt down in the snow. Traveler whimpered softly and licked his hand.

"Is my dog gonna die?" asked William in a small, scared voice.

"Nah," Clay growled, "he's not gonna die. Are you, girl? That's right . . . come on, nice and easy, now. Let's go . . . upsy-daisy." He lifted Traveler carefully into his arms.

When they got to the car, Carolyn opened the back door and Clay leaned in and laid Traveler down on the seat. William, not about to be separated from his dog for a minute, ducked under Clay's arm and scrambled across to the other side of the car.

"You drive," Clay shouted to Carolyn as he slammed the passenger door shut and climbed into the back seat. "I'll take care of things here."

"I'm from California," Carolyn protested. "I don't know how to drive in the snow!"

"Don't worry about it — this car's better than a tank. Just take it slow — and don't get us stuck when you turn around."

"Thanks," said Carolyn dryly as she slipped the Lincoln into low gear.

"What's wrong with Traveler?" William

asked in a small, worried voice. "Why's he bleeding?"

"Because . . ." said Clay, and then for a few minutes he was too busy to answer.

"Atta girl . . . good girl . . . you're doin' fine." And then, very softly: "Congratulations . . ."

William seemed all but speechless. "What is it?" he whispered finally, watching Traveler lick and nuzzle the tiny, wet thing squirming on the plush upholstery next to her belly.

Clay chuckled. He felt warmth and light spreading all through him, as if the sun were coming up on his soul. "It's a puppy, son," he said softly. "Traveler's just become a mother."

"Oh God," Carolyn burst out from the front seat. "I don't believe this!"

Clay sighed. He could see he was going to have to get used to tears.

Nobody got much sleep that night, at either Clay's house or Carolyn's, but it didn't seem to slow down the Christmas festivities one bit. The snow stopped before dawn, and melted off the roads by mid-morning. Members of Clay's family and Miss Leona's started arriving shortly after that, stomping in red-cheeked and sparkly-eyed, bearing gifts and bundled-up babies and exclaiming over and over again about the snow.

The older children tumbled out of their cars before the wheels had even stopped turning and fanned out over the farm, making snowmen and throwing snowballs and looking for anything they could convert to makeshift sleds. Much too excited to eat, they spent most of the day trooping in and out of the house, banging doors, leaving trails of mud through the kitchen and hallways and soggy clothes in the bathrooms, getting yelled at by adults too busy eating and visiting and having a good time to follow up on their threats.

The phone call came in the late afternoon, when everybody was just sort of sitting around groaning about how much they'd eaten and trying to decide whether they could manage one more sliver of pie. Nobody heard it at first, the conversational level was so loud. When they did, everyone just looked at each other, wondering who in the world it could be since everybody that might be calling on Christmas Day was already there. Clay gave Carolyn a look and went to answer it.

When he came back there was a strange, bright glitter in his eyes. He made straight for her, ignoring everybody's questions and curious looks, leaned over and whispered in her ear.

"That's it — she's signed the papers. Merry

314

Christmas, California."

Carolyn's mouth went dry. She sucked in air but there wasn't nearly enough of it. Clay must have seen the panic in her face, because he suddenly took her by the hand and pushed back her chair.

"We have to talk about this," he said grimly, ignoring his family's interested glances. "Where are the kids?"

The room around them was utterly still, everyone listening with open and avid curiosity, but they might as well have been alone in it.

Carolyn shook her head, her gaze clinging to his face as if it were a lifeline. "I think they went home," she murmured, "to check on Traveler and the puppies."

"Come on," he growled, pulling her to her feet. "Let's go tell them."

But once they were in Clay's pickup and heading down the lane, neither of them seemed to have anything to say. Or perhaps there was too much to say. Carolyn felt tense and trembly inside, her mind flitting around like a nervous butterfly, afraid to light on the sweet possibility of happiness. Afraid to *hope*.

Finally, when they were almost to the dirt driveway that led to the summer house, Clay spoke without turning, with an odd vibrancy in his voice that suggested he was as tense and uncertain as she was. "Well, California?

What are we gonna tell 'em?"

She shook her head, unable to say a word.

"Dammit, Carolyn," he said angrily, "you know we have to do this thing together. The facts are, you don't have a house, and I'm a single man. It's going to take the two of us, or the court'll never approve it."

"I know," Carolyn whispered. Her throat locked, and she swallowed audibly.

Clay threw her a quick frustrated look. "What the hell's wrong with you? I thought this was what you wanted. The kids are okay with it — you saw them this morning. That just leaves you and me."

She nodded miserably. "You said I'm not selfish, but I am. I must be. Because —" She drew a long, shuddering breath. "I just don't think providing a court-approved home for a child is a good enough reason for two people to get married."

"A good enough —" The pickup jolted to a stop in front of the house and Clay turned to face her. His eyes were bright and clear as the winter light. "You told me you love me." He sounded out of breath, almost angry. "Last night. In the car."

"Yes," she said softly, her eyes shining like candle flames. "I did."

"Well, then?" he demanded. The silence lengthened. And then suddenly the light dawned. Clay threw up his arms the way he'd seen his father do so many times before and shouted, "For God's sake, why do you think I've been putting myself through all this? You think I'd go through this if I didn't —"

"How can you? You haven't known me long enough." She didn't seem to be breathing; her face looked fragile and transparent as blown glass.

"Well, shoot — you haven't known me any longer."

She smiled very faintly. "Oh yes, I have."

He studied her for a moment, wondering if there was any way he could ever tell her how he felt about her — about the way she made him feel like he was coming home after a long hard journey.

At last he caught a quick breath, narrowed his eyes, and said, "Remember that morning, when I met you on the bridge? I didn't remember seeing you before, but I thought somehow I knew you." He paused and looked away, trying to get his voice under control. "Now . . . I think I must have known you all my life."

She didn't say anything, just went on looking at him with those confounded eyes of hers, like lanterns to his soul. Until he couldn't stand it anymore, until he had to get out of the car and fill his aching chest with the cold, sweet air and the poignant smells of soggy leaves and last-melting snow.

". . . But I *do* like the rock collection," Jordy was saying when he walked into the bedroom. "I told you — I'm sorry I threw it. I didn't mean to."

"Well," said William, "that's okay, you can keep the puppy anyway."

They were sitting cross-legged on the floor, one at either end of Traveler's bed of old quilts and towels. Jordy had a puppy tucked in the hollow of her neck, nuzzled right up under her chin. She held it up for Clay to see, while Traveler watched anxiously, licking her muzzle and thumping her tail.

"Look — William said I could have one, and I picked this one. Isn't she beautiful? She looks just like Traveler — see her white feet and her little white face? And the widdle white tip of her tail . . ."

"Are you sure it's a she?" Clay asked dryly as Jordy lapsed into syrupy babytalk. He hunkered down beside the dog and her three fat, brown, featureless puppies, now contentedly nursing. "She still just has the four, huh? Yeah . . . pretty puppies." He chuckled as Traveler nervously licked his hand. "It's okay, girl, I won't hurt your babies."

He sat there for a minute, balanced on his

heels, arms resting on his knees, not sure quite how to say what he had to say. He wished Carolyn would hurry up and get there. She'd know how to do it better. But he waited and she still didn't come, so finally he cleared his throat and said, "William, I've got something I'd like to ask you."

"You want a puppy?" said William eagerly. "You could have one. Carolyn, too. That still leaves one for me and Trav."

"Thanks, but that's not —" He cleared his throat again, and glanced up as he heard Carolyn come into the room. That curious warmth and light poured through him again, as it seemed to do whenever he looked at her. She smiled slightly and nodded, and he drew a deep breath and turned back to William. "What I want to know is, uh . . . how'd you like to come and live with . . . well, with Carolyn, and Jordy —"

"With us," Carolyn said softly. He felt her hand on his shoulder.

He thought his heart might burst. "Yeah," he said on a long exhalation. "With us — Carolyn and Jordy and me."

William was watching his own hand as it idly stroked Traveler's neck ruff. He seemed not to breathe at all. "You mean . . . forever?"

"Yeah," said Clay. "Forever."

William's hand moved slowly, slowly over

the dog's thick fur. "Traveler, too?"

"Sure — and all the puppies."

William's hand paused. A frozen second passed . . . then another. His eyes flew upward, alight with hope, to fasten first on Clay's face, then Carolyn's. And all at once he launched himself at Clay, bestowed a strangling hug on him, then hurled himself into Carolyn's arms.

"Oh brother," Jordy said, leaning back against the side of the bed with the puppy on her chest and trying her best to look disgusted. "Well, that settles it — if he's going to be my brother, he can't possibly be an angel."

There was so much going on — a lot of laughing and crying and everybody talking at once — that for a few minutes nobody heard the new sound.

Then Clay said, "What in the heck is *that?*" and everybody froze.

"It can't be," Carolyn whispered.

Jordy said, "Oh my God —" Her eyes got big and round.

"That's a cat," William declared, leaning back to look up at Carolyn.

It sure was — a hungry, out-of-sorts, bad-tempered, and thoroughly pissed-off cat, by the sound of it. There was only one cat in the world it could possibly be.

"Harriet!" shrieked Jordy, trying to rise. "Oh my God — what if she sees me with this? She'll have a fit —" She was suddenly in a panic, looking frantically around for a place to hide the puppy.

"Wait a minute," said Carolyn shakily, extricating herself from William. "Just hold it right there. Don't move. Traveler is going to be a member of the family, and Harriet is going to just have to get used to it. Whether she likes it or not." She threw Clay a look and headed out of the room.

He got up and went with her, slipping his arm around her waist as she opened the front door. The cat began instantly to yowl and twine about their ankles.

"I don't believe this," he muttered in disgust. "She's not even damp."

"Where do you suppose she's been?" Carolyn asked in a wondering tone.

Abandoning them suddenly, Harriet stalked into the house, nose in the air, tail waving like an imperial banner, and headed straight for William's bedroom.

"Oh my God," Carolyn said, looking at Clay. "The puppies."

"Don't worry," he said grimly, "she'll have to go through Will and Traveler first."

Carolyn gave a little snuffle of laughter. "And Jordy — don't forget Jordy."

They stood together, arms around each other's waists, holding their breath as Harriet marched right up to Traveler and the puppies. The children sat like statues, apparently mesmerized. Traveler bobbed her head, stretched it protectively over her babies, nose quivering.

Harriet ignored them all. With royal disdain she sniffed each puppy . . . then took two steps and sniffed the one in Jordy's hands. She recoiled, hissed, and spat. And then, having expressed her opinion on the whole lot of them, she turned and sauntered into the living room, indignantly demanding her dinner.

"Well," said Carolyn faintly, "that went well."

"Yeah," said Clay. "At least she didn't eat 'em."

They turned toward each other, their breaths expiring in gusts of relieved, giddy laughter.

"Hey, come here a minute," Clay murmured, pulling her through the door and out onto the porch.

"But I have to feed —"

"Let Jordy do it — it's her cat. There's something I have to do first."

"What —" And then his arms were around her and he was kissing her, and the earth spun slowly out from under her feet.

"I've been wanting to do that for ages," Clay said huskily, resting his chin on the top of her head. "This seemed like the appropriate place for it."

"Mmm," she murmured, blissfully listening to his heart, knocking against her ear. "Why's that?"

She felt his face move and change shape with his smile. "You kissed me for the first time, right here on this porch."

"I did?" She pulled back a little to look at him. "I *did*. I'd forgotten that."

He chuckled softly. "Well, you kinda took me by surprise. I'll do better . . ."

"Clay," she whispered after a while, weak and dizzy with wanting. "We can't — not here — the children . . ."

"I know." His hands skimmed down her sides, restoring her clothing to roughly where it belonged. He sighed. "What are we going to do? We sure won't find any privacy at my house."

"Well," said Carolyn, "there's the barn."

"With all those kids running around? Somebody'd walk in on us for sure."

"What about Miss Leona's car?"

"After what Traveler did to the back seat? I don't think so." They collapsed against each other, helpless with laughter and frustrated passion.

"You know," Clay said presently, when they had their breath back again, "that's the trouble with big families — no privacy. You best keep that in mind."

Carolyn drew back to look at him with wide, innocent eyes . . . intoxicating as warm brandy. "I never said anything about —"

"Yeah, but I know what you're thinking. I know all about that Look."

"What look?"

"That one . . . right there. My dad never expected to have a big family, either. Then my mom would give him the Look, and the next thing he knew there were seven of us."

"Well," she purred, leaning back against him, nuzzling the base of his throat like a kitten, "then they must have managed to find *some* privacy . . ."

"This really is a nice bed," Carolyn murmured sleepily.

"Yeah," said Clay, tipping his head back in order to look at the old iron bedstead propped against the sloping, roughboard wall. "Too bad it doesn't have a mattress."

"Who needs one? I'm comfortable — aren't you comfortable?" She squirmed a little, nesting herself more cozily against him, and ran her palm slowly upward over the plain of his belly to the sensitive places along his ribs.

He captured her hand and held it over his heart. "I'm comfortable," he whispered, his voice becoming groggy with desire all over again. Well, he thought as she lifted her mouth to his kiss, maybe comfortable wasn't quite the word . . .

It was warm in the attic. The late afternoon sunshine sliced through the louvers and splashed across the floor where they lay on folded quilts, covered only, in various and intriguing ways, by each other. Down in the yard people were beginning to leave. Voices drifted up to them like the cries of birds, calling to each other, scolding children, saying good-byes. Doors slammed, car engines fired and growled away into the distance.

"It's over," Clay said on a long exhalation, running his hands lightly down Carolyn's back. "Another Christmas, come and gone."

"It's been some Christmas, hasn't it?" Her soft, ironic laughter puffed warmly into the hollow of his neck. "I can't believe —" She lifted her head suddenly and gazed down at him with stricken eyes. "I can't believe I forgot your present." She rolled off him and sat up. "I got you one, and I forgot to give it to you."

He watched her, marveling at how beautiful she was, feeling stirrings of desire he knew he'd have to put on hold for a while. "I didn't get you anything," he said regretfully, propping his head on his arm. "I wanted to. I just . . . couldn't seem to think of the right thing."

She touched his lips with her fingertips. Her smile was soft, tender. "How can you say such a thing? You've given me . . . the most wonderful gifts I've ever had. You gave me William, and" — her voice broke and she finished in a whisper — "you gave me my daughter back."

Clay caught her hand and pressed her palm against his lips, wondering if he could ever find the words to tell her about the gifts she'd given him.

"Clay?" Carolyn said slowly, hesitantly. "Do you believe in angels?"

Her hand covered his smile. "What?"

"I was wondering. You grew up with Sunday school and all that stuff, right? So . . . do you believe in angels?"

He could see that she was serious. "I never thought much about it," he said, struggling to sit up, leaning on one arm. "I guess. Why?"

"It just seems so strange to me . . . the way everything happened. William turning up in my basement like that. *Mine,* of all places. Of all times, when things were so . . . when we needed . . ." She stopped, looking embarrassed. "I don't really believe in things like that," she said, shaking her head and laughing softly at herself. "But it's almost enough to make me wonder."

"I know what you mean," Clay grunted, looking around for his pants. "But if you ask me, I think it was Miss Leona."

"Miss Leona!"

"Sure, why not?" He glanced up at her and grinned. "I think she planned the whole thing — put food out to lure the kid, then sent me over to make sure you had everything you needed . . . And that pageant —" He stopped, thinking about it. "I wonder if those wise men really had the chicken pox."

"Oh, you don't think —"

"Wouldn't put it past her. Wouldn't put much of anything past Leona — not even being an angel."

Carolyn watched him stand up to pull his pants on, marveling at the beauty of his long, lean body, the set of his shoulders and the fine, strong column of his neck. Marveling, too, that the sight of him could make her stomach turn flipflops, even after the way they'd spent the last couple of hours.

He looked at her, caught her watching him and grinned knowingly. And suddenly there he was — the young man on the hillside, brash and self-confident, master of himself and all he surveyed. She caught her breath and in an overwhelming rush of emotion blurted out,

"You know what I believe in? I believe in you."

His eyes softened. He held out his hand, and when she took it, pulled her to her feet. "You know something?" he said in a voice full of wonder. "So do I." He gazed at her as if she were something precious and rare, then kissed her and whispered, "Thank you."

"For what?" she asked, trembling with all that was inside her.

He kissed her again. "For this."

"*Sex?*" she teased him wickedly.

"You know what I mean . . ."

She sighed. "Yeah, I do. I just wish —"

Clay shook his head and murmured, "It just sounds so sappy to say it."

"It's okay to be sappy," said Carolyn. "It's Christmas."

He lifted his head, as if the thought were altogether new to him. "Yeah," he said in a voice full of wonder, "that's what Christmas is all about, I'd forgotten."

"What?" she whispered, teasing again, basking in the security and the unspeakable joy of knowing without being told. "Being sappy?"

"You know what I mean."

"Then say it."

He closed his eyes and laid his cheek on

the top of her head, wondering when and how it had come to be damp. A great sigh shook him as he finally whispered, "Merry Christmas . . . love."